HELL TO PAY

HELL TO PAY
DARK ANGEL MERCHANT MARINES™ BOOK TWO

MICHAEL ANDERLE

This book is a work of fiction. All of the characters, organizations, and events portrayed in this novel are either products of the author's imagination or are used fictitiously. Sometimes both.

Copyright © 2022 Michael Anderle
Cover copyright © LMBPN Publishing
A Michael Anderle Production

LMBPN Publishing supports the right to free expression and the value of copyright. The purpose of copyright is to encourage writers and artists to produce the creative works that enrich our culture.

The distribution of this book without permission is a theft of the author's intellectual property. If you would like permission to use material from the book (other than for review purposes), please contact support@lmbpn.com. Thank you for your support of the author's rights.

LMBPN Publishing
PMB 196, 2540 South Maryland Pkwy
Las Vegas, NV 89109

Version 1.02, June 2022
ISBN (ebook) 979-8-88541-181-3
ISBN (paperback) 979-8-88541-180-6

The Zoo Universe (and what happens within / characters / situations / worlds) are Copyright (c) 2018-22 by Michael Anderle and LMBPN Publishing.

THE HELL TO PAY TEAM

Thanks to our Beta Team:
John Ashmore, Rachel Beckford, Kelly O'Donnell

JIT Readers

Peter Manis
Dave Hicks
Jeff Goode
Diane L. Smith

Editor

SkyHunter Editing Team

DEDICATION

*To Family, Friends and
Those Who Love
to Read.
May We All Enjoy Grace
to Live the Life We Are
Called.*

CHAPTER ONE

"Mugh-9 isn't the weirdest planet I've been to but it's certainly in the running," Lombe told them. "If it were anywhere else, they might have simply bombed it and made another couple of attempts to terraform it. So many coriostorms and unstable tectonic plates resulted in a shitload of swamps and as many dangers, but the Salifate discovered a whole slew of valuable minerals in the scans and decided they would keep the whole place to make themselves rich off a planet they didn't need to share with anyone else. Any questions?"

Daria tilted her head and took a swig from the cold, bottled stout that had chilled in a small, portable cooler she'd brought to the cockpit. "Yeah, I have only one."

The captain tilted his bottle back for a slow sip before he grinned at her. "Tell me."

"I merely wondered...who the hell asked?"

She turned to Jozzun, who had struggled to stop himself from laughing until she delivered the punchline of her joke. Until then, she hadn't realized that the Xi-Trang had picked up on the question she had in mind but when his feathers began to shiver with the effort of keeping that knowledge to himself, she knew.

"I thought you didn't read people's minds unless they consented to it." Daria closed her eyes and leaned her head back. "It's rude."

"It wasn't rude." Jozzun threaded his fingers through his feather crest. "But sometimes, I can't help myself. Besides, we've worked together long enough now that there's at least some consent implied there."

"That will not stand in any court of law and you know it." She narrowed her eyes at him. "Well...most of them anyway. Now, I think our good captain here planned to give us a nice, long, boring lecture on the history of Mugh-9. We're supposed to be very, very interested because this is a vital part of doing business with the Salifate in this part of space."

The Xi-Trang shook his head. "It might not be wise to pester our captain like that while in the cockpit of his ship. It's a good way to get kicked out."

"I would never kick the two of you out," Lombe protested and shook his head. "You're practically my family at this point and yes, I do understand that Daria has only worked with us for less than a month. That should tell you all you need to know about how much of a relationship I had with my actual family. On that note, I would not be above hitting your bunks with a stink bomb moments before I decide we need to head out on a month-long ride on the Lanes for some smuggling work, so...keep that in mind."

"You know I would merely sleep in the docking bay, right?" Daria laughed. "And then find a way to retaliate in like fashion to make you regret a large percentage of your life choices."

He nodded and took another sip of his drink. "Anyway, back to the lesson—which is very necessary since we still have a fuck-ton of resin in our hold we haven't been able to find a buyer for, even after the couple of weeks we spent off planet to let the situation settle. I've come up with a way we can make our cargo a little more attractive."

When his two ship's officers settled their attention on him again, he continued. "Mugh-9 provided one of the richest deposits of valuable minerals and they wouldn't risk having all those changed or dropped deep under the planet's crust after the terraforming process. Instead, they brought it to about as close to terran-ready as they could and began to drop mining parties down. This was…about two hundred years ago if I don't have my dates wrong."

"How likely is that?" she asked

"Not particularly," Jozzun interjected before he could answer. "The captain's good with dates."

"Thanks. You've been around long enough to know that the Jindahin truly do like their shinies, and a fuck-ton of those were found on the planet. But they also found something else even more interesting—very rich streaks of silicon and more importantly, its friend silicon dioxide. This was all too plentiful where we came from but is surprisingly hard to find in a useable state anywhere else in the universe. Prepare yourselves for some deep history, but Old-Earth tech was mostly reliant on silicon as an electrical insulator for micro-electronics and that is how our tech advanced as well."

Daria closed her eyes, snored as loudly as she could, and popped one eye open when he stopped talking. "Honestly, if I wanted schooling, I would have gone to a fucking school."

"Well, school is in session, and if we want to earn our place on this damned planet, we have to find out exactly why the Salifate spends so much money to keep it viable. But chemistry lessons aside, Mugh-9 is the source of most of their finest and most elaborate pieces of jewelry and decoration, which we know is a vital part of every Jindahin who has a mind to flaunt their status. Aside from that, there are the natural elements with both conductive and insulative properties that are incredibly valuable to their military tech, which has begun to get more important while the Jindahin fight wars with their philosophical rivals, the Perdahin."

"I thought they were only called the Jindahin," Daria commented and shook her head. "Or do they come up with new names for the people they don't like and call it a day?"

"The race is called the Dahin," Lombe corrected her. "Their...religious order, I guess, is called the Jindahin, and Perdahin are the new order. Both sides believe they are in the right and the other guys are the heretics. See, this is why a little schooling is necessary before you have to deal with them again."

She rolled her eyes at that. "So...aside from silicon, what the hell can they be mining here that's so fucking necessary? Metals, minerals, or whatever?"

"I guess whatever is the most accurate. This came as

something of a shock to me but it is the gases released by the mining process. I think almost every human has heard about Mistquik. You know, all the signs that tell us to wear full protective gear."

"Oh, yeah." Daria chuckled. "That guy...I forget his name. 'The only thing 'quik' about it is how quick it kills you.' I loved that guy."

"Right. The chemsaws and augurs they use to excavate the minerals and metals from the rock create the gas and send it to the air filters, where it's harvested, pressurized, and mixed with the Trangian resin. That's the whole process of how they create the lightweight, strong plastics that are vital for various construction pieces on human and Xi-Trang worlds. Now do you have a decent idea of what we're doing here?"

While she had never been burdened with an overabundance of schooling, she did have a decent mind for business.

"I guess that means we won't unload the resin here, right?" she asked and raised an eyebrow. "For us to get top dollar for trading it in human space, we'd need some of the 'quik."

"Right. Kiloliters of it, from what I was told. It should be simple enough to purchase it here since it's essentially toxic waste from the Jindahin, but there are a couple of complications."

"Let me guess. While it might merely be a byproduct of their mining on the planet, our fishy friends know what it's worth on the open market and they demand more creds so they can support the war efforts. Basically, it's an ongoing game of goose on pricing between buyers of the Mistquik and the Salifate."

Lombe reached into the cooler, took another bottle from inside, and tossed it to her. Two bottles of malt liquor in and she still caught it smoothly, although if she hadn't, their engineering trio would throw a fit and probably make her clean it all up. If nothing else, it meant she was motivated to make sure that not a single drop was wasted.

"Well done."

"Well, I might not have read many books as a child but I do know the basics of economics in the galaxy."

He nodded. "Interestingly enough, the second problem is also possibly part of the solution. While the mine overseers are Jindahin Salifate officials, the actual miners are primarily Perdahins sent to this side of the empire to isolate them from the rest of their people. That would make Mugh-9 something of a penal colony, and while the Perdahin miners are interested in undercutting their masters and selling Darkquik—the going term for Mistquik sold on the black market—they are limited in their ability to do so. Their overseers hunt the dealers ruthlessly and they make a point of punishing any of the smugglers they use."

"Something tells me we'll go ahead and try anyway," Jozzun muttered and shook his head.

"Which brings me to the third issue we'll face." Lombe paused to pick up another drink from the cooler and check to see how many they had left.

It was a meeting in the cockpit for the three of them, which meant the doc and their engineers didn't need to attend. Lombe would generally recommend their absence very casually during the times when they discussed possible jobs because that way, they weren't a part of the criminality committed. This meant that if they ever fell foul of the law, they could probably invoke some kind of plausible deniability that would make sure they weren't punished as severely as the rest of the crew.

That was all well and good and she both understood and agreed with it, but Daria couldn't shake the feeling that something bad would happen to the bots she had begun to grow attached to. Maybe a little too attached but she would cross that bridge when she reached it.

"And the third issue?" Jozzun asked and raised an eyebrow. He wasn't asking what the issue was, of course. He and the captain knew each other well enough that he didn't have to ask for access into his mind but it was still a decent way to remind Lombe that he'd gone a little off-track.

"Right. The third issue is with the planet itself. They did a bad job with the terraforming and as I said, storms out there have mostly turned it into an uninhabited waste."

The Xi-Trang nodded slowly. "Those coriostorms are chock full of acidic winds and static bolts that would turn almost any above-ground structure they encounter into another part of the storm. It means that the land above-ground around the equator and along the tectonic lines is essentially uninhabitable. Even the mines have to be careful, and they need to keep an eye on all the warnings for an earthquake in the region. They even have a system of satellites that monitor for virtually everything that might interrupt the mining processes."

"Is that the problem?" Daria asked and leaned a little

closer. "Those satellites will identify smugglers trying to get in and out of the planet, right?"

"That is a problem but not *the* problem." Lombe scowled and focused on the screens. "I know how to avoid them for the most part. They follow the major storms and the tectonic plates so we avoid them and the sats. On that note, only a couple of ports of call are above-ground on the planet at both poles, the most stable areas of the planet. Everywhere else needs to be underground, and the major ports of call are the underground-slash-underwater cities with interconnecting tunnels made to accommodate vessels even as large as the *Atalanta*."

"Can the poles dock larger ships?"

"Sure, but they still need to fly in on a shallow orbit. Larger cruisers sometimes need to circle the planet a couple of times before they can get close enough to land, which is not an option on this planet. That means smaller cruisers only."

"You'd think they would set up an orbital port for the whole planet to use," Jozzun muttered.

"And make things easier for people like us?" Daria countered. "No, I have a feeling the Salifate intentionally made sure that docking on this planet was as difficult as possible. It makes it easier to keep track of the people who do make a landing."

"She has a point with that one." Lombe smiled and leaned over to tap his bottle to hers. "It's the point of many of the mining planets, especially those that are basically penal colonies. You know how much they hate having Sentient Being Rights groups running secret studies on them."

She rolled her eyes. "What's the third issue? And hopefully, the point of this little history lesson?"

"We have a better chance of dealing with the mining colonies that are a little farther-flung. It's easier for smuggling in general out there but they can only be reached through some of the smaller passages or their vents to the surface, at least unless we want to be seen by the sats. This also requires shuttles or similarly-sized craft that not only have limited cargo capacity but are also more than a little vulnerable to the erratic and deadly weather conditions."

"Which is why you should let me handle the negotiations in this case," Jozzun insisted—not for the first time and certainly not for the last. "All your Jindahin contacts are mine and they all prefer dealing with non-humans anyway. When things are this…uh, delicate between the Jindahin and the Perdahin Salifates, you should keep everything as neutral as you possibly can."

Daria shook her head. "I suppose humans have earned that type of reaction. But honestly, there's a petty, annoying overall shittiness from all the humanoid species. It's not exclusive to the human civs."

"Nope, but we're the ones who are famous for it," Lombe pointed out. "The rest of them are merely following our example, I guess."

"So you agree with me?" Jozzun asked and sipped his drink. It wasn't the same stout the two humans were drinking. From how he explained it, Daria assumed that most Xi-Trang were allergic to the fermentation process humans usually followed but numerous beverages were available for his kind.

"In a manner of speaking. Most of the humans who

come to the planet are mercenaries brought in as a security force against the native species and…I guess, the help. This means they see all humans as the same kind of rough and tumble people—and it's not like we do much to change their minds about us. It does tend to push negotiations distinctly toward an unhealthy level of competition for all parties involved."

Daria nodded slowly. "Then again, we tend to inspire that kind of reaction from many of the different civs. Maybe it is our fault."

The captain nodded slowly. "Yes, and they tend to be a little more tolerant of teams with a Xi-Trang among the members. Human-only crews usually make people think of the purist movements you see on many of the human-run planets."

"Careful," Jozzun warned him with a grin. "That almost sounds like it's the only reason you brought me onto your team."

"I'll be the first to admit it was one of the many reasons why you're on the team. Of course, I'm also sure there were many reasons why you wanted to join our particular crew."

"There was only the one reason, to be honest."

"Oh, right."

Daria narrowed her eyes at them. It hadn't been long since she'd joined the small team and as much as she had begun to feel like they were growing closer by the minute, there were still many things she was out of the loop on. The story of how Jozzun and Lombe started working together was among them.

Fair was fair. Given that they had looked at her sheet before they recruited her, there wasn't much about her criminal career they didn't know, whereas she was still in the dark over various details of how they had started on their paths. Still, she didn't feel like prying too hard into their lives.

It wasn't a lack of curiosity on her part but in the end, pressing for knowledge they did not want to provide would either result in them shutting her down or they would simply provide a version of events they wanted her to see. It was much better when details were offered spontaneously, which generally required them to be about fifteen different kinds of drunk.

That was about three or four bottles of stout away from where Lombe was. She had no idea what Jozzun's tolerance level was since this was the first time she could study his drinking habits.

"Of course," the Xi-Trang continued and sipped his drink again, "I don't mind taking a look into your mind and I happen to see that you're coming up with more than a few opportunities based on your schemes. It's a little offensive that you haven't thought to use me in your previous schemes."

"How is it offensive? People generally want to deal with the captain. I merely never thought of calling on you to pass yourself off as the captain in these cases."

"Exactly. Offensive."

Lombe pushed from his seat and looked like he was about to address the accusation directly before he realized that the Xi-Trang was yanking his chain.

"Fuck you."

"It took you a little too long before you realized that, captain."

Daria leaned over, tapped her bottle to Jozzun's, and watched as the AI began to bring them down through the cloud cover overlooking the desolate landscape of Mugh-9. The planet was revealed slowly through the storms that still whipped across the surface. It was safer to let an AI navigate them through the tough weather and it gave them a few hours to come in from orbit and start their landing process closer to the poles.

"You know, you're a little psychotic," Jozzun pointed out and shook his head at the captain. "Your adventurousness will get you killed one of these days."

"Humans, in general, are a little too reckless for our own good," Daria reminded him. "It's not like he can help it. It's in his nature."

"Of course, I know that about you, although saying you are 'a little reckless' is understating it somewhat. Especially when speaking of the captain. He's pushed things to the level that suggests it might be a chemical imbalance."

"Once you two are finished talking about me like I'm not in the room with you, maybe you want to start thinking about what kind of chemical imbalance it takes for two people like you to join my idiocy on a regular basis."

"Naturally." Jozzun nodded. "We are as disturbed as you are."

"Speak for yourself. I'm only here in a desperate attempt to keep myself alive and my mind unscrubbed," she reminded them. "I don't know what kind of excuses the two of you have used."

"She makes a good point," Lombe admitted.

"And with that in mind"—she pushed from her seat—"it

looks like we're coming in for landing. I think it's high time I get the Hounds ready for our descent."

She noticed the Xi-Trang was watching her closely. The feather crests on his head and neck vibrated gently the way they did when he looked into her mind. It wasn't quite the unpleasant experience she had grown accustomed to when she had been in one of their prisons, though. They could make the experience agonizing when they wanted to, but that was usually only when they had a particular reason for it.

In this case, he seemed to try his gentlest touch as if he didn't want to intrude but was somehow compelled to.

"Whatever hell the for?" he asked when he realized she was looking at him.

Daria tilted her head, narrowed her eyes, and tried to decide what the hell the Xi-Trang was asking. After a moment, she put all the words together in something that made sense.

Jozzun shook his head and his expression turned both sheepish and apologetic. "Sorry. I...crude vocalizations were never something I enjoyed but they happen when we are startled and reply without thinking. I guess I must have slid into instinctual habits without realizing it."

"Right. The Xi prefer to communicate empathically and telepathically. I understand that wires could be crossed here and there." She shrugged. "And to answer your question, as inappropriate as your mind-reading was, I'm doing it just in case."

It didn't quite look like he believed her but there was something else to it. Maybe he understood that it didn't have all that much to do with the fact that they were touching down soon. He might well have sensed her concern for the mechanical members of her team and felt reluctant to broach it openly.

What was the point of being a psychic if he couldn't tell what she was up to?

CHAPTER TWO

"Are you sure you trust an AI to run this whole situation?" the Xi-Trang asked warily.

Lombe looked at him as if to decide what he was talking about. "Of...of course. When did you start to question whether or not we should use AIs to fly us through the storm?"

Jozzun shrugged and ran his fingers over his feather crest. He'd noticed that he made the gesture regularly and almost compulsively. It was comforting and soothed the clusters of nerves collected directly beneath the skin.

He would never understand how the Xo were able to sear that part of themselves off. It required the kind of deeply-rooted hatred for their own kind that he would never feel. As much as he felt certain frustrations with his people from time to time, it never reached the point where he would remove that part of himself.

It would have been akin to humans cutting their fingers off—or maybe their tongues—which would prevent them from communicating in a natural way with others of their race. He shuddered at the thought of having to interact in the galaxy without the psychic ability. How did humans and other species manage full, well-rounded relationships—business or otherwise—without it?

"You merely don't trust AIs that much, is that it?" Lombe suggested after a few crackles of static bolts that arced across the sky ahead of them.

"It's not a matter of trust and you know that. I'm more than happy to work with them to protect the *Atalanta* when we're in the air, but I prefer to at least have a finger on the pulse of the ship. What happens if the AI miscalculates or makes a poor judgment or something like that?"

"Between you and me, I'm probably more likely to make that kind of mistake. Of course, such a thing should never be said aloud and certainly not in front of our mechanical crew—Forrest especially. We don't need the bastards to grow anything like an ego. That's how wars like the Foxholes get started."

The whole ship shuddered suddenly as they continued to descend through the cloud cover and the winds began to whip as if in an attempt to throw them off-course. The shields were still engaged and the bright silver glimmer materialized every time they encountered a gust of acid wind that tried to cut into their armor.

"With that said..." The captain's voice trailed off as he leaned over to pick his headset up from where it hung next to his desk. "Klyz, Kliz, Kleiz—you three had better be working on those port thrusters assuming you don't want us all to plummet to our deaths about five thousand meters down."

"Working on it, captain," one of them answered. "One of them got caught in the last static arc but we're bringing it back online. You might want to compensate a little in that direction."

The AI had already picked up on that, but the drift was a little difficult to compensate for. Since this was the part of the planet that was the least affected by the extensive instability, Jozzun could understand why they hadn't fucked around with trying to get a smuggling operation established yet. It would require someone to pilot the shuttles through these types of storms.

There was bravery and then there was simply not caring if one happened to live or die. Or plain stupid people. He couldn't rule that out.

"It's interesting that the three of them think I'm piloting through weather like this," Lombe admitted. "And maybe a little flattering."

"Could you pilot through this weather?"

"I have before." The captain shrugged. "This is far from my first visit to the planet, but when you can get an AI with a full connection to the ship and its status without risking any kind of distractions, it's always in my interest to admit that I'm not the best man for the job."

"So if the AIs were knocked out by an unlucky static bolt strike…" Jozzun let his question trail off so the man could fill in the blank.

"I would be there to pick up the slack. You don't need to worry about that shit."

He shook his head. The captain didn't lack confidence, of course, and it wasn't purely arrogance. Lombe was one of the most skilled human pilots of his generation, and perhaps what made him one of the best was his willingness to admit when something else out there could do his job better than he could.

Of course, a little of the captain's laziness couldn't be entirely discounted, although he wasn't alone in it. It was a particularly human trait that also seemed prevalent in most of the humanoid species.

A few specialists in the matter suggested that humans were the source of the humanoids that spread across the galaxy—with a handful of exceptions—although no one took them seriously. While that might be stretched as a point for debate, too many out there thought humans were being left behind by the other humanoid species. Evolution was a little more natural for the rest of them, while humans seemed stalled by their inherent need to pretend they were the superior species.

Fortunately, not all humans felt that way.

The whole ship shuddered again.

"Shit," Jozzun exclaimed when he realized that the disabled port had come online in time for one of the starboard thrusters to go down. The vessel began to list to the right before the AI corrected the imbalance of the ship's movement.

"Physics is a cruel bitch," Lombe remarked in response. "Coming in for a straight landing with a full ship requires us to traverse hundreds of klicks across the planet's atmo. This isn't too much of a problem on most planets, even those prone to storms, but whatever happened to Mugh-9 has turned it into a potent and unpredictable nightmare with limitless things that could go wrong."

"Of course," the Xi-Trang countered, "most planets like

that usually maintain a port base in orbit or on a nearby moon that allows easier access, if indirect. My homeworld has such a system."

"True," the captain retorted, "although it's mostly because the Xi-Trang don't like having foreigners on their planet."

The Jindahin Salifate chose the expedient of simply leaving the planet as unhospitable as possible as a way to keep people who didn't need to be there away.

Jozzun pulled himself from his thoughts and looked to where Lombe chuckled as he kept an eye on the cameras to see what was happening elsewhere on the ship.

"What's got your attention?" He could simply have peered into his mind for a direct answer but it seemed oddly appropriate to ask the question. While not entirely sure why he'd been prompted to do so, it felt right.

"It looks like our first officer might have done better if she'd stuck around on the bridge," the man answered and turned the screen for him to see that Daria looked like she was about to be sick on the decking.

"Humans and your inner-ear-based balance." The Xi-Trang shook his head and checked on her to make sure she didn't need medical attention. Having to look through the ship required a little more focus from him, but Lombe could keep an eye on anything else they needed for the moment.

Satisfied that she seemed like she would be fine, he shrugged. "She needs to find something to do with her hands. That would help to distract her from the discomfort."

His mind returned to her decision to check on the

Hounds but he honestly couldn't understand why it unsettled him. Context was one of the most challenging parts of looking into someone's mind and while he could go digging for some frame of reference, he was aware that it would cause her more than a little discomfort if he did. This reticence surprised him a little too, although he generally restrained his psychic abilities as far as she was concerned.

The Xi-Trang frowned. He felt a little conflicted but decided concern for her outweighed his reservations. A quick surface probe would be sufficient. *I would almost say...something linked to the feeling that prompted her decision has made her sick, but from a psychological standpoint.* A reminder of a hurt—he thought it might be betrayal—touched his senses and he winced before he withdrew from her.

He decided against trying to make any deeper exploration while he didn't have her consent to do so. It was more or less implied between him and the captain now, but something about humans was so fucking alien.

"Well, it doesn't look like she'll be sick," Jozzun reaffirmed with a smile. "Although that might change if we encounter more turbulence out there."

"It shouldn't be a problem," Lombe answered, took one last swig from his bottle, and lobbed it into the recycler in the cockpit before he moved to another two screens that gave him a decent view of what was happening outside. "We're out of the cloud layer and unless I miss my guess, out of the worst of it all."

The cloud layer was where most of the danger was.

Arcs of lightning still struck the ground, although most of it was picked up by the antennas spread across the landscape. It was an effective method to collect the static charge to power whatever was happening underground. The swamps across the planet still managed to sustain some form of life against all odds, although from what he'd heard, these were mostly pests and insectoids that made the mining operations even more difficult.

Still, there was an odd beauty to the planet that the Xi-Trang wasn't sure how to explain. It was like he looked at the primordial ooze all their ancestors had crawled out of at some point or another.

The feeling disappeared when they slipped into the underground caverns used to protect all the ships that managed to maneuver through the storms. From that point forward, automated systems took over the parking of their vessel, brought them into port, and automatically assigned them a docking port.

"See?" Lombe leaned back in his seat and kicked his feet up on the console that effectively ran on its own. "Nothing to worry about. It's merely a little more exciting than our other landings."

"Well...most of our other landings."

"True enough." The captain sighed and shook his head. "I can't explain it but I do like this little slice of planet. Something—"

"Primal," Jozzun finished his thought for him as they began to touch down and connected their airlocks to one of the docking ports. Daria entered the cockpit with them.

"So." Lombe looked at her. "Were you sick? Did our

engineers bitch at you over how you messed up the loading bay?"

"No such luck," she answered but still looked a little green. "The Hounds are ready to go if there's any trouble waiting for us in there."

"Why would there be any trouble waiting for us?"

"Because I'm looking at mostly human cruisers there." She nodded at the screens to indicate what she'd seen. "A shitload of human corp is doing business around here, don't you think?"

"Not any more than usual," he responded. "Well…maybe a little more than usual. From the chatter I've picked up, they've brought large numbers of mercs in to deal with some insectoid infestations down south, which means we're looking at small armies patrolling around here. That always brings more business in. They gotta keep all those humans fed, watered, and supplied with weapons and other equipment they need for a long-term stay on an alien planet."

"Not any O2 imports, though," she commented. "The planet's atmo appears to be optimized for humanoid living, which means your regular distribution of nitrogen and oxygen—hell, it looks like a little more oxygen than usual. Almost thirty percent."

"Which means any humans we run into ground-side will be more hyper than usual." Lombe tilted his head. "Do…how do Xi-Trang deal with O2 anyway?"

Jozzun sighed, ran his fingers through his crest, and enjoyed the tingling sensation that went down his spine every time he did that. "We're much different than humans in that respect. The Jindahin, on the other hand, absorb most of their oxygen through their skin, although that usually only works when there's enough humidity in the air to enable them to do so. They can survive in much higher concentrations than thirty percent and even thrive."

"I guess that's why they walk around with those ridiculous water tanks," the captain muttered and pushed from his seat. "It's probably a good thing there are so many humans around here, even if they are mercs—and tied directly to the corp running the mining on the planet too. I noticed some from the Angelus Dominion, Flymmien Combineran, and the Gallian Enterprise. The big three—it's not usual to see them rubbing elbows."

The human civs were as hostile to one another as they were to every other civ in the galaxy, at least from what he knew of their histories with each other.

"Do you think they're here trying to start a fight?" Jozzun asked. "The *Atalanta* is registered under the AD so we might end up as a target for mercs hired by the other two."

"That's what our first officer and the Hounds are for," Lombe answered and patted Daria on the shoulder. "I believe she can stand up against the best anyone can bring against us. But it is a little weird to see them all here, and if they're bringing an armed presence in, it could be that they're pressing the freelancers out and applying pressure on each other."

"How well will your papers hold up under scrutiny?" she asked as they approached the airlock and she checked her weapons again as the doors hissed open.

"They're some of the best on the market," he assured her and Jozzun agreed. He'd been a part of acquiring them and while it had set them back a hefty amount, they were worth every mic so far. "And if they fail, we have some backups in place."

"I did a little digging and it seems dual citizenship isn't allowed for citizens, but it is allowed for ships," Lombe explained as their side of the locks opened up and left the work of the port's airlocks opening to whoever was on the other side. "We have codes that'll pass the *Atalanta* off as Gallian too, which means we fall very neatly in the gray area between true freelancers and chartered corp mercs."

"Still," Daria whispered as the last of the locks on the other side of the docks began to release, "I think it would probably best if we kept a very low profile while we're here. The Hounds can stay onboard on standby in case we need them in a hurry. There's no point in arousing the suspicions of anyone who might be able to see through whatever paperwork we might fly under."

It sounded distinctly like she was speaking from experience, which made sense. Jozzun didn't need to read her mind to know she had extensive experience with criminal elements, and that was enough to tell her that loud criminals ended up as dead criminals.

Fuck, he knew that much and he liked to think of himself as only a dabbler in such things. The other two members of the crew were the real professionals.

"Oh." Lombe cleared his throat and motioned for the Xi-Trang to take a step forward. "It's probably best if you're front and center for this in case some people have questions."

"Right. Good point."

It was simple enough for him to pick up the message the captain wanted him to pass on to the port official who waited for them as the last of the locks lifted and the doors opened.

Two Jindahin stood there and studied the data being transmitted automatically by the *Atalanta*, although they would still ask a handful of questions he needed to answer when they approached the dock.

"Good afternoon," one of them muttered from his fish-like lips, his gaze still focused on the data before he turned to the trio who had debarked. "Do you have any hazardous material or imported goods to declare?"

"Not a thing." Jozzun spoke calmly and confidently.

"What is your business on Mugh-9?"

"We're here at the behest of Matrox Vahir Nowas and have commissions to transport some personal effects relating to his pending transfer off-planet."

The officer checked everything he said. It was an efficient system enforced by the Salifate across the planet to make sure everything could be checked and verified easily. Generally, it cut down on the kind of red tape smugglers like them usually loved to see.

Thankfully, everything would be confirmed the way they wanted it to be. The officer would be listed as being transferred to one of the nearby moons, which would justify him calling in a freelance frigate to transfer his personal effects off-planet.

Still, the Jindahin took a few seconds longer than he needed to, checked every single detail down to the letter, and darted his gaze sideways a few times before he nodded and motioned for them to move on.

"We didn't even need to pay him off," Lombe noted once they were out of the officers' earshot. "This is a very business-friendly planet."

Daria shifted uncomfortably. "I don't particularly like Jindahin planets. They are always more humid than is comfortable for human skins. I suggest we finish this job very quickly."

"Agreed." The captain loosened the top button of his shirt and looked distinctly uncomfortable, although Jozzun could tell there was another reason for the man to feel unsettled. There was no need to point it out, of course, but he seemed unusually concerned about the potential trouble that could result from so many mercs on-planet at the same time and the overriding sense that something resembling a military campaign was in motion.

"Why are we meeting the Matrox in a bar?" he asked as they proceeded through the brightly lit tunnels. Signs were positioned every ten feet or so to tell them where they were and where each of the branching tunnels would lead them.

"Bars are always a good place to make a first connection, especially when you initially touch down on a strange planet," Daria answered, which came as no surprise. "It's a good place to get a feel for the planet without looking like you're prying too much, and a nice, public venue to learn how the rest of the planet feels about your arrival. You're also in a good location to hear about local news that might be relevant and to top it all off with a cherry locket, it's somewhere you can get a decent drink and a meal if you hold the meeting there."

Lombe chuckled. "Well...yes, all that. Although it should be noted that the Matrox suggested the bar as a way to pass the time. It's close enough to the port to make it a good location close to where we have to meet our man and it's a merc bar too. You always get the best drinks in those, no matter what your species."

The Xi-Trang certainly felt like there was a difference in experience between himself and the other two. Daria spouted the reasons like they had been drilled into her head as an operational code, which made him wonder exactly how many of these meetings she'd been a part of.

All things considered, it wasn't like they knew much about what she had done during her prior career as a criminal since all that was on her sheet was what she had been caught doing. *All the more reason to dig a little, but I'll have to hold back a while longer. It would work best if she trusted me to do so.*

"We'll meet the Matrox in a couple of hours," Lombe told them once they stepped through the doors of the bar. "So we might as well get a drink and a meal and see what we can discover about the situation here."

"Why don't you get us a table and order something?" Daria suggested and patted him on the shoulder. "I'll get a lay of the landscape and see if there's anything we should know about from the locals."

"You do that."

She had become more comfortable in her role as the ship's first officer. Getting a lay of the landscape, as she called it, was a good way to make sure no hostiles were waiting for them. Jozzun liked to think he could have picked up on any aggression directed at them, but this would only be possible if there was an imminent threat. In that case, the chances were that once he detected it, they wouldn't have time to retreat.

Lombe guided them to a booth that had a clear view of the entrance and most of the rest of the room, although the bar was packed with local mercs. Jozzun assumed these were who Daria referred to as locals since there weren't many Jindahin present. Their table made it easy for them to keep an eye on their first officer as she scouted the room.

It wasn't long until she started a chat with the folks at the bar itself and it sounded like she was commenting on the sports game on the Broadcast Feed over their heads. The Xi-Trang didn't recognize the particular sport but it looked like a favorite among the humans. From what he could see, people walked around with large aluminum clubs and swung at balls thrown at them at perilous speeds.

She laughed loudly and shook her head as drinks were poured for them. He tried to get a feel for what was said, but there wasn't much about it on the surface level of her thoughts and certainly not enough to make it worth a little deeper exploration.

It seemed like she merely absorbed as much intel from around her as she could, processed it quickly, and set it aside while she stuck with their cover story of merely being new arrivals who wouldn't be docked for very long.

"She's good at that," Lombe commented. "It takes skill to fit right in with the mercs like she's fought alongside them the whole time. What are you having?"

The Xi-Trang glanced at the captain, who scanned the menu projected on the glass plate next to their table.

"What do they have that's Trang-friendly?" he asked and leaned a little closer.

"Uh...it looks like only the fruit platter. They claim the fish is fresh but I wouldn't trust anything that has to be flash-frozen and shipped out here."

"Indeed. The fruit platter sounds like just the thing," Jozzun answered and shook his head. The chances were that the Jindahin-appropriate fish dishes wouldn't be palatable for him anyway, no matter what the menu said. "And a tea, I think."

The captain nodded, tapped the choices, and completed their order before he sent it to the people working in the kitchen. He'd ordered for Daria as well. She made her rounds through the room quickly before she walked to their table and slid smoothly into the booth across from Jozzun and next to Lombe.

"What did you learn?" the captain asked as the waitress arrived with their drinks orders. From the looks of her, she was a young human female but maybe not a pureblood. Her eyes didn't look it, anyway.

"The planet's hot," Daria whispered, sipped her stout, and winced visibly. "Boatloads of mercs have been imported, all paid for by the Salifate. From what I was able to glean, it sounds like they're having a problem with some of the local pests. The mercs talked about monsters in the tunnels, although from what I learned from a group called the Bugzzappers, it sounds like it all started because a rival corp tried to force the others out. Mercs were brought in to defend the miners and the merch."

"That doesn't explain why they've brought a fucking army in," Lombe retorted and shook his head. "I noticed some tank transports out there, freshly arrived. It looks like someone's planning a fucking invasion."

"That's what I heard." She beckoned urgently to the waitress, who carried their food to their table. "Another group mentioned how one of their captains was tapped to lead a full military campaign to reclaim parts of the mines that haven't been used for decades since a horde of the pests took them over."

"That why they're bringing tanks in?" Lombe asked.

"It sounds that way. They want to make a show of their firepower so they get the contract."

"Nothing's decided yet, then. That's good for us."

Jozzun couldn't claim to pay attention to either of them. He had been curious as to why Daria was so insistent that the waitress move a little faster, but he realized now that it was because she'd seen the beginnings of a fight brewing on the other side of the bar.

While it was likely that it would start and end quickly, there was always the chance that it would spread across the entire bar. A full-scale brawl would leave the staff no other option but to close themselves in the safe zones and let the mercs fight it out while they called the local authorities.

Which wasn't that great for them, but Jozzun had a feeling there was no reason to worry about it. Their paperwork was all in place and for the moment, there was nothing to contradict the story they'd chosen.

Daria looked like she had planned to dig into the platter of various cuts of meat that had been ordered for her but appeared distracted as she watched the fight develop and begin to escalate.

Sure enough, the staff had already retreated behind the bar and sealed it with the bulletproof glass that would keep them safe while the mercs fought themselves out.

"You know," she muttered and looked at Lombe, "if they get a little too close, they might fuck our food and drink up. Management probably won't refund us for what we have to eat off the floor. Do you want me to…uh, you know, head the fighting off?"

"You merely want to get in on the violence," Jozzun chided her, although he and Lombe both smirked.

"It's been a little too long since I've been in a real brawl. You don't want your first officer to go blunt on you, do you?"

"No casters," the captain warned her. "We don't need that kind of attention from the local coppers. Keep it to fists, nice and clean-like."

"What do I look like? A barbarian? I know the rules of a bar fight."

The Xi-Trang didn't doubt that in the least. She was probably the only one who adhered to the rules anyway, but it was a good way to make sure none of the authorities thought she was playing a little too rough and needed to cool off in one of their isocubes.

With that said, she was probably the only one in the room who didn't need to break any of the rules. She was fast on her feet and immediately stepped in to level one of the men with two punches that made him stagger back into a group of mercs who attempted to wrestle one another to the floor. A swift kick to the solar plexus made another double over when the breath rushed from his lungs.

Daria shouted a warning to one of the mercs, a shorter woman with a clip in her silver hair, who immediately turned to meet the threat of a shorter male merc with blond hair.

"You have to wonder how the most promising candidate from one of Lamusa's finest schools is ducking drinking vessels," Jozzun commented and took a bite from one of the exotic-looking fruits from the platter before he grunted in appreciation.

"Wait—what?" Lombe frowned at him in confusion.

"Didn't you read her sheet?"

"I…skimmed it. The point I came away with was that she was an orphan without much in the way of means."

"Well, yes, that was early on. She was given an opportunity to attend one of the planet's finest academies but she left without much of a reason why."

"Huh—oh…ow!"

A sudden rush of empathic pain made Jozzun turn to see what was happening with the fighters. The silver-haired woman had brought her knee up between the male human's legs and he fell and curled in agony as Daria pulled away from the fight.

"That has to hurt," Lombe whispered as his hand moved instinctively between his legs where his human reproductives likely ached out of empathy for his fellow human male.

"Has it?" Jozzun narrowed his eyes. "Well…I suppose it would for human males. Xi-Trang males have most of our vital reproductive parts contained inside our bodies where they cannot be attacked so easily."

"Yeah, well… Imagine it as someone grabbing you by your crest. That's the kind of pain you can imagine when a man is kicked there."

"Oh. Ouch indeed." Of course, Jozzun knew it was one of the many weaknesses of humans, but using that kind of feeling to describe it helped to make it a little easier to associate with it. Still, there was probably not much to compare between the two kinds of pain. Or maybe there was.

He smiled at the thought that researchers could attach probes to the males of each species and find out which hurt more—although finding willing test subjects for such a study would be difficult.

Lombe bounded suddenly to his feet. The Xi-Trang's train of thought ended abruptly and he looked around to where the captain stepped in to engage one of the mercs who tried to attack Daria while her back was turned.

Fair was fair, and Lombe didn't attempt to engage in an honest fight with the kind of man who would attack someone so sneakily from behind. His cane was already out and the stun function activated when he buried it in the merc's stomach. The man fell with a scream and grunt of pain and the chair he had brandished landed on his head.

"I may not be a barbarian, but barbarians always cause the best fights," Daria declared with a grin as she settled into her seat again. Jozzun tilted his head, studied her for a moment, and wondered if it was appropriate to point out that she was bleeding from her nose and had been spattered with the blood of one of the poor fools she'd had the opportunity to introduce to her fists.

He would have disagreed with her assessment that she was not a barbarian since she looked the part in every way, especially with her red hair and the evidence of the brawl.

Thankfully, she caught sight of her reflection on one of the platters and snatched a napkin to clean herself between mouthfuls of her food.

"Did you get that out of your system?" Lombe asked and raised an eyebrow when whistles from the entrance alerted them to the arrival of the local cops.

"I wouldn't say out of my system entirely, but it's good to release all the energy early once you touch down on a new planet," Daria answered and winced as she dabbed at the swelling that had begun to appear on her bottom lip. "It's yet another reason why it's a good idea to go to a bar first and foremost. I firmly believe it's always best to get the post-travel jitters out by pounding someone's face in so you're a little calmer for the rest of the job. Do you want to get involved, Jozzie?"

"I'll pass, thanks," Jozzun answered with a polite smile and chose to ignore the name-shortening. "I'm not sure I get these...uh, what did you call them? Post-travel jitters?"

"Lucky you, I guess." She shrugged, took a swig of her stout, and winced again. This time, however, it appeared to be the result of the cold liquid running over her injured lip.

Still, she certainly seemed a little calmer now that she'd had the opportunity to release some of her pent-up energy. She relaxed and smiled in her seat as the cops began their rounds to make sure everyone was more or less intact. It was their job to identify anyone who looked like they needed medical attention too, since people dying as the result of a fight would be on their city's overall record.

This was generally a bad thing. The Xi-Trang were, by necessity, a very empathetic society, which tended to lean toward the extreme in that respect. But there were religious reasons for the Jindahin to hate murder and even violence. Although they engaged in it often enough when they had to, there was a reason why they called human mercs in to deal with their problems planetside instead of using their troops, which would have been the cheaper option.

The fruit platter was surprisingly tasty, and it wasn't long before Jozzun sipped his cooled tea. He watched the staff clean up after the fight, set the tables and chairs up, and let their patrons return to eating and drinking in peace now that the brawl was over.

He paused, looked at the glass menu next to the table and made a note of the time, and transferred the mental image to the captain's mind's eye. The man needed to be reminded that their meeting time was almost at hand.

This wasn't quite the way they wanted to meet the Jindahin. Jozzun and Lombe looked about the same as they had when they first debarked, but Daria proudly bore the marks of the brawl. She'd cleaned the blood but her eye and lip were still swelling, and she pressed the cool stout glass to her eye with a soft sigh.

Jindahin were obsessed about appearances and they expected the same kind of standards from the people they did business with. Maybe the Matrox would have lower expectations since he knew he was dealing with criminals.

"It's a good thing the fight came to an end when it did,"

the Xi-Trang muttered as he finished the last of his tea. "It's not the best way to start negotiations with our new client, although I probably could have sent a pulse to get all the fighters to sit the fuck down."

Lombe shook his head. "That would have been a bad idea. I'm very sure that sending a pulse to that many people would have put you to sleep but fast."

"Sure, but—"

"Remember the real purpose of this little expedition. I need all your faculties working at full strength."

Jozzun scowled and ran his fingers over his crest. "Right. We should get moving, I suppose."

"That sounds like a plan. Are you good to go, First Officer?"

Daria looked up from where she still pressed her glass to the side of her face. "Oh…do you need me to swing at people?"

"Probably not but you never know. It's always best to have you around."

She sighed. "Fine."

The Xi-Trang was the first one to move to the door. He took the lead while the other two fell in behind him almost as though they were well-trained minions.

He was glad to have Daria take on the work of first officer, and something was interesting about how she carried herself around the galaxy. It was like it didn't owe her anything and she didn't owe it anything either, which meant the two could avoid each other as much as possible.

Even though he still thought he should take point in the negotiations with the Jindahin Matrox, he wouldn't feel too bad about having her there. Their contact had worked around enough humans to know they were a violent sort. Having one like Daria in the team would tell him that while the Xi-Trang wasn't likely to engage in any violence —even if necessary—the humans would not hold back in a similar fashion.

CHAPTER THREE

Jozzun had halfway forgotten that the meeting would be held in the bar, mainly because he'd been distracted by the explanation that bars were good places to meet. Still, he'd realized the error quickly enough when the captain checked the directions and led them purposely toward the small group of offices in the massive caverns system.

Perhaps this is why he doesn't give you the lead more often. There are benefits to working with a Xi-Trang in these situations, of course, but I relaxed and let my guard down. It was a small oversight and of no real importance, but it could have been critical.

It surprised him that he might have become overly reliant on non-verbal communication and maybe even allowed it to cloud the spoken information. This was certainly something he'd have to look into.

Maybe if Daria could bring herself to adjust to having him as a crewmate, she could take on the lead role. He could continue to relay what needed to be said between her and the captain.

He snorted inwardly. *And that would make everything even more confusing for everyone. Don't the humans have some weird saying about how broken telephones—no, don't go there. You don't even know what the fuck a telephone is.* Trying to identify Old-Earth devices would only add more confusion.

Although a part of him still believed they should start acclimating her to the process. It was almost seamless between him and Lombe, but it had taken them years to get used to working with each other. Even then, however, it seemed the captain had made the right choice—to pool each of their abilities to support and supplement his as the leader.

The business complex hung from the ceiling and looked almost like it had been carved out of a massive stalactite. That wasn't likely to be the case since there was probably not much in the way of structural integrity there but the idea was appealing.

Still, the similarity in shape was intentional enough, which meant the Jindahin officers inside wanted some kind of point made about their status and authority over the mercs in the region. Most of the fighters looked like they were making themselves comfortable in housing on the surface.

While the accommodations would be adapted to the conditions, they would still be a little less than inspiring.

Lombe cleared his throat softly and the Xi-Trang realized he'd stood in front of an open door for a few seconds, lost in thought. He was coming to realize that this was one of the problems that came from his species interacting with others—he lived a little too much in his head.

As they entered a small elevator barely large enough for the three of them and no doubt designed to carry only one Jindahin at a time, his first question was simple. The captain looked at him and narrowed his eyes in unspoken expectation, ready for him to ask it.

What do you hope to learn from the Matrox?

The answer was returned faster than he expected. *Mugh-9 has garnered something of a reputation as a mysterious place—much like the Old-Earth legends of the Bermuda Triangle.*

Jozzun frowned since he'd certainly never heard the legend or the name before and had no clue what it meant.

Lombe didn't need him to convey his confusion and hurried to explain. *According to the stories, it was a roughly triangular area—I imagine that's where the name came from—where vessels and even aircraft sometimes vanished, never to be seen again. It's relevant because recent scuttlebutt suggests that smaller operations have had whole ships go missing without explanation from time to time. I merely want to chat to a local who can tell me more about it and give us a sound indication of what risks it might pose for our little operation.*

At least he now knew what the name meant and could loosely understand what scuttlebutt was, although he'd like to explore them in more detail. It would have to wait, however, until they were somewhere away from where dozens of eyes—and possibly ears—were focused on their small team. His focus should not be on satisfying his curiosity but on discerning any potential threats they might encounter.

His determination to focus on the matter at hand was immediately challenged by his sudden interest in the fact that Lombe's mental voice was a good deal deeper than his actual speaking voice. Thankfully, he managed to wrench his attention to the silent message quickly enough to acknowledge the reminder that he needed to be extra vigilant. "You two are doing it again," Daria muttered.

"Doing what?" the captain asked and tapped his lips and then his ears innocuously before he glanced around the elevator as they stepped out.

She still looked confused and Jozzun decided to see if her awareness of their mind communication meant she was somewhat attuned to it. *The Jindahin are growing increasingly paranoid these days, which means we should expect unwanted interest and attempts to discern our purpose here—both verbal and non-verbal and almost anywhere.*

Daria appeared to receive something from him but still needed a moment to assimilate it. She finally understood and tried not to make it too obvious as she looked around the hallway they followed into the building. Her sheepish expression suggested that she'd not considered that it was advisable to avoid normal conversation around the location of the meeting.

Of course, she was right. They had done it again. Having a conversation that seemed to isolate her intentionally was probably not the nicest thing to do. At the same time, it was an integral part of how they worked as a team and she needed to somehow come to terms with it.

"You do realize," he told her in almost a whisper since telepathic communication wouldn't work for an ongoing conversation with her, "that if you want to be involved, all you have to do is get a little more used to the fact that you work with a psychic. If you can move past your reservations, you could be a part of every conversation."

"You know where my reluctance comes from." Even with such a low tone, she sounded a little defensive. "Being imprisoned by the Xi-Trang Authority leaves a very nasty taste in one's mouth. It's not something I can simply spit out and glibly move on from."

He could understand, of course, and even help where he could.

"I hope you can come to see that being a Xi-Trang does not make me one of them," he told her as gently as he could. "If you are ever ready to talk about what you endured while under their control, I would always be willing to hear you out."

She fixed him with an expression that was part disbelief and part rejection and he wondered if he'd pushed a little too hard despite his genuine intentions. "Then again," he quipped to ease the conversation, "I might not be so willing to do that if you call me Jozzie again." He'd never been called that before and something about it irked him.

He hadn't intended to mention it—at least not there in a Jindahin-controlled environment—but perhaps it might help her to see that he had foibles too, or maybe she also did things that might offend others.

"You do know it's a part of building rapport, especially among humans, to establish nicknames and the like?" At least she'd not veered toward taking umbrage at his comment.

"I understand that much about it but Jozzie simply does not appeal to me. Surely, as much as you are entitled to come up with various nicknames for me, I am also entitled to turn those down if I happen to dislike them."

At least, that was how he assumed the situation worked but he didn't have much to base this on. For the longest time, Lombe and the doc had been the only humans on their little squad. Although they enjoyed each other's company and had a vital and efficient interaction—something very close to what he thought of as family, although that could be confusing too—he realized that there was little in the way of comradery there. He was surprised by this insight since he had never considered another possible dimension to relationships between the species.

Ishima had once been an army medic, which meant she was more than comfortable in combat situations, but they weren't quite comrades in arms.

The Xi-Trang wasn't sure how that worked precisely, but it had something to do with their relationship as doctor and patient. There were certain things about Lombe that she was aware of that he wasn't quite as comfortable sharing with the rest of the crew, and that made any conversation between the two a little awkward. This sentiment was missing when he talked to Daria. There was a familiarity there that he hadn't seen in most of Lombe's interactions with the crew.

It seemed like something for them to talk about but it would have to come later. Lombe had spoken to him the entire time while they walked down the hallway and despite the Xi-Trang's distraction, he'd fed him with loads of information he had available regarding the planet that could make their efforts more difficult.

Of course, unlike the humans, he could process input

coming at him from a variety of different sources when he wanted to. It was simply a matter of what information he would process at any particular time, and he could sift through what was streamed into his head either from his body's senses or from what his feathers were picking up.

Daria had a habit of assuming it was always an intentional act on his part but most of the time, it was purely instinctual and there were releases he had no power to avoid. *I imagine it must be like when people yell or something smells very bad. She can't help but pick up on that information.*

The worst part was that most of the time, it was disjointed thoughts, random numbers, words, and images he would never have any chance to decipher unless he dug a little deeper.

Of course, humans wouldn't understand how he managed to filter through all that. They were only concerned about what was relevant to their little group like picking up anyone who intended to attack them or something like that.

This situation with Daria has made me confront questions I didn't know I had. If I'm honest, I wouldn't be able to explain how it worked either.

Filtering through the data to find what was relevant had become a matter of habit and practice but even then, he had to admit that he couldn't guarantee he would pick up on what they needed every time.

Jozzun groaned softly when he realized what Lombe was trying to get him to think about and Daria scowled again when she realized they'd slid into their non-verbal space again.

"I'm not sure if you intend to clog the connection," the

Xi-Trang stated to bring her into the conversation, "but I can't ignore the fact that your mind is awash with ideas of wild, dangerous exploits."

The captain grinned unashamedly. "All of which could result in elaborate payouts, despite the fact that numerous ships out there go missing and are never heard from again after sending maydays and calls for help. Or not, in some cases, depending on who tells the story."

Their first officer's scowl deepened. "I'm not sure any of this is a good idea. I know we often wish we could simply disappear, but I'd prefer it to be not permanent and something we have control over."

The Xi-Trang made no effort to hide his sigh. "This is the point, Captain, where I need to remind you that our most recent expedition took us into the depths of a derelict space station with the help of some less than trustworthy pirates. Despite the fact that we almost lost our lives and the *Atalanta*, it wasn't nearly as profitable as we had hoped."

"We still have to determine what can be sold," Lombe countered.

"Indeed, but it certainly won't make us rich. My point is that the risks hopelessly outweighed any possible return." Jozzun faced the man's stare firmly.

"Don't be too quick to write it off. Like I said, we don't know what we found yet. Only the software upgrades the engineers managed to install in the Hounds already justifies a little effort."

Daria snorted. "Yeah, but maybe not quite the effort we put in at the station. Still, you're not entirely wrong. Upgrades like those in the Hounds generally go for tens of thousands of creds."

"Fair enough," the Xi-Trang conceded with a shrug. "But I still don't think it was worth putting our lives on the line, almost being torched by thousands of pirates, blowing the station, and running from the blast through a debris field. We made it out but the kind of damage we took while doing it was expensive to repair too."

Lombe made no effort to refute this but still, Jozzun knew it wouldn't temper his enthusiasm. Daria had told them about the treasures in the vault. While they weren't the precious metals they'd expected, they would have been far easier to move. Relics and old, precious items always had value no matter what planet they were on.

She had taken what little she could carry so they could still make some profit from the station but it was not worth the risk. *And who knows how many of his insane schemes would simply result in our lives being wasted in a ball of fire?*

A couple of Jindahin officers waited for them when they finally reached the office of the Matrox. These weren't high-ranking at all but they still managed to deck themselves out with as much shiny shit as they could. It was a little foreign to Jozzun but it was a cultural obsession among the Dahin.

Many jokes were made about how the fish-faces liked having shiny objects, but too many jokes were made about his people as well—the bird-faces. He never thought they were funny but he wouldn't deny anyone their need to feel superior by making fun of the appearances of other races.

The gleam off what should have been utilitarian military uniforms merely made him wince when he saw it—although thankfully, neither of the officers noticed.

"Captain Lombe, here to speak to Matrox Vahir Nowas," the captain announced as curtly as possible. Establishing his position was important when dealing with the Jindahin. He had to ensure that even though he didn't have as much shiny on his uniform, they knew he was there for a meeting with their superior.

As expected, it worked. Both officers had appeared ready to challenge their arrival before he spoke, but the inclination evaporated quickly and they motioned for the trio to step inside.

It helped that Daria rested both her hands on her gleaming, pearl-handled casters. She also looked like she was ready to address any problems they had with either her weapons or her fists—which wouldn't be a good look for any Jindahin officer, no matter what the situation.

Her bruises plus the full-sleeve tattoos exposed by the armored vest she wore as well as the seam of silver that glinted in her cheek were equally convincing. They told the story of someone who had no issues landing the first and last blows in a fight.

Besides, she probably still had a little fight left in her, and Jozzun would bet on her every day of the week against Jindahin soldiers. It was less of a statement on the soldiers and more about what he had seen of their first officer's skills in a fight.

Thankfully, those skills would not be needed in this particular situation. The Xi-Trang was the last one through the door that was held open for them. He made sure his two companions preceded him before he advanced toward the large, gleaming desk that filled most of the office. It was perhaps a little too exaggerated—not a common fault among the higher classes of the Jindahin unlike their obsession with baubles. A little more subtlety could be found in the surroundings of those who had established status.

Everyone else needed to go out of their way to make a show of who they were.

"Matrox Nowas, thank you for taking the time to meet with us," Lombe said politely and bowed his head in respect to the officer who rose from his seat.

The Matrox was a little taller than most of his kind, with a slim build. His pale-green skin glinted in the humid environment and was matched by the gleam of the adornments on his uniform. A handful of those appeared to be military honors, but Jozzun had no idea what each medal meant.

He bowed his head in response to the greeting and subtly activated a noise canceller over the office once the door was closed behind the three new arrivals.

"You're late," the Jindahin stated brusquely as he gestured for them to sit on the uncomfortable-looking stone seats in front of his desk.

"We most certainly aren't," Lombe answered and sat calmly.

"Excuse me?"

"We could have been here hours ago but you chose the time that suited you best. You even suggested we kill time at the bar while we waited. Then you messaged me to bring the meeting forward by half an hour and we arrived here less than ten minutes after you sent that. I guess this means you might want to throw off any local cops who might have caught wind of it but here I am, an accommodating business partner."

He motioned for Daria and Jozzun to sit beside him. The Xi-Trang complied and fed lightly into the Matrox's ego to suggest how much he impressed them—and because they were so accommodating, he could trust to be good business partners.

Keep it light, Lombe urged him.

The warning was well-meant but unnecessary since subtle influences were all he would dare to attempt. Fortunately, it appeared to work as the Jindahin leaned back in his seat and relaxed his shoulders enough to make it clear that they didn't need to get confrontational.

"I was merely a little concerned when I heard about the fight," he answered with a smile that displayed his needle-like teeth. "Many of those hired to respond to civilian disturbances look for ways to improve their position and status. Any one of them might have shown inconvenient interest in you and your purpose here, which would have drawn attention to me. And yes, this is the same reason why I did not want to meet you in the bar at all. I can only hope your…first officer was not the one to start the brawl?"

Lombe looked to where Daria shifted uncomfortably on her seat. "First Officer Hughes? No, you have nothing to worry about on that score. We had ordered food and drinks and when the melee moved a little too close, she helped to guide it away. You can look into the footage at the bar if you want confirmation. We would never endanger our business relationship with you that way."

"I don't think that will be necessary." Appeasing the

man's ego was doing wonders to settle him, and the captain was quite happy to do his part to further Jozzun's effort.

Daria merely wondered what the hell was happening around her since she knew that behind the spoken conversation, her two crewmates undoubtedly shared an ongoing non-verbal conversation she wasn't a part of.

Hopefully, she trusts us enough to understand what we're doing. If they needed her to do something, they would let her know in a way that left no question about their intentions.

That was one of the things he admired about her. She might not be psychic like him and didn't have much openness for that kind of thing, but she had a keen eye for reading people of all backgrounds and species. This meant she didn't have to be a psychic to tell when problems would present themselves. *She might not always get it right, but she's way ahead of most others. I wonder if the need to survive has played a part in developing that.*

Lombe removed his top hat and inclined his head to the Jindahin with a smile. "Now, shall we talk business? I don't think you'll want us to be seen to speak to you for too long."

"No, I would not. While I would normally charge a much larger fee for dealing in this type of thing, I've already moved most of my assets off-world. I don't need those kinds of questions asked about me at this point either."

That wasn't quite a lie, but someone who wanted to put the screws on the humans he dealt with could always find a way, usually by passing the fees to another officer who would owe them for it for a later payoff.

The fact that he didn't push them for more money was no doubt the happy result of appeasing his ego, as debasing as it felt in that moment.

"We'll already bring work to your family," Lombe pointed out to drive the point home that they didn't need to be antagonized any further. "Your cousin is running this in Sector Thirty-eight, if my memory serves?"

"That is correct. He has some Mistquik he wasn't able to ship out and it's burning a hole in his stores. Of course, he could always simply wait for the next shipment, but there's no telling if it'll be any good by then. That will be enough for them to drop the prices for it."

This explains why the offer is suddenly available to us. I suspected as much. Lombe's thought sounded smug, no doubt because he'd been proven right. *And it's a dangerous shipment so there will hopefully be limited buyers out there. It's losing the owner money the whole time it sits in his storehouses. He'll want to offload it as soon as possible.*

Not only that, it will probably be one hell of a trip to get to Sector Thirty-eight, although I'd need to check a map before I can say that with any degree of certainty.

Which makes the buyer pool even smaller.

And our task even more difficult, the Xi-Trang retorted sharply.

"Of course, between the two of us, we know that sector has a weak stream of low quantity gas," Lombe commented for the Matrox's benefit and scratched his jaw. "It makes me think you might be trying to pull some kind of silk over our eyes."

"What is that supposed to mean?"

"I mean there might be a reason why your cousin wasn't

able to get the gas in his tanks on the last shipment, and there might be a reason why you're trying to pass it to your smuggling connections."

Maybe Lombe was playing a game Jozzun couldn't see, but he felt something prickly in his connection with the Matrox that said the man probably didn't appreciate being called a cheat in this particular case.

It now took all he was capable of to try to influence the official's mind into thinking the statement wasn't quite as offensive as Lombe probably meant it to be.

"The best mining locations have already been redistricted to favor the larger corps," the Matrox stated bluntly, "and now that they're bringing their own mercs in, they're buying larger contracted access to the best areas. All of them are looking to stockpile the Mistquik to drive the prices up before they sell in bulk. This is one of the only sources of it still available on the market but if you don't like it, you might want to consider asking the corp for some of what they have."

The captain leaned back in his seat and looked a little too comfortable in it before he exhaled a long sigh.

"Well, if it's the only source of Darkquik out there, we might as well snap it up before someone else does. You already have my contribution, right?"

"If I did not, we would not be speaking."

"Right." Lombe pushed to his feet with a polite smile. "We need to get the ship ready for the trip. I'll let you know if we need to talk again."

"You do that."

The terse turn the conversation had taken was about as good as Jozzun could manage to keep the two from starting a brawl right then and there in the office. Daria would probably have enjoyed that, but there would be consequences to assaulting a Jindahin officer, even one as annoying as the Matrox appeared to be.

The captain motioned for them to join him as he strode out, walked down the hallway, and made sure they were out of earshot of the guards who waited outside the office.

"We have to find another source of Darkquik," he stated, shook his head, and scowled down the hallway they had just come from.

"You know the consequences if the Jindahin catch us," Jozzun reminded him as they stepped into the elevator. "We're already facing some serious trouble in Xi-Trang Authority space, so we'll run out of friendly skies to fly in —unless you want to start working in human space."

That was always a gamble. The space occupied by the human civs was where most of the good money was, especially for someone of Lombe's particular talents and propensities. Unfortunately, it also meant the competition was fiercer and they had more people to fight off for every mission.

The captain had a talent for sneaking their crew into the kind of work that would pay well while it enabled them to avoid crossing paths with the other merc groups that could muscle them off any particular job.

It didn't always work, but there was no need to stick around any particular work for their egos' sake. This meant they weren't quite desperate enough to charge headfirst into a job that was certain death.

Most of the time. As for the other times…well, it

brought them neatly back to the captain's impossible leanings toward anything that redefined crazy.

"What do you suggest?" Lombe asked and shook his head. "Merely taking whatever garbage they happen to pass onto us isn't a good way to make money."

"We can try not to make ourselves wanted in every fucking territory we do business in. In simple terms, it means we try to find work without pissing everyone off."

Daria shrugged. "I can't...uh, disagree with that. I like a good fight, but being on the run from every fucking agency out there is not appealing at all."

The captain sighed again, closed his eyes, and rubbed his temples before he replaced his hat. "Fine. We play nice —for now."

"I'm so glad you agree that we shouldn't get ourselves killed." The Xi-Trang sounded smug.

"Fuck you, beak-mouth."

It was another insult he didn't quite understand, but Lombe was angry, annoyed, and frustrated. Jozzun didn't mind giving him the opportunity to vent it now instead of when he could end up angering the wrong kind of people.

CHAPTER FOUR

It didn't seem like Lombe's mood would improve as they began to return to the ship. Jozzun knew better than to try to influence it at this point, especially given how well the captain could recognize the effects almost immediately.

He wouldn't be happy about it, which in turn would defeat the object of the exercise. *Perhaps our best chance to get the captain back into a good mood is to let him drink a little before he begins to explore the options.*

At the same time, though, it wasn't that he didn't trust Lombe to make the right choices. The man would always think about his crew above his feelings. The paradox—and the inevitable conflict that created most of the problems—was that he also had a certain vanity to him that made him crave heading into the fight instead of running away.

But he ultimately chose the crew over himself every time. Jozzun, above all others, knew how much it pained the man to make those decisions. Because of this, he took it upon himself, as the ship's emissary, to try to help the man feel a little better about it when he could.

"There won't be many openings for us to work with," Lombe pointed out as they stepped onto the walkways suspended over the mines below them. "Nothing will come easy on a planet like this. The opening we do have available is from the Matrox. He supposedly has property held by his cousin for us to purchase and we're cleared to head out there with some shuttles to collect it. Since it's owned by a member of the military, it won't need to be checked by the regular customs assholes."

He paused in thought for a moment. "Of course, it doesn't mean someone won't see right through it and decide to blame us while they let the Matrox off scot-free. Fuck, he might decide to turn us in if he thinks we're any kind of threat to his plans, so there's no point in hanging around here any longer than necessary."

The Xi-Trang nodded agreement but an odd awareness pricked at the back of his mind. Something was wrong, and he knew he was about to find out what it was.

Daria had suddenly turned tense and quiet with nothing to add about being in and out quickly. *She didn't even voice the fleeting inward joke about Lombe having a little too much practice in that regard when it came to his sexual partners, which is entirely out of character.* Instead, she pushed it quickly out of her mind when something appeared to distract her.

He turned to look at her and tried to determine what had caught her attention. Her gaze was directed at a small group of mercs that moved toward them from the other end of the walkway. There was enough room for an AGtruck on the suspended surface, and it was strong enough to hold all their weight without giving them much to worry about.

Oh dear. I'm afraid the logical deduction is the right one. Her attention is focused on the men themselves.

They all wore armor—which wasn't that unusual since they were supposed to represent their corps while out and about—and nothing in particular about the group set them apart from the rest. He knew the emblem they wore on their chests belonged to the Red Crows corp. There were enough of them around to make them the type of group that anyone should be wary of as a matter of course.

Daria's reaction, however, appeared extreme. She stared daggers at them and had settled her hands on her weapons. He didn't need to be a psychic to know she was preparing for violence, although it looked like she would be the one to start it.

The mercs, on the other hand, didn't even seem to notice the three members of the *Atalanta* crew. They laughed and looked a little drunk as they moved toward what appeared to be some kind of afterparty that waited for them in one of the barracks set up to house them.

A moment later, however, one appeared to register her relentless glare.

"What's the matter, Red?" the man asked and stopped a few paces in front of her. "Do you see something you like?"

That drew a smirk from Daria. With her hands still on her casters, her shoulders relaxed into what the Xi-Trang sensed was a ready pose. "I can't imagine you've ever heard anyone seriously answer that question in the affirmative.

At least not when they weren't trying to pilfer your money out from under your nose."

"Now, now—there's no need to be rude."

"No. I think there's very much a need to be rude."

The man smirked in response but it wasn't quite as smooth as hers. "You don't want to mess around with us, love. Step down now or I'll grind your bones to make my bread."

"You know, it's not every man who has the courage to admit that he looks, smells, and acts like a fucking ogre. I guess that makes you brave, doesn't it?"

He immediately took a step forward, his fist drawn back, and readied himself to launch forward to deliver a punch to her face, but she moved as well. She almost looked like a dancer as she swayed back, watched the fist miss her by centimeters, and continued forward to stamp hard on his instep. He slipped and fell to one knee.

Her knee rose to drive into his face and broke his nose with a soft, wet crunch. Before he could react, she caught hold of him by his thinning, greasy brown hair and thunked the side of his head into the railing of the walkway.

The impact was hard enough that Jozzun could feel it, although from what he could tell, the blow didn't kill him. Still, he was unconscious and would likely need some medical attention. Hopefully, this might convince his teammates to focus on the need for treatment rather than the brewing fight.

It didn't look like the other Red Crows were on board with that particular plan. A dozen of them were still on their feet and they were all drunk and violent enough to not care about anyone's injuries or that they were about to get in the middle of a fight they would pay very dearly for, even if they won.

The first one had drawn a knife and his first swing at Daria was clumsy enough that she didn't even need to move away to avoid it. Instead, she closed the distance and drew her caster with her left hand. She pressed the muzzle under the jaw of the first attacker and something wild and insanely calm gleamed in the redhead's eyes.

"You and your little buddies will help your unconscious friend to leave, or he'll have to carry those few of you still alive out of here when he wakes. If he wakes."

The woman has a way of making peace by being prepared for war. Jozzun would give her that much, but these were fighters with their inhibitions lowered. They wouldn't back down from a fight when they thought they had the upper hand, despite the fact that she had gone out of her way to make sure that one of them had thrown the first punch.

The Xi-Trang wasn't quite so stupid as to think she hadn't caused the fight in the first place, which begged the question of why she wanted to pick a fight with the group. *What does she stand to gain from it?*

"Do you think you can do anything?" Lombe whispered, grasped his cane a little tighter, and watched the mercs trying to decide if they would back away from the confrontation or get more involved.

"They're drunk and they're looking for something to hit." Jozzun shook his head. "I can do something but it'll only influence one or two of them. The others will notice and take that as a way to start the—"

He was cut off when the captain suddenly bounded away and caught one of the mercs who had attempted to sneak around Daria's peripheral vision to knock her on the head and end the fight then and there.

It wasn't a smart move, but there was a lack of inhibitions in the area for the moment and none of them looked like they intended to back down.

A wet pop confirmed that the merc who had her caster pressed to his jaw was now missing a chunk of his skull. *Well, this isn't quite the way the day was supposed to go, but our first officer seems to be in something of a mood.*

So were the rest of the mercs, unfortunately. Ten of them were still standing, with one having the top of his skull blown off by the caster and the other nursing the spot where Lombe had struck him.

This certainly hadn't been an outcome any of the *Atalanta* crew had anticipated.

Daria turned her weapons on the rest of the mercs as they moved to take cover behind the pillars supporting the walkway they were on and which connected it to the ceiling. They weren't quite fast enough and one of them sagged as he clutched his throat where she'd shot him.

"What the hell's gotten into you?" Lombe shouted. It was their turn to take cover when the Red Crows began to return fire. None had any coil rifles, thankfully, but their casters were as deadly and forced the three of them to hide for a moment while they decided what their next move would be.

"I've run into the Red Crows before," she answered calmly and checked the batteries on her casters. "They would have caused trouble. I merely stepped in and made sure I could control it."

Before he could answer, she peeked out from behind cover and took a shot with one caster and then the other before she scuttled to the other side of the walkway to hide behind another of the pillars.

There had been two shots but the Xi-Trang heard only one thud, which said she'd made sure she had a killing shot. It looked like she had hit the merc in his armor, knocked him out from behind the pillar he was hiding behind, and finished him off with a shot to the head.

That much was easy to pick up on from what her mind projected. *But below the obvious...I could almost swear to the fact that she is lying through her teeth. What makes it interesting is that it is a very good lie.*

From what he could glean from her memories—those that swam very close to the surface—was that the Crows were the violent type and liked to pick fights with almost anyone they thought didn't belong and probably didn't have any decent protection.

Logically, this meant their culture would practically demand that they start a fight with the new freelancer arrivals merely to swing their supposedly massive reproductives around.

But something else is most certainly there. I can't sense what it is since she won't let me see it, but it's personal and very visceral.

Jozzun realized she was staring at him. Or, more likely, he was staring at her and she had noticed. Maybe she knew exactly what he was trying to do but instead of shouting at him for invading her privacy, she shook her head.

Don't be a feather-crested fool. Common sense alone should warn you to not piss the woman off when she is in a killing mood. Still, they needed to finish this fight quickly or law enforcement officers would arrive. They likely wouldn't appreciate the fact that they were pissing the mercs off given how good they were for the local economy.

We need to get the hell out of here before anything like that happens, and I have a good idea as to how. Jozzun closed his eyes and reached out the minds of the humans on the other side of the firefight. It never felt like he was leaving his body the way humans seemed to think his powers worked. He smiled at the fleeting thought, momentarily entertained by how little they understood of the Xi-Trang. It faded as soon as he remembered that he probably had as little understanding of them.

His ploy was a simple one made much easier by them being drunk, angry, and distracted. *They are all Red Crows, right?* The power of their party seeped through their veins at his urging. *You need to end the fight quickly. Crows can fly and there is no reason why Red Crows should be any different.*

It wasn't quite something most humans would believe but he pressed the idea into them, and drove it home repeatedly while he appealed to the very human desire to fly. *You want to and need to fly. There's no need to fear it simply because you've never done it before. You simply need to do it. Fly. You can. You know you can fly.*

There were many ways to resist his kind of barrage on their minds. People could be trained, a handful of helmets out there could help, and some people were naturally resistant to his compulsion. Still, he didn't need it to affect all of them, only a few. That would be enough to distract the rest.

"No! Get away from the edge!" one called to a teammate.

"I can get in there to flank her! I know I can."

The Xi-Trang didn't need to look out from behind his cover to see that at least three of them were affected by his control. These were ready to jump over the edge and stood on the railing while the other six tried to talk them down.

A moment later, he realized that only four of them were more or less unaffected by his compulsion. The last two had difficulty stopping themselves from climbing on the railing and were in no position to help the others who needed it.

One of them jumped before his teammates were able to stop him, and Lombe narrowed his eyes as he tried to understand what was happening. Daria didn't stop to consider the possibilities. She stepped out of cover and sprinted to the other side of the firefight.

Her nature was such that she wouldn't wait to consider the philosophical problems of killing men who struggled under the effects of his mind control.

It's a battle, the Xi-Trang reasoned, *and if they had the same advantages as she has, they would make the most of them. Shit, there are already too many of them to even consider making it a fair fight, but she will no doubt even the odds.*

Another jumped from the railing and disappeared into the murky darkness below. The third had tried to jump but was held fast by three of the mercs while a fourth reached for him.

Their first officer didn't even hesitate. She fired at those who were distracted by the one man hanging from the railing after his sudden break with reality. Her accuracy with the ancient casters she liked to carry was a little too chilling, and two of them were dead before they even realized the shooting had come much closer than they would have liked.

She stepped forward and almost blasted the head off a another before she kicked the last man holding onto his comrade and launched him over the railing.

Lombe approached quickly with the intention to help as the last three struggled to recover their minds. He saw no need to kill them, and three quick strokes dropped them to the walkway before they had the opportunity to raise their weapons.

They probably wouldn't have done the same thing had their situations been reversed. Still, Jozzun still didn't feel too comfortable executing the three who had put up such a strong fight to stop him from sending them into the depths of the mines. *Killing unarmed and mostly disabled mercs feels like something that will come back to bite us in the ass in one way or another.*

In this situation, I firmly believe it is best to not tempt fate.

"That went much better than we could have thought," Daria whispered as she changed the batteries on her casters with those on her belt. "Still, we should probably get out of here. There's no telling how the locals will react to this little shindig."

Lombe nodded. "Right. And then you can go ahead and explain to me what the fuck you were thinking."

"I told you, I know these assholes. They would have attacked us the moment they knew we were unaffiliated, probably stolen our ship, and integrated it into their fleet. This way, we make sure they know we're not to be fucked with, especially since they need all the people they can get to bolster their numbers in the mines."

The captain looked at Jozzun and the Xi-Trang was tempted for a moment to tell him there was more to it than merely a bad feeling about a group of bad moranges.

The urge passed quickly, however. He knew Daria wouldn't cause him any grief over telling the truth, but something in her needed to be taken out on the cretins. And it had helped them, besides, although it could very easily have gone the other way. Still, it needed to be made clear that he would not condone her simply attacking anyone who triggered her aggression.

"Right," Lombe muttered once they were on the other side of the walkways and realized that alarms and bells now rung to alert people to what had happened. He'd tried to ask Jozzun for clarity on his first officer's behavior, but all that had been passed back was confusion. The simple truth seemed to be that the Xi-Trang couldn't determine why she needed them dead.

"It doesn't look like anyone's following us," Daria said as they continued at a good pace and avoided anything that might slow them on their way to the ship.

"Okay, but we need a few ground rules for this kind of situation." The captain caught her by the shoulder, brought her to a halt, and turned her to face him. "From this point forward, we leave the premonition about who might prove to be trouble to the actual psychic in the group, understood?"

She looked at Jozzun and he couldn't help but run his

fingers over his crest to calm himself. It took him a moment to realize that she didn't look angry or even like there was any imminent violence in her. *She seems more apologetic than anything else, but there is also no real remorse for what she has done. Only some regret over what the consequences could be and how they would impact her crew.*

"Yes, Captain," she answered simply, cleared her throat, and placed her hands on her casters.

"Good. Now, let's get out of here before anyone starts looking for witnesses."

CHAPTER FIVE

They were all a little on edge and it filled the air like static electricity. Lombe was piloting and he was suspiciously silent after everything that had happened. His stiff posture and frown said clearly that he was running his mind over the events of the day in an effort to come to terms with them.

At heart, the captain is a good man with a conscience and doesn't like the idea of executing people, no matter what the reason is.

He wasn't an innocent, of course. He knew they would encounter problems in their business that would call for violent reactions. Still, what had happened nagged at the back of his mind and he hadn't yet resolved the numerous questions he no doubt had.

Daria, on the other hand, doesn't look like she particularly cares about what happened. She knows enough about human body language, however, to realize that Lombe hadn't quite bought her story. That explains why she's remained so quiet—to make sure he doesn't feel encouraged to voice those questions.

At least it looked like she had her story straight, and he could concede that the lie—or deliberate omission of the full truth—was a good one. It didn't make it right, though, and he felt like his silence was a little complicit.

Is that why this situation has left me all prickly like I have a nagging worry I can't pinpoint? Am I concerned about what the captain will think if he finds out I've held back?

He'd honestly never had that kind of thought and it threw him a little with its suggestion of…well, humanness.

Maybe Daria had a good reason to attack the Red Crows and maybe she didn't. The main reason why she had been brought in as first officer was because Lombe wanted someone with a particular set of skills to head up what they needed in that department. That said, the Xi-Trang knew the man hoped she would abide by the same rules he lived by despite how complex and hard they were to explain .

Or, he thought hopefully, maybe Lombe was a little too focused on flying them through the tunnels toward Sector Thirty-eight. It was a nerve-wracking flight and one that required them to take one of the shuttles since the route was a little too narrow for them to bring the whole ship.

That in itself was enough to make the captain nervous since it meant they had very little in the way of armor. Worse, there was nothing in the way of weapons for them to use.

We're already taking a risk with this purchase, but now we're forced to move slowly and carefully through the dark caverns and deeper into the mines that crisscross the whole planet. As if the damn tunnels aren't extensive enough, the Jindahin continue to dig even deeper for the vital minerals and metals they need.

"You do remember that little something something about how these tunnels are supposedly infested with thousands of insectoid mutant monsters?" Daria asked once it was obvious that no one would break the silence that had fallen over the three of them. "It's nothing much to worry about, I'm sure, but shouldn't we have taken a few precautions? Maybe found a way to arm the shuttle somehow."

"Arming shuttles is illegal," Lombe reminded her shortly.

"Arming a ship like the *Atalanta* is supposedly illegal too but it doesn't stop people from setting ships like it up with as much firepower as they can afford. In this case, it seems like the people who are being paid to handle the menace have started to arrive, and they did so with fucking tanks and artillery. That kind of firepower makes me question why they don't simply hit the whole planet with an orbital strike and start again. But we have to navigate through it with an unarmed shuttle."

The captain nodded and negotiated carefully around a tight hairpin corner. "This might not be the best choice, but even if we were to find a way to arm the shuttle for this kind of venture, we would have the cops crawling all over us. It's best to simply take our chances. And the shuttle has some sensors that will be able to pick up on almost anything out there before we come in contact with it so maybe we'll have some warning, at least."

She leaned back in her seat, tilted her head, and still looked like she didn't quite approve of their whole approach. Be that as it may, it was exactly as Lombe had pointed out so succinctly—they didn't exactly have much of a choice.

"If they wanted to make this planet livable, they would have installed some kind of pacification resonators. It would be easy enough to tap them into the rocks around their mines," Jozzun said almost before he realized he'd intended to speak at all.

"Pacification resonators?" Daria asked and glanced at him.

He sighed, relaxed, and ran his fingers through his crest while he told himself he would have to consciously control that tic before someone decided to use it against him.

"Yeah," Lombe responded. "I heard that was something they used around the Xi-Trang worlds. It is a way to let them settle on the terraformed planets without having to cull the local wildlife. I was always under the impression that they weren't quite as effective as anyone thought they would be."

"They are effective," Jozzun assured him. "But there are limits. For the most part, it prevents non-sentient species from being too hostile, but they will attack if they start to feel threatened so you need to keep your distance, even if one is active. All it does is stop the native species from hunting the Xi-Trang before they can set up proper defenses and the like."

"It might be better to simply find a way to stop the creatures from approaching at all," Daria suggested. "Canids and leonids don't like anything to do with fire. At least that's what the stories say. In the early days, back when they would merely drop settlers on planets with nothing but a few blankets, tools, and maybe a herd to get things started, they had problems with the local wildlife so they built these...uh, fire walls. Like...they dug a trench, filled it with some kind of oil, and kept it burning until they could build their defenses up."

"I somehow doubt that would work with insectoids." Lombe scoffed. "Have you ever heard of the term like a moth to flame?"

The Xi-Trang smirked. "Well, it worked out well on my homeworld. We live in something like peace with all the local wildlife in and around the Saffron Sea. Of course, the Xi-Trang have another word for it, but the humans called it that because...well, the wind that whips across it and blows inland always smells of saffron. They installed the pacificators in the water. Somehow, that helps to spread the psychic energies over a larger reach. We lived in peace inside the borders and there was no unnecessary killing of non-sentient creatures that didn't know any better."

"That's the consequence of having a whole species out there with a connection with almost every living thing they come across, I guess," Daria suggested. "You can't help but be empathetic, even to a fault. Of course, there are the psychopaths among you, but then I haven't seen a species that doesn't have its worst representatives. At least you Xi-Trang have the good sense to keep yours in a prison settlement. Of course, they happen to be running the settlement, but...you know, semantics."

Jozzun chuckled softly and shook his head. "I am sorry about what you went through."

"It's not like you filled my head with torture that would be all kinds of illegal if they did it to my body."

"Hey. I was tortured a little too, you know," Lombe

pointed out. "Not for as long as she was, of course, but still. I had myself a tough time when I went in there to get her out. I'm only saying I might be owed an apology too."

Jozzun laughed in response and shook his head. "Fine. You have my sincerest apologies."

"Thank you."

The Xi-Trang nodded. "The resonators weren't always quite as effective at keeping the creatures docile, but those it didn't were kept away. I think here of the Wave-Prowlers—massive ocean creatures that would crawl onto land at night to hunt and then return to the sea before the sun came out. It burned their skin otherwise. I remember them because they never so much as came close to the pacificators. The elders always said it meant that the creatures it drove away were sentient and didn't like having any psychic energy playing with their minds."

"Hey, I can see the appeal of that," Daria commented and leaned forward when it looked like they had begun to approach a small enclave. It was tucked away inside the caves where more transports pulled in and out. "It's weird to think that a terraformed planet would simply evolve sentient beings, though. What were these creatures like?"

"Uh…massive, for one thing. Five or six times the size of most Xi-Trang. They had eight to twelve limbs and had no bones at all. This meant they were able to move across the ground without too much trouble and used those limbs to drag people into their mouths. Either that or they kept them trapped in their tentacles using the suckers on the bottom side. Those allowed them to grasp almost anything they took hold of. They were able to change their skin color to match their surroundings as well so they were almost invisible when they were underwater and definitely invisible in the dark of night."

"I think I know of that kind of creature," Lombe interjected as they began to descend outside the mine they were approaching. It was clearly marked with the number *38* carved into the stonework above them. "But those on my home planet were generally much smaller. Well, those that came to the surface, anyway. They were about twice the size of a human hand. Deep below was where you would find the larger ones that were able to drag whole boats into the depths, or so the legends said."

"That's interesting." Daria frowned in thought. "I always thought there was a difference between the planets that Xi-Trang and humans terraformed, but I guess there is always something that guides them toward a design that's more or less the same."

It didn't sound like either of them knew much about it. The process of terraforming was highly technical, to the point where people who hadn't spent decades studying it mostly had only a basic knowledge of how it worked.

Besides, it didn't matter at the end of the day. Finding planets in the so-called Golden Zone was always a big deal and generated intense bidding between the different civs over who would terraform it to their specifications. After that, it still took decades for a planet to form completely to the specifications of the civ that ordered it.

Even then—as Mugh-9 stood in a testimony—there were always unexpected side effects to the process. No one planet ever required the same process as another.

"Did you see one of those creatures yourself?" Daria asked, unbuckled from her seat, and stood to make sure all was well with the area where they landed. "Those...Wave-Prowlers, I mean."

"Not personally, but I did see holos of them when I was a kid. Usually, the warning vids told us why we were never allowed to leave the zones set up for us on the planet. I can still see them simply appearing out of nowhere in the darkness. Two eyes and an amorphous blob suddenly reached out for me with a dozen tentacles to grab, squeeze, and tear me apart, then dragged me into its beak-like mouth."

"How...how would they even get vids of that?" Lombe asked.

Jozzun shrugged. "Mostly by setting animals out as bait for the creatures to attack while they filmed. It wasn't the kindest way to dispatch the animals, of course, but we needed to know how the Prowlers hunted and that was the safest way for us sentient creatures. Why do you ask?"

The question was directed at Daria, although she needed a moment to realize he was talking to her.

"Hmm? Oh, I merely wondered if we would see something like that coming out of the darkness of the mines. A big, huge, amorphous blob that filled our viewscreen moments before it devoured our ship."

That was one hell of a visual. He wasn't sure he liked the idea, given that the Prowlers had always been something of a phobia of his. Although everyone said they needed to stay out of the sun and in the water to survive, a planet owned by the Jindahin would likely be humid enough for them to live in the open. And, he reminded himself, there was no sunlight in the tunnels.

Fear rippled through him and he realized that both Lombe and Daria shivered at the same time and turned to look at each other in confusion before they focused on him.

It was purely accidental and he'd never intended to spread the empathic fear of the monstrous things from the deep to the minds of the people around him. Embarrassed, he smiled and showed his teeth.

"I'm truly sorry about that."

"Yeah," Lombe muttered as they moved to the bay doors. "I always thought it was a serious faux pas to share your mind accidentally like that."

"Although it does present a slight evolutionary advantage," Daria interjected, clearly trying to make him feel better. "If you live in a flock like the Xi-Trang do, it's always a good thing to make sure the rest of your people can see and hear any dangers you pick up on, right?"

He'd heard that kind of talk before and as much as he appreciated her attempt, it didn't soothe him the way she might have thought.

"We don't live in flocks. Well, not anymore and not for thousands of years. These days, it's considered rude—almost to the point of…uh, farting in public or vomiting on someone. The usual response you get from that kind of thing is disgust. It makes people think maybe you're rude or sick and in need of medical help."

"Do we humans ever do something like that?"

"In a way but never to the point of what you just felt," Jozzun admitted as they approached where they could see a group of miners that had gathered and were now directed to different transport shuttles. "Most sentient minds have some type of empathic connection, which is what communicates with me through my crest.

But unless you have a crest too, it'll never be strong enough to project your sensations, feelings, and thoughts to another mind with the same level of impetus as we can."

"Well, you never know what the techies will come up with next," she quipped and motioned for Lombe to take the lead when the Jindahin supervisor noticed their arrival and moved toward them. "The next thing you know, I'll be fitted with an artificial crest and will bombard your mind with all kinds of unseemly thoughts."

"I'd take it as a kindness if you didn't."

"Fine. But I'd do it to the shits running that prison, whether they took it as a kindness or not. In a fucking heartbeat."

"If you did have one fitted, there is a level of…well, control that you would need to exercise to stop yourself from doing what I did by accident. I would imagine you would be embarrassed if you found yourself broadcasting almost every thought that came to your mind like a newborn might."

Lombe motioned them to quiet as the supervisor approached. Like most other Jindahin, he was dressed in as much that glittered in the light as he could carry. In his case, though, it looked like he wore it because he was comfortable with it. From what Jozzun knew of the species, it meant he was probably old money.

What interested the Xi-Trang more, however, were the other Dahin. The miners who worked there wore coveralls that hid most of their bodies. A survival kit was connected to each one in case they reached an area of the mines that was a little too dry for them to breathe. None of them had any of the brilliance on their clothes that would indicate that they had any status to speak of.

Although if I had to guess, I would say it isn't their choice to be dressed like the dregs of their society.

He assumed these were the Perdahin prisoners, members of their own species forced into what was essentially slave labor to prevent them from rising against the Jindahin status quo.

Defenses were present—tanks, turrets, and even drone stations were set up and ready to keep any monsters that attacked at bay. Everything was vibrantly colored in the way the Jindahin preferred, but something was garish about the brightness of it all.

The Perdahin were being loaded into the tanks and yelled at by the Jindahin, although he couldn't tell what they were saying. It sounded like a string of curses, and it was accompanied by enough physical abuse to make his blood feel like it was boiling.

No, not my blood, he realized a moment later. *Daria's blood, and she's holding her weapons like she is ready to draw them.* For now, though, it seemed like her self-control still held strong. She knew better than to get into a firefight out there. It was odd how powerful her psychic projection was—for a human, anyway.

Besides, all that abuse was a show put on for the benefit of the newcomers. Jozzun could see that much. It was mostly a display of power to make sure everyone knew how things worked in their little mining colony.

"You must be Captain Lombe," the Jindahin stated when he reached them.

"You can call me Travis if you like. This is First Officer

Hughes and Emissary Jozzun. You must be Masetrox Warro."

"Ugh." The Jindahin groaned. "The lowly officer ranks never suited me but my family thinks I need to climb them before I'm allowed to join them on the more civilized planets. Having to sift through the filth around here is bad enough, but I suppose there are perks as well."

The captain shrugged. "I feel for you, I truly do. I assume you only get promoted once you make enough money to buy your way through, which is why you're selling whatever sparse quantities of 'quik you can spare?"

"Yes, but I still have a quota to meet for the people who run these mines." Warro gestured for them to follow him and headed to what looked like an office with a thankfully small desk inside. "What they leave behind is what I can sell but in the end, it's usually what they wouldn't be able to sell any other way. Or, at least, what would be cheaper to simply leave in my storerooms to take up space. I have eighty liters and not the good stuff."

Lombe scowled and Jozzun could see why. *Eighty liters, likely of diluted 'quik, wouldn't be worth the effort or the fuel it has taken us to fly to the area. It isn't quite the way we wanted to start our day, but I can see that Lombe suspected this would be the case.*

"I can take it off your hands but not for the price you quoted me," the captain told him bluntly. "You wouldn't be able to sell it any other way and like you said, it's taking up space until you have to pay someone else to come in and dispose of it for you. And here I come, stepping in to save you all that cost and even pay you for the trouble. Let's say…a third of the price you quoted me per liter."

"The going price is a hundred and fifty per. You want to make it fifty?"

"It's a bargain if you ask me. How much would you pay to have it moved out of your stores to clear the way for new inventory?"

The supervisor smirked and nodded slowly. "I think we can make a deal. But I have a feeling you want a little more from me along with that kind of friendly price."

"I was a little transparent about that, wasn't I?" Lombe smiled easily.

The Jindahin studied the three of them before he motioned them into the office. "Let's discuss this in private."

CHAPTER SIX

"You know, there was a time when they wanted to man all these mines with bots."

Jozzun looked up and realized that the Jindahin was still speaking to Lombe as they settled into his office.

"It seems like it would be much cheaper these days," the captain responded and folded his arms.

"That depends. The Salifate likes the idea of these penal colonies on the less-established planets as a threat to keep the people in line. It's effective enough and makes sure the heretic layabouts know they'd better not try to push against the rules or they'll be expected to start pulling their weight in our society."

There was nothing for them to do other than keep their mouths shut while they had to deal with him—and even more so these days when the conflict would push people into the uncomfortable choice of one side against the others. People in the military especially would be expected to hold to the party line or their loyalty to the Salifate would fall into question.

It's something most humanoid species have a problem with and honestly, I've long since given up any attempt to understand it.

Of course, Lombe already knew most of this and while he wouldn't state it outright, these kinds of situations made people like them fall under suspicion. While Jindahin space was still wide open to them, if their planets were the stage for an intra-system war, now was the time to either establish themselves as working with or for one of the sides or get out.

The captain was aware of that as well but it seemed like he wouldn't make a decision one way or the other for the moment. They were there for a job and what they'd collected already wasn't enough to justify the effort and time they'd put into it. Besides, they had a crew to pay, and they wouldn't be happy about having a percentage of zero creds to split up.

"It's getting worse too." Warro continued with his complaint. "The fucking shits think they can increase their resistance to working their fair share and they claim the reports of the creatures deep underground are becoming more common. They're trying to get out of working, even though we've sent them in with proper guards.

"These are old excuses, but now that people are making a fuss about the fucking Bugz, they see it as a way to try to avoid the work they owe the Salifate. All the while, I'm the one blamed for their lack of production. Honestly, I cannot wait for the day when we decide to simply send these shits elsewhere and let us work with bots. They say it would cost more to repair and maintain them, especially if we pay the mechanics top dollar, but in the end, it will result in more production and more efficiency in the long run."

He showed no inclination to finish anytime soon and as much as Jozzun wanted to intervene, his tentative probe showed him that his effort would be pointless. The Jindahin as a species were far more difficult to influence with his abilities and some—like Warro had now proven to be—were particularly resilient. It wasn't necessarily because of anything in their genetics but they were merely more alert to what was happening in their bodies and they picked up on smaller changes that attempted to influence them from the outside.

Some studies said the Jindahin had a higher percentage of their population who were completely shuttered against the effects of the Xi-Trang psychic abilities. There were always questions about those studies since it wasn't like the Jindahin agreed to be test subjects.

Occasionally, the odd rumor would surface that in the distant past, abductions, interrogations— both psychic and verbal—and even vivisections had been performed by the Xi-Trang to understand the source of the phenomenon. However, no real evidence had ever emerged about the experiments, which would certainly have resulted in permanent damage to the relationship between the two species. Fortunately, neither of them was willing to act without any verifiable proof one way or the other.

Thankfully, time and commerce inevitably overcame the unease these rumors caused, but the Jindahin nevertheless regarded the Xi-Trang psychic abilities with a large degree of suspicion.

Still, there was enough evidence to support the assumption that they were resistant, at least in part, right in front of him. *I could probably find a way to communicate with the Jindahin idiot but honestly, it would be like whispering through a crack in a concrete wall.*

He turned his focus to the Perdahin outside but even that took a little more effort, no matter what he attempted. While he could try different angles of approach, the harder he tried, the more obvious his efforts would be.

The Perdahin he had touched with his mind seemed to realize that something was happening but his attempt didn't trigger the protest he expected. She remained calm as she looked at the office and her eyes narrowed when she saw him.

It wasn't much of a connection but enough to allow him to reach out to her. *Carefully, Jozzun. You don't want to send her into a panic.*

His first sensation was of a great deal of pain, which wasn't surprising given that she had received most of the abuse when they had approached. It was interesting that she seemed well aware of his presence there. The picture formed by what she shared was different than the impression he got from the Jindahin in the office with him.

I do not wish to harm you or your people, he assured her. *We merely wish to understand and learn about your situation without alerting the Jindahin to our interest.*

After a long moment, she responded and he was surprised by both her willingness and how easy she seemed to be able to use the connection. The miners, it appeared, were on a work-release program. This meant they owed a certain amount to the Salifate, which was determined by the amount of work they did in the mines.

A sum was deducted from the total amount they earned toward their release. It was a brutal scheme designed to get the most work out of people who had been forced into it.

Something else pushed through, however, and he let his mind sift through the messages.

We are only too anxious to get back to work but our hours had been cut, not by the supervisors like Warro but thanks to orders directly from the Overseers.

But why would they do that? he responded. *Don't they wish to increase the turnover?*

Word is that too many miners have gone missing, which is generally not much of a problem since they don't give a Bugz' balls about us. The real issue is that the gear and tools they had been sent out with proved to be a little too expensive for them to justify their loss.

What about the guards? I thought they were always here.

He was a little impressed that she even managed a telepathic grunt of derision. *That is true, of course, but their responsibility is to make sure the Perdahin don't sneak off with any of the materials we mine or smuggle 'quik to bolster our release accounts. When miners began to disappear, the guards didn't go looking for them. They merely told everyone to pack up and head back to camp.*

"Well, I'm already here picking up what you wouldn't have been able to sell otherwise," Lombe pointed out and distracted the Xi-Trang momentarily as changed the subject of the verbal conversation as subtly as he could. "This is the point where you help us by telling us where we might be able to find other camps that might want to unload their product."

The captain had picked up on what Jozzun sent him, that much was clear. The thought of how the prisoners were treated made him grasp his cane a little tighter than usual but otherwise, he showed no sign that he possessed information he shouldn't have.

This was different than the knowledge that Warro had already made an order for mercenaries to come in and support his sector, which was less expensive than arming and training his security force a little better. Time would tell if the savings were worth the hassle, although that came from the Jindahin himself.

"No offense, mind you, but having humans around is always a good way to show that sentient creatures are better at being violent than the non-sentient. But people who sign up to be mercenaries in the private sector are generally a step above what we've come to expect from the rest of your race. Still, we don't ask them to do much more than flush out the trouble instead of solving it completely."

Jozzun realized that the Jindahin they spoke to had begun to annoy him more than most. It was no secret that the Perdahin he'd been in touch with felt a very strong loathing for her superior and it was enough for him to take a risk.

He shifted his main focus to her. *Do you know of anyone who is selling some of the Darkquik that would make up for the pitiful haul we'll walk away with here?*

She turned to look at the Xi-Trang and studied not only him but also Lombe and Daria. He merely waited while she tried to decide if there was anything trustworthy about them that would justify sharing that kind of information. *Given that there isn't much in it for her, I couldn't blame her if she refused, and if we reported her to the superior, she would be in serious trouble. In all honesty, there is more than enough reason for her to simply lower her head and say nothing.*

He projected as much and showed her that they could afford to filter some bribes to her if she helped, which they were allowed to do anyway. People could feed into a prisoner's release fund without justification, although it usually came from family and friends who wanted to get people out of prison quicker. It was a system that allowed parties with money to get their privileged individuals out of serving any time at all without needing to justify it.

This particular broken cog would help them in this case, and the Perdahin nodded her assent before she resumed work on loading one of the tanks to head out.

She impressed him again when she continued their conversation while she seemed entirely focused on her task. He could only assume she'd had some experience with other Xi-Trang, for which he was very grateful.

I don't know of any specific locations that would have what you needed but I know of a place in the nearby port city where you could find someone who would get you what you want—a full damn cargo-hold full of Darkquik.

It was thin enough that even she knew it wasn't information that would bring her much in the way of a nondeclared bonus, but the Xi-Trang looked at Lombe, who still nodded and smiled while their host continued to bitch. The captain knew better than to make a physical sign of another conversation in progress but he answered in the affirmative.

The money wouldn't be too hard to get, and the amount the young Perdahin asked for made it a good enough deal that would at least get them within spitting distance of the people who could help them.

Images of the place didn't mean much to him, but the female's memories would help them find it. Jozzun transmitted them to Lombe since he wasn't sure the first officer would be willing or able to receive his message. He carefully made sure the fourth person in the room could not pick up on what was said, although it was unlikely he would, even without his caution. This was one of those instances where the Jindahin's mental block played in their favor.

The location appeared to be some kind of brothel and he imagined this would amuse Daria when she found out.

"I appreciate the intel and I'll look into it," Lombe said. "Unfortunately, we have a living to make so can't chew the fat all day, as the old saying goes."

"Is that an old saying?"

"An old human saying. It's probably from something violent in our past, I'm sure." He patted the Jindahin on the shoulder with a smile. "I'll let you know when we get through to your contacts, and we can find a way to do business in the future."

"I'll look forward to it."

Lombe motioned for the team to return to the shuttle and they moved quickly. There was no point in playing games when the clock ticked on when the locals would simply toss them off the planet, with or without their ill-gotten goods.

"Did you get anything of worth from Warro?" Jozzun

asked once they were in the shuttle. "I didn't pay all that much attention to what he was saying."

"Most of it was endless whining about why a rich little boy has to play at working before he can take his rightful place at his family's side—nothing worth our time, honestly," Daria answered as she strapped herself into the co-pilot seat. "What part of the other important conversation did I miss?"

"Jozzun made a connection with one of the Perdahin prisoners who gave us a location to start a search for a cargo-hold of what we need," Lombe answered. He made sure that what they had paid for was loaded before he sealed the door. "It's not much to go on but it's a start and better than having to deal with the corrupt officials on this fucking planet. Did you get her name?"

The Xi-Trang nodded. "Mar'fena Tafful. Do you think you can find her fund using only the name?"

"I'm already on it." The captain powered the shuttle on.

"Why...why are we paying for this intel anyway?" Daria asked. "It's not like she can turn us in if we fail."

"Well, there's the fact that I like to think of myself as an honorable soul," Lombe said and rolled his neck. "Besides, this is the way you cultivate connections for the future. You fulfill a contract when you don't necessarily need to and make them think you're trustworthy about shit. And it's not even that much in the bigger scheme of things."

"Three hundred creds is enough to take a month off her contract," Jozzun pointed out. "This is one of those situations where the worth of the creds is subjective."

"Right. It's not that much to us is what I meant. And in the future, if we need a contact among the Perdahin, we might be able to start with her. Think of it as more of an investment than anything else."

Daria sighed and nodded as the shuttle elevated.

"Besides, that moves us directly onto the next topic of conversation." Lombe grinned at Jozzun. "I told you we would have to tap the Darkquik market."

"Didn't you also tell me that it is very irritating to announce when you knew events would turn out a certain way?" Jozzun countered smoothly.

"That…" The captain paused, looked sharply at him, and scowled. "That only applies to psychics because you literally know what will happen."

"It doesn't quite work like that."

"Whatever. You peer into the minds of the people around you and judge the most likely result and so far, you've never been wrong. I'm only saying that it's different when a human does it based on our much more limited knowledge base."

"That's because it's based on coincidence rather than a knowledge base, no matter how limited."

"Exactly. Don't be such a know-it-all."

"Captain? You'll want to see this," one of the engineers called.

The *Atalanta* had begun to feel like home. Jozzun had never thought he would feel so comfortable in a home that moved, but everything about it—from the creaks and sighs of the external armor heating and cooling, to the stale smell of the filters in the atmo scrubbers—had begun to feel as comfortable as his childhood home.

It had been many years since he'd seen it, of course, and the chances were that the building had been replaced and rebuilt a dozen times over since he'd left. This meant that the *Atalanta* was home now, a realization that made him feel oddly secure.

Even the people he shared her with only made it feel more comfortable despite the irritations that touched them from time to time. These were merely small inconveniences and would always occur when people lived in close quarters with each other for extended periods of time.

He looked around and noticed that their three engineers had scrambled into the cockpit and seemed excited. Or at least that was what he could pick up on. The short, stubby mechanics were of a species that didn't use body language to convey what they wanted to say.

Their methods of communication with their species were similar to those of the Xi-Trang but fundamentally different. *Possibly even primitive by comparison*, he thought without any conscious attempt to be supercilious.

They were some of the finest engineers in the business, however, and he discovered that he had a few warm and fuzzy feelings about them as well. It was almost like they were his siblings, although the fact that they were mated made that comparison a little troublesome.

Even worse, they were psychologically so similar that it made it difficult even for him to tell the three apart, although he liked to think he was better at it than everyone else on the ship.

Lombe looked up from the screen and narrowed his eyes. "What have you got...Klyz?"

"I'm Klyz," the one in the middle corrected cheerfully. "Kleiz was the one who found what you'll be interested to see."

"It's from one of the items Daria found on the derelict station." Kleiz stepped forward and connected a node to the screens in the cockpit. "It looked like only a simple line of coding—which is why we missed it the first time—but we connected it to a multi-system program which allowed—"

"With some preparatory modifications," Kliz added.

"—a ship to emit an altered signal," Kleiz finished without so much as missing a beat despite the interruption. "Sensor readings and ident codes too that match any cataloged ship."

Daria tilted her head when she saw how impressed Jozzun and Lombe looked at the information the engineers shared with them. "Wait... This disguises our signal? So it lets us travel through almost any port of call without raising alarm bells?"

"As long as the vessel we choose has been cataloged, sure," the captain answered with a smirk. "We'll have to be careful when we use it, of course. I'm sure owning software like this is illegal, but provided we don't try to enter a port by using the identity of a ship that's already docked there, it should be simple enough for us to use."

The Xi-Trang nodded. "It's what happens when most ships don't usually come in close enough for them to see each other. Passive and active sensors would only be able to pick up on what's being actively broadcast—identity and allegiance codes for the most part. There's also the ambient information emitted by the other ship—engine bleed off, shield energy frequency, exhaust trails, and so forth."

"Most ships aren't picked up on visual scans until they're almost close enough to crash into each other," Lombe explained. "If we were to change even one or two aspects of our ship, the reality is that even the most rudimentary sensor system would identify the ruse. Even if you altered multiple points of identification, the precision required to mimic another ship's identical info ranges is complex. Failure to fall into those exact cataloged bands would at least register as an error and draw attention to the aberrant signal."

"Which you wouldn't want to do if you were broadcasting a pirated signal in the first place," Jozzun added, although he could tell that Daria was getting a little annoyed with them speaking to her as though she were a child.

Still, she didn't say anything since it was a vital part of their life and she was ignorant about it. As much as she was irritated by her lack of knowledge, there was only one way to correct it.

The captain leaned closer to make sure she understood what they were talking about before he continued. "Anyway, this code—"

"The Doppelganger Code," Kleiz interrupted.

"The...what?"

"That's the name of it," Kleiz explained.

"Written into the code," Kliz interjected.

Klyz took a step forward. "Seems like there might be

some history to it, but we'll have to do a little research before we make any definitive statements."

"But true enough."

"Might want to hold off on using it."

"At least until we know if dock protocols already have it flagged."

It was a little annoying when the three engineers did that. Each one finished the others' sentences, which made it much more difficult to tell them apart, but Lombe didn't seem to mind.

He cleared his throat and waited to make sure they didn't have anything else to add before he spoke again. "Anyway, the Doppelganger Code…" He paused and studied the screen for a long moment. "From what I can tell, it allows for almost perfect imitation. Unless there's a significant difference in size—think several magnitudes like a 'vette pretending to be a heavy cruiser or a battleship, for instance—it should hold up under even the tightest of scans."

"But like our engineers pointed out, the software might be flagged so we might want to run a quick check on our next port of call to make sure they don't have firewalls looking for something like it," Jozzun added.

Lombe smirked and nodded slowly. "It can't hurt to check but I've never heard of it, which means there's a good chance that no one's run into this code—or not for decades anyway. It isn't a bad discovery, all told. You never know when it might be a useful little something for a group of smugglers to have up their sleeves. And I have the perfect way to run a test on it."

The Xi-Trang could already see what the captain

wanted to test the code for and he narrowed his eyes and ran his hands over his crest, annoyed by the tic when he could see Daria had noticed it too.

"I don't think that's a good idea, Captain," he protested warily.

"Well, we've considered how to head to another port on the same planet. We're docked here as the *Atalanta* but we can dock somewhere else on the planet as a whole other ship. Unless someone's actively looking for us, they won't give a shit that a new group of freelancers has made planetfall, looking for work."

"Since we're already plugged into the dock's network, I'll be able to run a couple of tests to check if they already have flags on our software," one of the engineers pointed out. "We probably shouldn't switch the signal over until we're off the network, though."

Lombe tapped his forehead as he had already begun a few tests of his own and also alerted the port authority that they were getting ready to cast off the planet.

Daria looked like she hadn't quite bought into the whole idea, although it was clear that she wouldn't raise any issues with them since it was well outside her wheelhouse.

A little trust was in order and it seemed she was more than willing to give the captain and their engineers the benefit of the doubt, although Jozzun already knew what she would ask when she turned to look at him.

"We're about to do something very stupid, aren't we?"

The Xi-Trang tilted his head, his eyes narrowed as he tried to think of the right answer. "It might be stupid or it might be a genius move on the captain's part. The execution of it will determine if it is the former or the latter."

"I had a bad feeling you would say something like that." She pushed from her seat in the cockpit. "I'll get the Hounds ready in case they lock us down in port and try to board us."

"You do that."

Truthfully, he didn't think it was likely that anyone would pick up on their probing search. As long as they kept their signal the same as it had been when they made port and covered their tracks while they probed, it would probably be all right. The real test of the code would be when they entered the planet's atmo again and had to submit their landing codes to the port authority on the opposite pole.

If they were blocked and couldn't land, they would know the code was dangerous to use. Still, that was the best-case scenario among all the possible worst cases. If they suddenly had to fight off a fleet of combat 'vettes, they would know the coding worked a little too well and had accidentally given them the details for a ship that had been blacklisted by the Salifate.

By all appearances, it looked like their probes had gone unnoticed and Lombe began to move them away from the port.

Hundreds of ships made planetfall every day, even on a location as isolated from the rest of the galaxy as this one. It meant that all they needed to do was get out of sensor reach before they switched their codes and descended again.

The *Atalanta* was a comparatively common ship among

freelancers, so the model wouldn't be flagged unless, as the captain had pointed out, someone was already watching them when they requested reentry.

Lombe tilted his head, which was the only visual cue that said he wasn't fully confident in the plan. They had tried to find a way to get onto the planet unnoticed but in the end, all the code would do was make their work a little easier and cut maybe three or four hours off the time they would need to head into space before they were able to return.

Still, he wanted to try it because if it worked, it would prove to be very valuable in the future. *Shit, if we decide to simply sell the code to someone else, it would be easy to ask for millions of creds. Any number of corp—legal and illegal—would pay that kind of price without blinking an eye.*

"It doesn't look like any eyebrows are raised," Lombe stated with a grin. "All in all, it looks like a successful test."

"They'll still need to integrate it into the rest of the ship's systems," Jozzun commented and looked at Kleiz, who had remained in the cockpit to monitor the status of their first attempt.

"Sure, but it doesn't look like the switch has raised any red flags, and no one will look too closely on an outpost planet like this anyway," the diminutive engineer answered. "Now that we know it works, I can begin to install it across the *Atalanta's* systems and get the AI's comfortable with it. Should take a couple of hours, which will take some of those systems offline or make them glitch a little, so…fair warning."

The captain nodded and let the AI take over landing them on the other side of the planet. They had only a couple of hours before they docked. "It shouldn't be a problem. Wait until we're on the ground and alert the port authority to tell them you're running some updates so they don't think anything hinky is going on. We'll be off-ship for that time anyway. We have deals with the Perdahin to make."

"Of course, Captain."

It was an easier landing than the first one they'd made on the planet. The weather was better at the South Pole than the north, although Jozzun assumed it was something that changed from day to day. Still, it wasn't long before they engaged with one of the ports that connected them to the city.

"Are you all ready to go?" Lombe asked and tapped his top hat with his cane. "It's time to visit a brothel."

"About that..." Ishima interjected as she stepped into the cockpit. "Daria told me about what you plan to do."

"We're only going there on business," he assured her.

"I'm sure that's how it'll start but I still feel it's my duty as the ship's medical officer to make sure you head in there with a full medical once-over. It means I'll know what your condition is before and after partaking in any sexual activity."

"You have a very low opinion of me, don't you, Giselle?"

She tilted her head and looked almost insulted by the assertion. "My opinion of you is about as high as it'll ever get. I'm sure that while the plan is to head in there on business, you have to admit that your plans rarely ever play out the way that you want them to."

"Sure, but you don't call for a medical once-over on any of my other missions," he pointed out bluntly.

"Your other missions didn't take you to a brothel. Captain."

"They didn't?" Daria asked, folded her arms, and grinned. "Well, that'll have to change from this point forward. You can look forward to a whole lot of brothels and a fuck-ton of medical examinations."

"Shut it," Lombe warned, only half-joking.

"I'll admit that the captain will have to be monitored but I'm also interested in finding out if there are physiological differences in a Xi-Trang's body post-coitus."

Jozzun gaped when he realized that the doc's whole plan was to study him like a lab rat.

"I—what?"

"Well, your kind don't share the particularly human trait of constantly being in heat and I've always been curious to find out what goes on in a Xi-Trang's body."

It was difficult to be angry at the doc. She was only doing her job, after all. Besides, knowing them as well as she did meant she could make sure that when they needed her services, she was equipped with all the knowledge she needed to treat them.

But there was also the fact that she appeared to think of them all as merely test subjects and would probably publish some kind of paper on their interactions and travels. Hopefully, this would be once they were all dead and she needed something else to do with her life.

And he could tell that her intentions were mostly pure

too, which meant feeling offended by the insinuations wouldn't help anyone.

"My mating cycle has already passed," Jozzun muttered and tried not to let his embarrassment show on his pale skin. "Although with how busy we have been on the ship, I've had to appease my body's needs on my own a few times to take the edge off."

Daria laughed at that. Ishima had no visible reaction, but the captain winced when he heard it.

"Shit, I didn't need to know that," he protested.

"Are you telling us that you've never needed to appease your body's needs on your own while we've been on the ship, Captain?" the first officer asked with a grin. "Especially since you haven't visited many brothels lately?"

"I already told you to shut the fuck up."

The doc sighed and looked disappointed by the news. "Oh, well. I'll still take a few vials before you leave anyway, just in case. This means I'll expect all three of you to visit my clinic before you head out."

"Yes, ma'am." Daria offered the other woman a mock salute as she headed out, likely to prepare the tests she needed.

CHAPTER SEVEN

The city at Mugh-9's South Pole looked like it was far more densely inhabited than the one in the north. Jozzun could tell that almost immediately when they emerged from the tunnels that led them to the port.

They opened into a massive chamber that was only partially underground from the looks of it. All the markers for a larger city were present. Aerial traffic was cordoned off to prevent any of the inevitable accidents from hitting the many buildings. More than a few of these were tall enough that they integrated directly with the ceiling of the chamber and if he had to guess, most of them probably extended above ground as well.

Openings in the cavern ceiling were marked as no-fly zones for the shuttles that streaked across the city's "skyline," and while it was open to the rest of the planet's atmo, shields were in place to stop the dangers of the weather from getting inside.

It seemed a little hazardous that they appeared to leave

the safety of the city at large to a few shield generators, but almost everything on the planet was a hazard anyway. Hellish weather abounded above-ground and monsters waited below.

Why would the hab zones on the planet be any different?

"This feels like my kind of place," Daria commented as they approached a shuttle that waited for passengers arriving from the port to ferry them all to the city below. "You know there's a thriving underworld down there that relies on the corruption of the city officials who only care about padding their pockets."

"How do you know?" Lombe asked and raised an eyebrow as they found seats on the shuttle and waited for it to move along the wire that directed it to the city.

"None of the larger buildings are up to any safety code I've ever seen," she answered with chuckle. "You can tell a lot about a city by how safe its buildings are. Most of the safety requirements are standard across the galaxy, so the only reason those aren't being enforced is because the city officials don't mind taking a payoff to let cheaper construction slide. In fact, they don't even care that it's visible to the rest of the city that they aren't doing their jobs."

Jozzun hadn't even thought about that. Whatever knowledge she lacked when it came to space travel, she certainly made up for it with her basic knowledge of how criminality worked from planet to planet.

He also noticed that she wore the node that connected her to the Hounds, although she possibly only used it for the benefits it provided when she was in a combat situation. She hadn't worn it when they fought the Red Crows on the other side of the planet, but she had clearly learned from that particular mistake and wouldn't be caught off-guard again.

It wasn't quite the attitude he would have liked to see from their first officer but given what she had said about the city's likely vibrant criminal underworld, maybe it was better to be prepared for almost anything. They could still hope they would be pleasantly surprised.

"Do you know where we're going?" Daria asked once the shuttle reached the bottom and the doors opened.

The Xi-Trang couldn't help but flinch at the overly ripe smell of the city that greeted them. It was the kind of thing that happened when thousands or millions of people of various species lived together in close quarters.

The situation was made even worse when the city's infrastructure was not designed to adjust to the uptick in population numbers. Inevitably, it became difficult for the people who tried to keep the city clean and habitable to keep up.

Still, given the almost overwhelming number of people living there, maybe the smell was merely something they got used to over time. He couldn't imagine that he would, but there were various ways to adapt even to that. A good gas mask would filter the worst of it.

"Yeah, I know where we're going. I looked up the location on the way down." Lombe gestured for them to follow him. "It's close to here too from what I can see. Still, we don't want to get lost, so we need to get in, make a connection with our contact, and get out as quickly as possible."

"I can agree on that point," Jozzun noted and cleared his throat.

Daria smirked. "Don't let anyone bump into you and if they do, be sure you have all your possessions on you when you break away."

"I've been around pickpockets before," the captain answered, rolled his eyes, and reached down for his tablet, likely to check his map and make sure they were on the right path.

He patted his pockets a few times before he turned to where she held the device up with a smug look on her features.

"That's not fair," he muttered and snatched it from her fingers. "I trust you enough to let you get in close enough to pickpocket me."

"Clearly. But don't extend that familiarity to anyone else around here."

If the Xi-Trang had to guess, he would have suggested that the city was exactly Daria's kind of stamping ground. This was verified by how comfortable she looked despite the abrasive sights and smells all around them. Her hands rested on her weapons and he knew she was a split second from having them drawn, aimed, and ready to shoot, but that didn't mean she wasn't also relaxed.

Shit, her most relaxed moment is probably when she is a split second away from blasting someone's head off.

"Are you sure you want to work with the Perdahin?" she asked as they continued to navigate the winding streets of the city. "They're not all that popular around these parts. Fuck, the Jindahin will probably go so far as to label them as terrorists in a not too distant future if they haven't already."

"One man's terrorist is another man's freedom fighter," Lombe commented. "As long as no one catches us working with them, we'll be able to open connections with the group without alienating our 'friends' among the Jindahin too. Working both sides is the best way to make money in a situation like this."

She snorted. "Right up until someone shoots you because they don't want you to supply their enemies with weapons or contraband cigs."

"We'll simply add them to the very long list of people who want to shoot us anyway," he answered and pointed a little farther ahead. "That's where we're going. Keep a low profile and try not to cause any trouble."

Daria snorted. "Why are you looking at me when you say that?"

"Because you're the one who got us into a firefight the last time we tried to keep our heads down and not cause any trouble."

"How long will you throw that in my face?" Her pout was almost cajoling.

"At least until the week is out," he retorted. "Provided we survive that long."

It wasn't much of a given at this point, although Jozzun didn't think he needed to add that to the captain's blunt reminder.

The establishment they were heading into looked a little more upscale than the buildings around it. Despite the untidy sprawl of slums around them, the brothel itself —creatively named the Come Right Inn—complied with all the city's standards for building safety. It was painted a rich purple that reflected all the neon lights around and it openly displayed the services offered.

On top of catering to almost every physical vice generally expected from a brothel, it also provided a handful of restaurants, a few gambling dens, and even hotel housing for those who needed it.

From what the Xi-Trang knew about such places, they usually lost money on almost all the amenities they offered to encourage their patrons to spend heavily on the services and vices that were offered at a severe markup in price.

The plan didn't involve them staying longer than it took to get a drink and some intel on a location for the 'quik they were looking for, but he could tell that Daria inspected the services on offer carefully and seemed more than a little interested.

Jozzun didn't like knowing that about her. *It's yet another reason why I shouldn't look into the minds of people without their permission. Private thoughts were exactly that for a reason.*

Still, she wouldn't act on anything that interested her for the moment. From what he could tell, she had merely made a mental note of everything so she could make use of it when they had the time.

"Did you find what you've been looking for?"

The voice startled him and he froze in place. He realized that they'd stepped into the building and the captain was already ordering drinks and a booth for them while they tried to decide what their next move would be.

Lombe would expect him to pick up on the people they were looking for. The fact that they were looking for

Perdahin did narrow their options a great deal since they need to find Dahin and the whole building was filled with almost every race imaginable.

It should have to be easy to to find them even with the crowd for but he was slightly distracted. He shook his head to clear it and turned his attention to the person who had spoken to him.

The Xi-Trang woman was almost as tall as he was, with the same slim look about her, but her eyes were a little harder. Their coldness drew his attention to how blue they were in sharp contrast to the bright red of her crest feathers.

"I'm sorry?" Jozzun almost coughed and noticed that the captain and Daria were already returning with drinks.

"It's not usual to see one of my kind this far from home," she answered with a smile.

It was unsettling to recall what it was like to be around his kind. For one thing, he had to recall the manners he should observe, especially when it came to scanning the locals. It was a little disconcerting to discover that he'd lost some that had possibly even been deeply ingrained habits. She would make his job a little more complicated than it needed to be.

"Nor I," he admitted, returned her smile, and inclined his head in a polite bow. "I'm here with the...the rest of the crew of my ship. Well, not my ship, but...uh, you understand."

A light touch on his consciousness was enough to tell him that she did understand.

"I am Yorua'fenn Palaza and the inn is my establishment. I trust you'll feel right at home."

The inn belonged to her. He found that interesting. *Of course, it makes some sense to have a Xi-Trang with her feathers intact running a brothel like this one. She would be able to look into the minds of the patrons and determine what they want almost immediately.*

It did explain the success of the establishment, at least.

"Hello," Daria commented with a smile. "It looks like Jozzun made a friend."

His eyes widened when he realized he had unintentionally reached out to his crew and made them return to him a little faster than they might have otherwise.

"My apologies," Palaza answered with a smile and a bow to the other two. "It is uncommon to see one of my kind in this area of space so I could not resist coming to make his acquaintance—especially one as regal-looking as…"

All three of them looked at him and he realized this was the point in the conversation where he was supposed to provide his name.

"Jozzun," he blurted and cleared his throat. "Emissary Nu'ach Jozzun, of the *Atalanta*."

"Wait." Daria growled and narrowed her eyes. "Regal-looking? Does that mean Jozzun here is a stud by Xi-Trang standards?"

The madame laughed. The musical sound made Jozzun smile before he even realized what he was doing.

"Yes, I suppose the mammalian comparison is rather appropriate," she answered.

"Sorry. Captain, Daria," he said hastily when he remembered his manners. "This is Yorua'fenn Palaza, the madame of the inn. Palaza, this is Captain Travis Lombe and First Officer Daria Hughes."

Palaza lowered her head. "You humble me with your presence in my establishment. I am sure you will find what you have come looking for, even if it is not advertised among the many services we provide."

She motioned for them to move to one of the more isolated booths and Jozzun realized that she had immediately discerned what the captain had come looking for. He couldn't, however, pick up any intention on her part to alert the authorities.

If he tried to push in more, it would be considered prying and since it looked as though she would help them with their problem, he wouldn't raise much of a stink over it. They should, however, proceed cautiously.

Lombe nodded at the message passed to him by Jozzun, although Daria seemed a little distracted, immediately and completely enthralled by the sight of a female Xi-Trang. Maybe she hadn't seen any of them while she'd been in prison. Or maybe she wouldn't have been able to tell the males apart from the females in there.

They settled quickly into the booth and the madame joined them and leaned a little closer.

"It is interesting to see a human so used to being around one of my kind that he is able to pick up messages sent," she noted. Jozzun realized that it was her way to be honest about what she knew, which he chose to take as a good sign.

"You don't miss a trick, do you?" Lombe asked.

"I do not. And you should know that what you've come looking for is very dangerous. Not only because of who you'll have to acquire it from but those you'll need to avoid while picking it up. Still, it does not look like you shy away from danger."

"We don't dive into danger without necessity if that's what you're suggesting," Daria interjected, leaned back in her seat, and sipped her drink, but one hand was noticeably absent from the top of the table.

He didn't need to read her mind to tell that a hand rested on the handle of her caster to be sure that if the madame posed them any danger, she would be ready to finish her off, no matter what kind of mess it would cause.

In the bigger scheme of things, murder charges were practically nothing compared to what would rain on them if it was discovered that they were associating with Perdahin. If they weren't careful, they would waste their lives away as prisoners in one of the mines.

Palaza appeared to realize how quickly her life would end if she gave Daria the wrong impression as well and she raised her hands delicately.

"Please note that I pose no danger to your endeavors," she said and kept her voice low. "In fact, I am the one your contact sent you to find. I regularly deal with the people who have what you are searching for. While they might be difficult to deal with, I can assure you they honor the deals they make, and what they carry will more than pay for the effort it will require for you to acquire it."

Lombe nodded and seemed to understand that she was talking about more than only money, although some of that would be required as well.

It didn't look like Daria would relax, no matter what assurances were made, but her attention had shifted to the rest of the room as if to make sure no one was listening to their conversation.

It wasn't one that needed to be held verbally and Jozzun opened the communication between himself, the captain, and the madame. Daria could listen as well if she wanted to, but she was more interested in keeping an eye on the rest of the room. She took her job as their muscle very seriously.

Palaza began to give the captain the lay of the land. *The Perdahin have a presence on the planet but they have to maintain a low profile, especially with the added mercenary presence being brought in. They are working to liberate their people and send them off the planet.*

Lombe shrugged. *While this kind of context is good to know and I'm not hardened to the situation they are in, I'm not sure how much it has to do with us.*

The madame met his gaze squarely. *How much would depend entirely on you, Captain. They already have contacts who assist them to ship their people off-world once they are liberated, but they still needed to be transported across the planet with as much protection as could be spared for them. It is a delicate and often dangerous process.*

Jozzun narrowed his eyes in thought. *I could have misinterpreted the message, but the deal appears to be that the Perdahin are willing to part with their stocks of 'quik if the smugglers were willing to work with them a little.*

"I think you have the rights of it," Lombe muttered from around the lip of his glass, leaned back in his seat, and cast a glance at Daria to make sure no threats had presented themselves before he turned to the madame again. "Do you think they would be willing to deal with us on this?"

"Given that you have already made the connection with one of their captive sisters, I don't see why not, especially since you kept your end of the bargain that was struck to direct you to me."

Lombe turned to glare at Jozzun, who shook his head sheepishly.

"I must apologize, Captain Lombe," Palaza continued hastily, "but you must understand that I needed to make sure you were trustworthy before I revealed anything to you. This required me to determine that the deal you made that brought you to my doorstep was honored. You can call it a test if you like."

It seemed as though the madame was more than merely a collaborator with the Perdahin—not quite a true believer in the religious beliefs that put them at odds with the Jindahin but something a little simpler. The slave labor employed on the planet was abhorrent enough to her that she was willing to help however she could.

Jozzun realized that she was looking at him and had shared that information openly. She kept her mind open and allowed him to look through to ensure that the trust cultivated went both ways.

He turned to nod at the captain, who relaxed a little more in his seat.

There was more from her mind than only what he was supposed to see to establish that they could trust her. As he touched on this—accidentally, of course—a strong spike of empathic desire seared through all his careful control. It was intensely hot and heavy and Jozzun realized his cheeks were a little flushed. Of course, he expected someone working in a brothel to say he was regal, but it was something else entirely to realize that she meant it and so much more.

Daria—of course she would—picked up on that immediately. No psychic communication was required to tell her he was embarrassed, although it had begun to exude from him before he could even try to stop it.

His reaction spread to her and the captain as well, and a visible flush appeared in their cheeks as the empathic connection shared more than he'd intended.

"It's been a while since you've been around one of your kind, then?" Palaza asked with a coy smile.

There was no way Daria would let him out of this situation without some severe mockery, and while he was a few months away from his mating cycle, he realized that he now entertained a slight hope that he could return to the inn to indulge himself in the future.

At least in this case, he was better at keeping his composure and his thoughts to himself.

"Back to business," Lombe insisted and took a sip from his drink to cool off. "Helping the Perdahin isn't quite what we're equipped for. If we aren't able to help them, would they be willing to deal with us anyway?"

"I see no reason why not, but you might find the drop in price for those who help their cause is significant."

"Is that why you're helping them?" Daria asked. "A drop in prices?"

"I have my reasons. The point remains that I've chosen to be their connection for anyone who might decide to help for pay or...other reasons. Whether you'll be willing to help or not is up to you, but I can assure you they will deal with you either way."

"Would you mind if I discuss this with my crew before we answer?" the captain asked.

"Of course. Call your waitress when you have come to a decision. Or if you need a drink or...any of the other services that we offer."

It was not lost on Jozzun that her gaze lingered pointedly on him with that phrase before she glided out of the booth and moved away to continue to tend to the booming business of the inn.

"What do you guys think?" Lombe asked and looked at each of them in turn. "It seems like we could save some money if we help them with whatever they need help for. And it would solidify us as connections for them to use in paying work."

Daria scowled and shook her head. "It's one thing to do business with them. That's what smugglers do. But if we're part of the process to jailbreak their people from the planet, the Jindahin could start to think we're more than merely business associates. They might think we're part of their cause, whatever the fuck that means, and it will lead them to treat us as enemy combatants instead of smugglers. Enemies instead of a necessary nuisance."

"That's assuming they can pin anything on us at all," Jozzun pointed out and raised an eyebrow as he threaded his fingers through his crest. "With the Doppelganger Code, we'll be able to keep them spinning in place even if we are seen working with the Perds."

She didn't look like she was entirely convinced, although it came from not knowing how effective the code was in the first place. He could understand where that came from too. She was used to relying purely on skills to get in and out of tough situations. To have to rely on software she knew nothing about was foreign and therefore frightening for her.

The Xi-Trang appreciated that she refrained from commenting on how she might have thought he had only agreed to the plan because he had the hots for the madame. It wasn't called for at all, and while she thought it, she wouldn't make that kind of comment in their current situation.

"It's your decision ultimately, Cap." She sighed and finished her drink. "If you're willing to trust the code and the Perds, as Jozzie here calls them, we might as well give it a try. A significant drop in the pricing means a bigger cut, and I'm sure you'll pay me a hefty bonus from the profits for dragging both your asses out of any fires we wander into."

"I think it's a risk but a worthwhile one," Lombe admitted. "Jozzun?"

"I'm not particularly fond of being called Jozzie, as you well know," he stated bluntly and shook his head. "But I agree with the captain. It's a risk but a worthwhile one."

"That means I'm outvoted," she answered. "Let's see what they want from us."

Lombe nodded and pressed the button that would summon their waitress.

Palaza knew what their answer was before she reached their table with a bill for them to sign for their drinks.

"Are you sure I cannot tempt you to stay a little longer?" she asked once she'd passed on the details of how they could contact the Perdahin and the job they were walking into.

"I don't know...maybe Jozzun wouldn't mind sticking around for a while," Lombe responded and nudged his arm. "We don't run into many Xi-Trang outside of business, so maybe you two will want to exchange stories about your homeworlds or something."

What surprised him most was the fact that the captain's offer was genuine. Maybe he only wanted to give him time to interact with a familiar face for a while. Or he thought he and Daria could do the job on their own, or merely that they could wait until he could join them again.

He had no intention to stick around, though. Given how few of his kind they usually encountered, he hadn't expected to run into a Xi-Trang. It had thrown him a little and he needed to get his head on straight again before he said or thought the wrong thing.

"I...uh, I might come back to enjoy the pleasures offered by the inn," Jozzun answered and maintained a firm grasp on his thoughts to prevent them from being shared, either empathically or psychically. "But for the moment, I will have to decline."

"Well, I look forward to the day you choose to grace my humble inn with your presence again." Palaza bowed her head graciously as they turned to leave.

Daria was practically bursting with what he knew would be her making the most of his discomfort but she had the good sense to wait until they were out before she spoke.

"I think our good friend Jozzun is in love," she whispered and punched him gently on the arm. "Who knew our ship's emissary was such a looker?"

"Well, I brought him on board for his mind but I guess I

could say I planned to use his good looks all along," Lombe quipped with a grin. "Maybe the next time we need to break someone out of prison, we could send him in to seduce all the guards so we don't need to fight our way out again."

"I don't think he has the stamina for that kind of thing, Captain. Maybe we need to send him to the inn on the regular to get him trained to seduce fifty or so prison guards at the same time."

He knew this was inevitable but he couldn't help but feel like they pressed him a little too hard. *Still, they are my friends so perhaps this is a kind of rite of passage. I need to look into human customs more since I have to interact with them all the time. Besides, maybe the time will come when Daria comes face-to-face with a human she is infatuated with. That would be my turn to tease her mercilessly and she wouldn't be able to complain either.*

Jozzun paused suddenly and harnessed his thoughts when he felt a prick of intensity at the back of his mind. His companions continued to find ways to tease him about his encounter with the madame, but it seemed that had distracted them from possible danger in their vicinity.

It wasn't quite clear where it came from so he kept his mind fairly open and waited for something to alert him to any dangers they might face.

He scanned their surroundings quickly as they returned to the shuttle that would take them to the *Atalanta*.

The source of the distraction was suddenly apparent. Dozens of mercs had spread across the streets, likely looking to spend their signing bonuses before they were sent to deal with what monsters could be found in the depths.

One particular group stood out thanks to the bright red bird displayed on the armor they still wore. Members of the Red Crows merc corp were out and looking to spend their creds.

That alone had been enough to catch Jozzun's attention. His mind had been open to any thoughts directed at the three of them in particular and in this case, it seemed the ten or so fighters so had recognized Daria.

It's a little too soon for the news to have spread that she attacked one of their groups on the other side of the planet, which begs the question of why these have recognized her.

They whispered amongst themselves but their thoughts were jumbled. There wasn't enough context for the Xi-Trang to know exactly why she had caught their attention, but he didn't particularly appreciate the fact that she had.

He reached out to the captain and Daria and interrupted what he was sure was some truly hilarious teasing on their end. Lombe sobered almost immediately but she needed a little more nudging before she picked up on what he was trying to send to her.

In the end, the image of a bright red crow projected directly into her mind's eye quieted her, and she flipped her hair with a laugh to make it seem as though they were still deeply engaged in the teasing. The casual gesture enable her to catch a glimpse of the mercs in question out of the corner of her eye without making it obvious that she had looked at them.

It was a smooth move on her part but the seriousness of

the situation was immediately imprinted on his mind by her reaction.

What the fuck do those bastards want? Will the assholes never learn?

It didn't bode well at all, especially given how the mercs now appeared to communicate with other members of their corps while they watched her specifically.

"Let's get back to the ship," Lombe whispered tersely.

CHAPTER EIGHT

"I'm not sure I like the idea of heading off to find these freedom fighters in the making without any real weapons," Daria commented and leaned back in her seat. "I mean, they gave us a timeline to work with. It's not like they could go anywhere until we arrive to save the fucking day."

She'd raised the point more than once and this time, Jozzun was on the side of getting the job done as quickly as possible before they left. Talking about weapons was merely something Daria did when she was bored.

It was a long flight across a planet they couldn't travel on the surface of, which meant they had to fly the shuttle through tunnels that were specifically designated for air travel. They had a map to tell them where they were going, but that was essentially all they had to work with.

Jozzun realized that their first officer had reached a point where she wished the insectoid monsters they had heard so much about would make an appearance. It seemed a little extreme but indicated how desperate she was to have something to do other than monitor the feeds.

"The whole point of the situation is that we're out here trying not to be seen by anyone," Lombe explained. "And if we attach a whole slew of weapons to our shuttle without any kind of contract to explain why, the wrong people will ask questions."

"She knows that," Jozzun muttered and scratched his jawline. "She's simply bored and wants to talk about something because we've been silent this whole time."

"Three points to Jozz—uh, Jozzun over there. There's nothing wrong with a little quiet time, but the fact that we have to be on the alert and wait for an attack that might never come makes it so much more depressing."

The captain nodded. "Well, we have our ship waiting for us under a fake name and the whole purpose of this mission is to make sure we can flit in and out of Jindahin space without them thinking we're helping their enemies. Honestly, the Doppelganger Code might be one of the best things to ever happen to our little crew. It's the perfect disguise for a smuggler."

"You're welcome." Her tone carried a little more snark than was possibly appropriate.

"Well, you didn't know what you were picking up in there. It's kind of a crime that we had to blow the whole fucking station to pieces, though. From what your HUD recorded, only one of the items we could have retrieved would have been enough to set us all up for a life of luxury or—at least less misery."

"The number one rule in any situation where you have to fight for your life is knowing you can't spend any fortune if you're dead. Living is the fortune you never stop spending," she responded glibly.

Lombe chuckled and shrugged. "I suppose that depends on what you're living—or dying—for. Perhaps some people don't want to live long enough to spend certain treasures."

"Sure. And many people wouldn't mind ending up on the wrong end of a caster if it means their families are able to live in luxury. The Pennington Brothers made quite a living out of that. They got innocent people to steal or kill for them by choosing names of the folks who were dying of terminal illnesses, then promising to pay money into a blind trust in their children's names or something like that."

"Right, the P-Bros. Do you know what happened to them?"

"Last I heard, they retired to Mansio, stage fights with retired Tekkans, and give the money to charity to rehabilitate their image or something like that."

"It's amazing what rich people are willing to forgive when you rub shoulders with them." The captain shook his head. "Is there anyone out there you might do something like that for? Someone you wouldn't mind dying for so they could have a comfortable life?"

"Probably not," Daria answered without hesitation. "If there's one thing I've learned while I've dragged my sorry ass through almost every ounce of misery I could stumble on, it's knowing that a comfortable life isn't quite what it's cracked up to be—especially if you find out that a loved one died to earn it for you. I think, if I was ever presented with that kind of choice, I would choose to stand with that loved one instead."

"What if you were already dying of something?"

"We're all dying of something. Someone told me that humans kill themselves by oxidizing their bodies repeatedly with every breath they take. That's another interesting thing about the situation we're all in together. No matter how rich and powerful you are, we all die."

"Sure, but if you're rich and powerful, you get to extend that somewhat limited life by seventy or eighty years. I hear a couple of corp heads these days are looking forward to celebrating their bi-centennial."

Daria laughed at that. "Can you imagine spending your life being so terrified of death that you'd do anything—and I mean anything, including and not limited to keeping yourself in a rotting body for over a century—simply to delay the inevitable? I tell you, it's people like them who always get cancer from the sheer stress of being terrified for their lives for decades."

Lombe snorted. "And you have another philosophy?"

"Sure." She shrugged. "Find ways to enjoy your life no matter what. Charge into gunfights, keep the bullets flying, always play the part of the person who doesn't care, even though you do. We all have that sword hanging over our heads, so we might as well make sure we don't have any large regrets when it finally happens. Besides, the best way to forget that you're going to die is when you stand over the bodies of fifteen people who tried to kill you. That or a nice hard dicking. Or giving one, depending on whether you're in possession of one or not."

That drew a laugh from Lombe, but Jozzun tilted his head as he tried to find a meaning in what she had said. *Given the experiences she's been through in her life, it sounds very much like a coping mechanism—almost like something she needs to tell herself to not only survive it all but to thrive in the lifestyle she has been compelled to choose for herself.*

He couldn't tell if his theory was correct or not. Looking that deep into someone's mind was something he would only ever do with their express consent since digging into the subconscious mind was a truly unpleasant experience for the person being dug into.

That was—as only one example—precisely why the Jindahin had developed such an intense abhorrence to this particular ability of the Xi-Trang.

"Do you think humans will ever find a way to avoid death completely?" Jozzun asked and folded his arms. He felt like it was a decent way to continue the conversation and get a sound read on what Daria felt as she answered the question.

"Well...it could happen. Medical advances occur every day. There's nothing more human than the need to avoid our last gasp and that, in the end, is what makes us what we are. Eventually, someone will find a way to integrate their consciousness into a computer server and use that as a way to live forever. Maybe they already have, or something else. But my theory is that the moment when we no longer have to worry about dying is the point where we stop being human."

Now that was an interesting theory and a thought that had never occurred to the Xi-Trang before. One of the driving impulses of mammals was to avoid death. Canids had a tendency to chew their leg off if it was caught in a trap, for example.

If there is no fear of death, is the creature that remains even human?

"I'm picking up on something," Lombe interjected and leaned forward to study the data. He overlapped the sensors to make sure what he had seen wasn't merely a blip that had nothing to do with their presence in the area.

"What might that be?" Daria asked and peered a little closer. "Please, oh please, let it be the underground monsters."

"There's an old saying about being careful what you wish for, but I fear that falls well short of what we need right now," Jozzun commented.

His responsibility was to reach out ahead to find out what the hell was moving around there. A brief sense of a large cavern was confirmed as they approached and the overlapped sensors began to provide them a decent view of the chamber that opened up ahead.

It had been on the map given to them, of course, but the word in the market was that the beasts known as Bugz liked to do a little digging to bring tunnels down and start new ones. They even had a way to build walls that required a special solvent or a considerable amount of potent explosives to get through.

Honestly, the more I hear about the creatures, the more difficult it is to understand why Daria is so anxious to run into them. Maybe she needs some kind of confirmation that they exist along with a hint of having the bragging rights of having killed one of the beasts herself.

The mercs he'd found who had encountered them had described the insectoids as tough, difficult to kill, and almost impossible to find unless they wanted to be found.

This usually resulted in a swarm that required a hasty retreat or that particular group of mercs would disappear.

Although it did create an excellent cover for the Perdahin who hid in the tunnels. Perhaps it wasn't quite something they wanted to be associated with, but it was always better to have their enemies assume the monsters had done the killing when a group disappeared in there.

These are certainly not monsters of any kind—depending on your perspective, of course. Non-sentient creatures were easy to distinguish from the sentient ones, and the signals he received from the group ahead of them were most certainly sentient.

Even worse, they were human—and lying in wait, so the monster definition might be moot after all—so any hopes that it was the Perdahin with an advance scouting team were soon dashed as well.

"We need to step on it." Daria growled her annoyance. "Those are AG bikes and it looks like they were waiting for us."

The question of how the Red Crows knew exactly where to find them in the mess of the tunnels would have to be addressed later. They were in a fairly open chamber at the moment, and the shuttle's engines were more than capable of putting some distance between them and the bikes. That would come to an end, however, and they would have to navigate through the tunnels with the bikers on their heels. The enemy vehicles were far better equipped to handle the tight turns and the narrow gaps left for them.

"Shit." Daria knew exactly where his thought process was leading them and she unbuckled herself quickly as

Lombe began to accelerate through the chamber. He pushed the craft toward the other side as fast as possible as the low howl of the bikes erupted behind them.

They were losing ground rather predictably, but they would surely know it wouldn't last. Maybe that was why they had brought the AG bikes instead of a shuttle. Of course, they knew the planet and the tunnels far better. The chances were they merely needed an inkling of where the *Atalanta* crew were heading for their knowledge of the subterranean passages to enable them to find a shortcut.

Those routes wouldn't be large enough to accommodate a shuttle like theirs, probably, and likely involved a fairly rough ride, which made him wonder why. What could they possibly want with Daria that would drive them to such lengths?

Revenge wasn't all that was on their minds, although he could tell that they knew about what had happened at the North Pole and wanted to make her pay for that too.

Something else drove them, however, and it went further back than Jozzun was able to reach for. He could with a little effort, of course, but he had a feeling they wouldn't have the opportunity for him to simply sit back and probe their minds for intel.

That would probably have to come later. He turned and watched them closing in on the tunnels again with alarming speed.

"I'll need your help with this one, Jozzun," Lombe admitted in the calm voice he usually used when he did some particularly difficult piloting and his mind was mostly on that. "We need to know where they'll attack from and how I can avoid it once we're no longer in the faster vehicle."

The Xi-Trang nodded, narrowed his eyes, and felt a prickle at the base of his spine when his body warned him that more energy rushed through his feathers than was comfortable for any of them.

"They won't try to bomb us out of the sky," he whispered, closed his eyes, and grasped the controls in front of him. "They want to board the shuttle while it's still running. Bringing it down will kill Daria and they want to take her alive."

"I don't understand why they'd go to all that trouble." Lombe didn't sound like he was devoting too much of his brainpower to the mystery. "If they want revenge on her for the fight she picked with them at the North Pole, they could simply knock our engines out and leave us to die here."

There wasn't much of an answer he could make to that —or at least not one that wouldn't reveal that there was more to this feud than what they had seen. He didn't feel it was his place to share that information and now was not the time for it either.

"I guess they might merely be looking for a little extra revenge," Lombe said finally. He came to that conclusion with a little help from Jozzun, although hopefully not the kind he would pick up on later. "She started it all so they want to get their hands on her and leave us to rot. Either that or they want to hire her and make sure she doesn't have any choice but to work for them. I guess we'll find out sooner or later."

That sounds like a good assumption on his part. Nothing in her record mentioned that she'd worked with the Red Crows before but the details were woefully incomplete. Maybe we will find out a little more when she is finally willing to give us a peek into where all this trouble originated from in the first place.

They were already in the tunnels and had to slow to navigate the tight twists and turns the miners had dug in search of whatever ore or crystals they'd been after in these mines. It wasn't like rapid movement had been on their mind while they worked, and the Xi-Trang could already hear the screams of the AG bikes closing in on them. The Red Crows mercs followed them closely but carefully too and made sure to not cause the shuttle to crash and put a stop to all their plans.

"Daria, get ready down there," Jozzun announced on the comms. "It looks like they're closing in on our port side. They might be—oh, look at that. A plasma torch to get them through the armor."

"Boarders. They are always fun to have. At least they're not trying to blow us up outright."

She made no complaint about their lack of weaponry on the shuttle, which wasn't the best sign. At least she was taking the attack as seriously as possible. They had left the Hounds behind because they assumed that if the Crows had any intention to attack them in retaliation, the best way would be to take their ship and wait for their target to return.

Of course, for all they knew, this was still a possibility. The mercs had enough boots on the ground to run two attacks at the same time in case one of them went wrong. Still, Jozzun had the feeling that if any of them did try to attack the ship, they would be in for the surprise of their lives.

Even if our first officer isn't on board, our engineers are more than capable of running the Hounds in an attack formation and can defend themselves very effectively too. Plus, Ishima would make sure the boarders were in for one hell of a shock if they made the attempt.

His attention was better focused on their current situation and not on outside possibilities, though.

"They're coming in through the airlock," he alerted Daria and clutched his seat when Lombe twisted them through another tight curve.

"Go on and help her," the captain muttered. "I'll be good here on the bridge but from what I could count, there must be at least twenty of the bastards trying to get in. We're not ready for that kind of company."

It was a good point, although the Xi-Trang didn't like that this meant he had to stand and walk around while they hurtled through the tunnels. His reluctance stemmed mainly from the fact that the only thing that kept his feet on the deck were the grav generators in the shuttle and the inertia dampers that stopped them from flying all over the place whenever Lombe encountered a hairpin.

The moment something went wrong, they would be flung in every direction and probably all die or be severely injured.

He toyed briefly with the idea of simply turning everything off so anyone who boarded them had to deal with being flung around the ship like ragdolls, but there was no telling what that would do to the shuttle's systems.

Besides, Lombe probably couldn't turn those systems off without far more work than they had the time for.

"Shit," Jozzun whispered. He'd only brought his caster and as much as he he was willing to be in on the fighting, all he could do was be there to help direct Daria to the best points of attack while he stayed alive himself.

A shower of sparks from the airlock told him the Crows were almost through the door and it would take considerable work and money to get the damage repaired. They could probably seal it with the ship but they wouldn't be able to use it as a shuttle outside in a location that had its own atmo.

The sparks were more intense as they got through the last few layers and all that kept the door closed was a lock.

"Where the hell are you, Daria?" he shouted. He could pick up her psychic signature but it was a little more difficult to pin down her exact location.

For all he knew, she was dealing with an attack from the other side of the vessel.

The lock opened and the door fell inward to admit two of the assholes. They wore full armor and looked like they were ready for a fight. The Xi-Trang opened fire and his rounds sank into their armor but did little in the way of actual damage. Still, the Crow he hit fell back with a gasped cry of pain. The round didn't kill him but thankfully, it hurt like hell.

Sometimes, feeling another's pain is immensely satisfying.

Jozzun immediately had to duck behind cover when the one that he hadn't hit began to shoot what sounded like a coil rifle at him.

"Look out!" the one on the ground shouted. "If you kill her outright, you're as good as dead yourself!"

"Stop being such an idiot! Did that even look human to yo—"

His voice was cut off by a wet choking sound. Jozzun looked around the corner to where the one with the rifle had fallen to his knees, a chunk missing from his armor that had not been made with a projectile weapon.

Like a shadow, Daria cut through the room and smoothly executed the merc on the ground by slashing his throat with the sword she'd retrieved from the derelict station. Despite how many items had been lost in the conflagration, she'd managed to claim a few treasures that had all proven their value.

The sword was certainly something he could see her getting attached to. With the antique casters she liked to use, it made sense that she would enjoy having an actual fucking sword in her hand. A little training was all it took for her to get the hang of using it, too.

She stepped into the gap where the door to their airlock had once been, her caster already drawn, and she opened fire. Her shots didn't appear to be aimed at anything specific but rather to cause as much damage as she could. Maybe two others were still on the bike, but she'd managed to force them back.

Daria charged one last shot on her caster and unleashed it, not at one of the Crows but rather at whatever magclamp they used to keep the bike connected to their shuttle.

A flash of light and the rumble of an explosion was all Jozzun needed to hear to know the bike was no longer connected to their ship. She paused and looked out the opening to make sure one of the assholes hadn't jumped onto the shuttle at the last minute.

It didn't appear that any of them had and she stepped back and looked at her crewmate.

"Are you all right?"

"I..." He shook his head. "I'm not too bad. How are you?"

She narrowed her eyes at him and shrugged. "I don't hear their engines outside anymore, so they must have clamped onto the other entrances. Is there any chance you have a lock on where they'll come from?"

The Xi-Trang frowned as he tried to keep up with where her mind was going. He hadn't ever been on a mission with her and the only real indication he'd seen of her fighting talents was when she was training.

Well, there was the skirmish at the North Pole city as well, but that seemed closer to a brawl than a proper engagement, although he wasn't sure what the particular difference was. She was a little faster and more decisive in ending a fight in an engagement like the one they were in now, while she seemed more willing to let a fight go on a little longer so other people got their punches in when she brawled in a bar.

"They're coming through the bay doors," he said quickly and gestured for her to follow. "All of them by the sounds of it."

Attacking through the airlock was a narrower entrance for them, that much was clear, but it gave them quicker and easier access to the cockpit. Maybe they's hoped they could simply grab her , drag her out, and let the rest of the Crows finish Jozzun and Lombe off when they were done.

Although it was interesting to note that Daria wasn't in the mood to offer much of an explanation for why they were attacking in the first place. Even her thoughts were on a strict lockdown like she knew she was teamed with a psychic and didn't want him to know about it either.

As much as Jozzun wanted to give her the privacy she wanted, there would come a point when whatever history she had with the Crows would be hazardous to the rest of the crew. That meant it would be his obligation to wrest the knowledge from her if she wasn't in the mood to share it.

It would have to come later, though. She had already begun to move to where they could hear the Crows inside their cargo bay. The boarders hesitated and looked around for any sign of the defenders. Daria narrowed her eyes and looked at Jozzun like she was trying to think of something to say when he suddenly realized it was an attempt to communicate with him.

She didn't seem to know how it worked, however, and her stare intensified as she tried to determine what she should do. There was no time for him to give her a decent lesson on how to communicate with him on a psychic level, so he resorted to a blunt explanation.

You only have to think something openly and commit the words to a voice in your head or an image in your mind's eye. From that, I will be able to sense what you need to tell me.

While it didn't appear to make much sense to her, Daria wasted no time and thought her message equally as bluntly.

I want to run a simple flank attack on them. Two doors access the room, one from the back and one from the front. I need you to move to the back.

The request delivered, she sheathed her sword, drew her other caster, and ran a mental list of the things she needed to do before she stepped into the firing line.

Jozzun's eyes widened and he shook his head, swiped his hand across his throat, and told her to cut the link off. He had what he needed from her and all they should focus on now was clearing the damn mercs out.

It wouldn't be easy, but if she was careful, calm, and collected, they would be able to pull it off.

He moved quietly to the door at the back, well behind the enemy lines. The shuttle's docking bay wasn't that large but it was enough for him to ease in behind them as he heard her open fire on the group below. She had some advantage from being above them and behind easy cover, but when dealing with sixteen of the bastards, maybe that wouldn't matter.

Of course, Daria had made the mistake of forgetting he was a psychic. *It's something she could probably make more use of and more often too but in the end, as long as I remember to help, I won't need to remind her of it at every opportunity. Hopefully she'll see the results and start to include it in her arsenal.*

They were all humans in full armor, and it looked like she had managed to wound one of them with her volley. It had also kept them behind cover and stopped their advance on the cockpit.

Lombe was still navigating through the tunnels although at this point, he probably wished he'd brought

Forrest in to do it. The Xi-Trang paused and suddenly realized why the captain hadn't brought the bot.

For situations like this, it only made sense to bring the bot that was more than comfortable flying their shuttles in and out of danger. It seemed logical that he'd want to keep them isolated from this particular job in case they were boarded by the Salifate. That way, there would be no chance that their hard drives would be swept for any illegal activity.

This was a reasonable decision, especially since what they were doing there went way over the line beyond illegal and into the realm that would classify them as an enemy combatant to the Jindahin. If that happened, the entire area would be sealed against them almost immediately, and that was assuming they managed to escape.

Focus, you feather-crested fool.

Jozzun shook his head and peered around the corner to where Daria still pinned the Crows down with pinpoint accuracy. Her rounds didn't do much other than damage their armor. There wasn't more she would be able to do beyond that until they came in a little closer and by then, the chances were that the fight would already be over.

He moved out from the hallway and onto the platform above the loading bay, kept himself low, and avoided making too much noise as he focused on one of the mercs. Affecting more than one was easier when he was able to influence them one way or another, but a direct psychic attack needed to eliminate them one at a time.

It's up to you now. You have to make the attack one that will ensure the merc doesn't go down on his own. If he can take at least one with him, that's a good way to lower the odds.

"Fuck, what the hell is that?" a man yelled.

"What the hell is wh—"

Before the other merc could answer, one of those who held the line at the back raised his rifle and opened fire on his comrade's back. The Xi-Trang had projected the image of a massive insect there with a stinger that looked all kinds of dangerous. The illusion was poised as if about to attack.

The image he projected jumped to one of the other mercs and landed on his head instead. Panicked, the man targeted by the attack continued to shoot, unable to realize that his bullets didn't damage the creature and instead, pierced through it and struck his people behind it.

More of the creatures began to appear and the merc screamed and maintained his fire. His barrage made the rest of them look at him while they tried to determine what was happening. It was clear that there was no love lost between them as they immediately retaliated.

Satisfied with the chaos he'd caused, Jozzun turned his attention to one of the others and the only one who had kept his attention on where Daria attempted to find a more efficient way to make her shots count.

The merc's hallucination likely felt like thousands of tiny creatures crawled through his armor while they bit, scratched and—from the way he ran, screeched, and ripped his armor off—tried to kill him.

Daria was quick to bring that particular feeling to an end and delivered a neat single shot into the man's head from over thirty meters away. It was impressive enough, but she didn't delay once she was assured that it had done its job.

She turned and opened fire on the rest of the mercs, who still had no idea why their people were hallucinating violently and trying to kill each other.

Jozzun was surprised that he didn't need to continue feeding chaos into their minds. She made it unnecessary when she jumped down smoothly, landed on the balls of her feet, and rolled over her shoulder.

As she came out of it, a smooth swipe with her sword severed the head of one of the mercs and she immediately attacked the others. Her deft strokes made sure that none of them was allowed to feel safe and she carved through the group with ease.

Two of them threw their weapons down and looked like they were about to surrender before she finished them with shots to the head. Up close and personal, there wasn't much their armor could do and they fell without so much as a whimper.

"You...didn't even let them surrender, huh?" the Xi-Trang called as he climbed down from his perch.

"These guys don't surrender," Daria answered with a firm shake of the head. "It's in their contracts, so either they would try to run away from the Crows, or they would wait for an opportunity to shoot us in the back. If they got back to their superiors, they would be gunned down anyway. Besides, it's not like we're taking prisoners here, right?"

That was true, and even if they did let the bastards go, they would either go directly to the Salifate to tell them what was happening or back to the Crows to bring in more people, even if she wasn't telling the truth. He could tell that she was, though, which made the point moot.

"I think we should have consulted the captain first, though," Jozzun pointed out as she began to drag the bodies to where they could be thrown out of the holes that had been made in the ship.

"Do you honestly think so?" Daria asked and gestured for him to help her.

"Well…yes. I happen to know that while he doesn't abhor violence, he does have something against it being used in a wanton fashion like you did."

"Seriously? And your little psychic attack—thanks for that, by the way—doesn't count because they committed the wanton violence? From where I stand, you pulled the trigger. They were merely the weapons."

He nodded. "Indeed, and I won't argue the point. However, none of those attempted to surrender. I'm talking about the violence that occurred after they were ready to lay down their arms."

"Oh… I guess you're right about that. I hadn't thought about it." She tossed the first one out, grasped the boots of the next, and made sure to check the weapons to see if there were any that were worth keeping. "I'll… Well, I'll be a little more alert to that in the future. Thanks for calling me out on it."

Jozzun was halfway suspicious that she was merely saying that to appease him, but a quick check on her mind said she was being genuine. She certainly remembered Lombe's reaction to her behavior at the prison during their escape, which would have killed any number of people—innocent and otherwise. It seemed she hadn't thought about it much until this particular moment.

"I appreciate that," he answered. "We'll probably also

have to talk about how you know so damn much about how the Crows operate. What you mentioned isn't exactly what people would call an outsider's knowledge."

"I told you already. I've worked with them before."

"I know there's more to it than that. You know I know. Besides, they attacked with the intention to take you alive, and that's not something they would do for anyone. You don't have to tell us now but the fact of the matter is that you'll probably have to confide in us eventually. Provided, of course, that you want us to be properly prepared for the next time they come a-knocking."

"Guys?" Lombe called on the comms. "It's very quiet back there and I hope that's good news. If it's not, I should probably go ahead and lock the cockpit door. A warning would be appreciated."

"We're here, Captain," Daria answered gruffly. "Jozzun and I took care of the boarders, no problem."

"Oh. Well, thanks for the heads-up, I guess. We're approaching the drop coordinates so you need to clean up back there before people come in and ask questions."

The Xi-Trang wondered briefly what questions Lombe didn't want them to answer to a group of recently released freedom fighters. Maybe he simply didn't want them to know that they had difficulties with a few of the locals. That generally made people nervous, especially those who tried to keep a low profile.

Daria tossed another of them out and caught hold of the next one before she shook her head. "I…I'll have to tell you guys," she told Jozzun quietly, "but it won't be right now. I have shit to sort out first."

"That's understandable, but we would appreciate it if

you could let us know before we encounter the Red Crows again."

"If we do, I'll be sure to get everyone on comms and let you all know the salient details."

"That's all I ask."

They cleared the bodies out of the cargo bay and then hurried to the two that had been left in the hallway where the first hole had been made. The atmo bubble still held around the shuttle, but a noticeable draft came in as they began to descend into an area that looked like an abandoned camp of some kind. It was difficult to identify outright, but as they approached with what they were looking for in mind, it became clear that this was where they should land.

That was confirmed when the guards stepped out and although they looked confused to see them at first, they almost immediately waved the shuttle down to where they were expected.

Lombe pushed of the pilot's seat and looked like he had sweated profusely for a while. He wiped his forehead with a handkerchief a few times before he put his hat on and stepped out of the hole that had once been their door.

One of the Perdahin noticed the damage almost immediately, although it didn't appear to slow the rest of the group they were there to pick up.

"Find the place all right, did you?" he asked and raised an eyebrow.

"It wasn't too difficult," the captain answered with a smile.

He didn't appear to be in a hurry to disclose their troubles and the Perdahin showed no inclination to ask any more questions. In minutes, the freedom fighters were on board and Lombe had returned to the pilot's seat to direct the shuttle to become airborne again.

"A fine bit of work if I do say so myself," he muttered and guided them out the way that they'd come.

CHAPTER NINE

"You did notice that you took some damage, right?" The Xi-Trang wasn't entirely sure which of their engineers had spoken.

"Do I look blind? Do you think I walk around without eyes and simply paw at the world I can't see because I don't have eyes or something?" Daria retorted.

Jozzun grinned, folded his arms across his chest, and watched her deal with the three Euchriens who examined the damage the shuttle had taken. Lombe was currently negotiating with the clients, who tried to find a way to get across-world on the *Atalanta* now as well.

It appeared that the ship they had intended to take had some trouble it needed to shake off before it could be useful again.

"Well, something's wrong with you or you wouldn't have returned the fucking shuttle looking like a child abused it with a hacksaw. Seriously, look at this technique. They probably didn't even have any training and simply put the plasma torch in the guy's hand and told him not to point it at people."

"Yeah, that's what I thought. Not the fact that twenty of the shits rode AG bikes and tried to shoot us all dead with their coil rifles. No, what was at the forefront of my mind was the fact that none of them seemed to know how to handle a plasma torch."

"You know, your sarcasm isn't helping matters any," one of them stated. It was probably Kleiz since he seemed to be the oldest of the three and was therefore the one who usually needed to calm things before they escalated into pointless bickering. "We can probably fix the damage, but it means the shuttle will have to be decommissioned until we get the parts to repair it. You'll have to use the other ones in the meantime."

"Honestly," one of the others pointed out and ran his short, stubby fingers over the damage. "How did they even catch you? Anti-grav bikes aren't even that fast, especially not compared to a shuttle that is spaceworthy. Why in the hell didn't you...I don't know, shake them off?"

"Shake them... Uh, simply...shake them off like it's no fucking big deal or anything." Daria looked like she was genuinely annoyed this time. "Yeah, we could probably have shaken them off if we were out in the open or maybe out in space where we wouldn't have needed to worry about fucking bikes at all. But instead, we were in the tight fucking tunnels that didn't allow for much shaking, if any."

The engineers were intentionally poking and prodding at her, and Jozzun was a little surprised when he realized that she was simply going along with their meddling. It was entertaining enough to watch and he was happy to see how well she got along with the three of them.

It seemed she had a knack for getting people of all races, species, creeds, and affiliations to like her. He had grown quite attached to having her as a member of the crew as well.

It seems like the type of skill that would keep someone alive while bouncing from party to party. Or maybe it isn't quite a skill but a survival instinct—a way to get people to think positively of her. It's intriguing, honestly. I might be able to look into the minds of the people she interacts with to see why they end up so fond of her.

Although Jozzun wasn't sure if his motivations in this case weren't merely fueled by him wanting to learn how he could get people to instinctively like him as they did her. *I wonder if it's possible to actively alter the person's brain chemistry to make sure they have a positive interaction no matter what I do.*

It was a matter for another time, however. He pushed it quickly to the back of his mind when Lombe approached down the narrow hallway to where they still bickered over the condition of the shuttle.

"Am I interrupting something?" the captain asked and raised an eyebrow.

"I believe our three engineers were questioning your skills as a pilot," Daria answered quickly before any of the three smaller creatures could. "They thought you should have simply shaken our attackers off."

"You did point out that we were in tight and twisting tunnels, right? The kind that are tough enough to fly a shuttle through even when people aren't hunting us?"

"Sure, but they think you should have anywa—ow!"

Kleiz—probably—interrupted her by kicking her hard in the shin. "Only a little gentle ribbing after a job well done, Captain. What's the word?"

"The word is that we were played, although not quite as badly as I first thought," Lombe admitted and placed his hands on his hips. "They've stored their 'quik in a warehouse closer to the equator where we wouldn't be able to go in a shuttle. It's the capital of the planet, as it were—which means it'll be easier for them to get their people off-planet—but they want us to transport them there."

"It would take…days for you to navigate through the tunnels to get that far across the planet," Jozzun pointed out and narrowed his eyes.

"It's impossible," the captain responded. "There are checkpoints along the route that we would need to cross that… Well, we wouldn't be able to get through them with our cargo, so we'll have to take the *Atalanta* up, change our codes, and head in again. The weather's decent so it should be smooth sailing. It would be foolish to make a target of ourselves at this point in the game, but the Perdahin said that would be where we need to pick their 'quik up anyway. We might as well ferry their people there for an additional twenty percent off their usual asking price."

"That's practically at cost for them," Klyz noted. "Still, it comes with a little too much work."

"Our savings can take the hit but we might need to hold off on repairing the shuttle until we get a full payout on the resin and 'quik mixed together. It's not the amount of work we'd want to go through to finally get some money from this deal, but making new connections always takes a few extra steps, right?"

Jozzun wasn't quite sure if all this was worth it, but from what Lombe thought, it appeared they might well involve themselves in a much more profitable form of smuggling so they could afford to take a few more risks.

He didn't particularly like that. They made enough money on the work they were already doing, which meant they didn't need to make any changes. But Lombe was ambitious, which meant the rest of his crew needed to be as well. The Xi-Trang would stand by his captain no matter what, but he would voice his issues with the decisions made too.

Lombe expected honesty from his crew as well.

"We'll break atmo soon so be ready to start switching the codes out," the captain said finally and Daria followed him, along with the three engineers, while Jozzun brought up the rear.

"I already have another coding set up and waiting," Kliz told them when they reached the cockpit as the *Atalanta* cleared the takeoff protocols. "After you said it was the Red Crows corp that gave us so much trouble, we looked around for one of their ships that we could sneak the code off."

"And we did!"

"A lucky break there too, although we were looking for ships that had been relegated to the decom list without ever having the paperwork filed. We found one of the Red Crows vessels that was the same make and model as the *Atalanta*."

"A little creative work means we don't need to worry

about anyone ever pinning this kind of work on us. We can simply make it all about them."

Lombe smirked as he dropped into the pilot's seat. "I do like that little irony there. Do you think they'll be able to pin it on the Red Crows if we are flagged? Because in that case, we might flash our asses at any Salifate 'vettes that arrive to make sure they take the blame for this."

"It's a possibility but not a likely one," Daria told him and shook her head. "The Red Crows have all the right connections in this corner of space. They might be asked about it but they've supported the Jindahin for long enough that their leader could merely shake his head and they'll make it all go away before it hits the caster nets."

"Oh, well. We might as well try it anyway." The captain grinned and began to bring the ship out of the dock and upward into the atmo before he handed control to Forrest.

The weather caught them immediately as they began to climb and forced the AI to adjust its path out of the planet's atmosphere at a sharper incline than they would have liked. Still, it meant they moved out of the planet's influence in under an hour to a position away from where the sensors could pick them up.

"How long will it take for you to settle the new coding?" Lombe asked their engineers.

"Shouldn't take more than a minute."

"All those upgrades we ran while the three of you went to the whorehouse were to make sure we didn't need much time to switch the coding out."

"Not much time at all."

The captain smirked. "What would we do without you?"

"Crash and burn, most likely."

"Which is a quick enough death if we're fair."

Daria sighed. "Why don't we simply transport the Perds to where they need to go in the first place?" she asked. "We're already out, free and clear. The Jindahin wouldn't be any the wiser if we transported them back to…wherever—their base of operations."

"Because the Perdahin don't trust us enough to tell us where they house their people," Lombe explained. "I suggested as much to them but they didn't like the idea enough to go for it. They might do in the future, though, and I believe the pay for that kind of thing comes directly from the people running the Perd operations. It's not a bad way to make money."

Jozzun opened his mouth to speak but shut it almost immediately. It wasn't the time to address the matter with the captain yet.

"All the codes are in place," Lombe noted and brought the ship's nose around to face the planet. "We're looking at a clear line of descent to the capital. Again, the ride will be a little bumpy so you had all better brace yourselves down there!"

He had addressed this warning to the freedom fighters they had stashed in the cargo bays of their other shuttles, positioned so none of them were out in the open where they could be tossed around if the *Atalanta* hit any particularly rough gusts on the way down.

It didn't seem like they would, though. The weather wasn't quite good but it was smooth enough as they headed to a city almost directly on the planet's equator as the sun began to come up on the horizon.

"I always did love me a dawn landing," Lombe whispered as they began their descent but not to the docks directly. Instead, they twisted and headed toward where dozens of smokestacks spewed an inky black smoke into the air and practically made a cloud of it. "I always felt like it was the planet's way to greet us while we approached."

It seemed like Daria agreed and Jozzun had to admit that even with the heavy pollution in the area, it was an impressive place to land, especially as the sun began to rise.

No landing spaces were out in the open and they had to enter the tunnel system with the *Atalanta* to find a place to land near the warehouses in the district. In this case, Jozzun was more than happy to let the automated functions take control because even with the captain's skill level, there was no way he would have been able to navigate the narrow corridors.

One twitch at the wrong time would have crashed them into the walls and brought the tunnel down on them.

Moving through the underground passages took longer than the landing but thankfully, it was something of a maze. They were guided deeper to where they could safely assume that none of the sats could pick up what they were doing.

If it happened that they did, it would be the end of their little plan to make a connection with the Perds.

The warehouse didn't look different from most of the others they'd seen on the way down, but Jozzun wasn't the only one to notice far more heavy security in the area. Turrets and drone stations stood in stark warning and he had a feeling they weren't in place to prevent the insectoid monsters from causing problems.

As the ship touched down, he could practically taste the

smell of the refined 'quik. It looked like most of the factories in the area were dedicated to exactly that—processing thousands of tons of it every hour to ship off in dozens of ships like the *Atalanta*. Their leaving with a cargo of it wouldn't raise any eyebrows at this point.

The warehouse doors were closed by the time the actual Perdahin made an appearance. There wasn't much of a physical difference between them and the Jindahin. They even dressed the same—like they needed to scream their position to everyone who came into their line of sight.

Still, he knew better than to bring that up to their new business associates.

"You were sent from the heavens to help us in this time of need," one of them stated as Lombe stepped out to make sure all went smoothly with the disembarking.

"Literally," Daria commented with a smirk.

"Yes. Hah, literally sent from the heavens. Messo must have known we were in trouble when he brought you to the planet to help us."

"Well, I guess Messo must have known that we don't exactly work for free," the captain answered. "I'm sorry to be blunt, but we've been on this—pardon my language—shitheap of a planet for much longer than any of us are comfortable with. We'd like to get off it as quickly as possible. Do you have what we came here for?"

"The Darkquik, yes. It's recently refined and lifted from the shelves of what comes away from the planet every day. They lose about twenty percent of what is transported off-planet and that is calculated into their profits here. It's mostly from it spoiling over longer travel times, but they also assume they might have some that leak from their containment units or are even stolen. As long as we keep the amount stolen to a reasonable amount, none are the wiser."

"I always did love a neat little scheme like that," Lombe answered. "How much do you have for us?"

"As much as you can carry and it is already being loaded into your ship's hold as we speak. Due to your help for our cause, we are more than comfortable deducting fifty percent from the original price of the 'quik.'"

"Fifty? We agreed—"

"We are aware of the blessing of your work, Captain Lombe, and we need to make sure there is enough that you know your efforts are appreciated. Fifty percent instead of the forty we agreed before is precisely that."

"I feel like this is you…uh, tipping us for a job well done."

"You can consider it so if you like. And know that there will be more work for the crew of the *Atalanta* should you find yourself available again."

"I might take you up on that." The captain extended his hand. "For the moment, though, we should probably get moving."

The Perdahin was not as comfortable with a handshake as Lombe was but he still took hold of the man's hand between his forefinger and thumb and shook it carefully before he snatched his hand away.

"Yes, you should," he whispered and glanced at the captain and crew. "And fly with haste. I think trouble might be heading our way."

"Shit." Lombe motioned for them to move into the ship and he hurried to the cockpit.

"He wasn't wrong," he stated bluntly. "We have a handful of Salifate 'vettes heading into the tunnels we came in through. It might not be because of us at all but at this point, I don't think we can afford to even be seen."

"He's right," Kleiz commented and looked up from one of the panels he was working on. "We can switch all the codes we like, but if they catch a glimpse of us, they might send pics to every friendly port to keep a lookout for certain markings. We could change the paint, but we would have to do that outside of Salifate space."

"All right, I'll take her up now."

The 'quik they'd ordered had been loaded quickly thanks to the automated systems already in place, and the freedom fighters they'd released were hurried into worker's uniforms. Those would hopefully put them beyond suspicion when they mingled with the others.

"The 'vettes picked up our signal," Daria noted. "They've sent a ping to notify us that we need to stop and be boarded. They have... Well, it says that they're investigating the area for possible insurrectionist activity."

"Fuck." Lombe hissed in frustration. "Okay, we have to get out of here and fast. Kleiz, get one of the AIs to move us out of these tunnels. Daria, do you think you can do something about closing the tunnels we'll travel through?"

She nodded. "I can hit a few of the supports with torpedoes. I think that'll interrupt the work they're doing here, which means we won't be a priority, but they can still send a grounding signal once we get out of the tunnels."

"Not if we changed the codes," he answered, already

working through the process himself. "Damn, I do love the Doppelganger Code."

It was a good place to test it, but they could only engage the code itself once they were out of transmission distance from the 'vettes that had already increased speed to intercept. The *Atalanta* was more than equipped to fight them if needed but in the end, if they had to fight, it would give the pursuers more than enough time for them to signal the rest of the defense forces on the planet. That would mean the end for them.

Daria seemed a little calmer than Jozzun felt. Even calmer than Lombe, who quickly picked up a new catalogue of ships for them to steal codes from.

"Supports coming up," she announced and looked around. "Are you guys ready?"

"We were born ready," Lombe answered with a grin.

"Yeah, well, that would have been about forty years too early, but I'm glad to hear about it."

"Thirty-six!"

"Whatever."

She chose her targets quickly and launched the torpedoes. The 'vettes slowed almost immediately, thinking they had been pinged for the attack, and by the time they realized that they were not, the supports had already begun to collapse.

"Check!" Lombe shouted and looked around as the ship shuddered when a handful of rocks came down on them as well.

"No damage to the ship. Shields took it all," Kliz announced.

"Signals?"

"Nothing coming up, captain. We broke their connection to us."

"Nice." He hissed in triumph and immediately activated the code changes across the entire ship as they emerged from the tunnels and moved up and away from the planet almost immediately. "It looks like we're in the clear, guys!"

He raised his fist in celebration and Daria bumped it with hers before she turned to offer Jozzun a bump as well.

"It looks like they're already flagging the Crows ship as being a part of the insurrectionist activity," the Xi-Trang commented. "But it's not what we're flying under so they're looking for any ships associated with the Crows in the area. It should be a nice little chase for them."

"This code, man," Lombe whispered and shook his head. "It's exactly what the doctor ordered."

CHAPTER TEN

A quick jump took them out of Jindahin space. Mugh-9 was on the borders of the planets they controlled, and as much they wanted to move directly to the part where they could sell their 'quik and get it out of their hold, a few more steps were required for a full success story.

"You always come here when you need some smuggled items legitimized," Jozzun noted and folded his arms as they approached the asteroid field. "Is it truly the best plan for us to be predictable like this? Or are you merely trying to get our enemies calm and collected to the point where they think they can predict our every move before we change everything and catch them off-guard?"

Lombe narrowed his eyes at the Xi-Trang and looked like he was trying to decide if he was serious or not. It was all Jozzun could do to keep his face straight for as long as possible while they moved steadily toward the space station.

It wasn't particularly difficult to find, even hidden deep

inside the field. The station had been set up on an asteroid that was about the size of most moons or even one of the smaller dwarf planets. It had been mined for all kinds of minerals it was rich in, and the corp that stripped the rock decided they wanted to make a little more money from it and settled on the idea of turning it into a market station between Xi-Trang and Jindahin space.

Like most places between one large government and another, it rapidly became the popular location for all types of interesting trades and created one of the best pipelines for contraband in this area of the galaxy.

This explained why Lombe liked to go there whenever he could. It was the perfect place to shake off anyone who might follow them, but connections could be made there as well—his favorite c-word as Jozzun rapidly discovered. Finally, it provided them with a nice haven to stop and collect themselves while they decided what their next move would be.

In addition, it was the perfect place to find buyers for their product but for that, they needed a fence. These individuals traded mostly on their reliability, which meant people generally got what they paid for when they went to one. Malova had proven to be the perfect combination of reliable and reasonable.

They would never be guaranteed a payout when they visited her, but if she was unable to help, she was always willing to suggest another buyer to make up for it without charging any of her usual fees.

"You know what I say," Lombe muttered finally and rubbed his temples when he decided Jozzun probably wasn't being serious in his line of questioning. "About a solid half of the galaxy's population is middlemen and they usually hate being cut out of it. Malova's reliable when it comes to getting us what we need, which means we have to be reliable in getting product she can move for us. Nothing keeps a fence hooked on us like giving her consistent moving fees."

"I know, I know. I merely thought there might be another reason you might like to visit her."

"Please. She's at least eighty years old and she's been a staple of the smuggling community for longer than either of us have been alive."

"And yet she doesn't look a day over thirty. It's impressive for a human."

"It means she's probably not all human. For all I know, she might have a whole bunch of teeth down there. It's always best to make sure."

"So you have thought about what she has down there."

Lombe shrugged. "Keep it up, buddy. I can always go ahead and change the subject to the madame on Mugh-9 who had your knickers in a twist."

"Ah, yes. She was exceptional. I think I'll pay Mugh-9 a visit when my next mating season kicks in. Assuming, of course, we're not flying away and on the run from yet another dangerous group of dastardly villains."

"Cops aren't dastardly. They might have followed the orders of a psychopath but it didn't mean they were terrible people. We merely needed to lay low and hiding out in an unknown area of space was the best way to do that. We might have had to do it for about a week until the mentions about us disappeared from the local casting markers. And honestly, I didn't know that time was when you were at your worst—biologically speaking—and I didn't want to know. So…when you do reach that point in your body again, would you please do me a favor, and…uh, not tell me?"

Jozzun chuckled. "Well, I guess I can do that, but you should know that while you are disgusted by my biology, that is the state most humans are in all the time. Imagine how disgusted you are, then consider that it's how I feel being around humans all the time."

"Well, in fairness…" The captain paused and tilted his head. "Nope, I don't have anything for that but I do feel sorry for you. I guess I would feel that way if I found out that any of our crew were bumping uglies, though. It's not the kind of thing a captain needs to know about his crew. I know it's there, of course, but as long as I have no actual frame of reference, I can pretend it isn't."

"I suppose that makes sense. In that case, I will make an attempt to keep you blissfully ignorant of my biological functions."

"That's all I ask."

Jozzun pushed out of his seat as they entered the pull of the station's grav. The people who ran the docks inside had already shown them a path and gave them a place to dock with the station. The AIs picked up the navigation and moved to the other side of the asteroid while they took care to ensure that they weren't coming into the path of any other vessel.

As belts went, this one was fairly unique since it was held in place by an odd white dwarf. Its gravitational pull worked together with an incredibly unlikely series of events that kept the belt around it. This drew in new bits and pieces of space matter and made it unusually dense when other asteroid belts had far more distance between the debris that orbited them.

Many attempts had been made to study the phenomenon but for the most part, it was merely interesting to wonder what the hell was causing this particular belt to work the way it did without needing to find as many answers as they could.

Maybe that was simply from the part of him that didn't quite understand the basics of physics, Jozzun decided. Perhaps if he applied himself and studied a little more, the questions that needed to be asked would be clearer and drive him to answer them to the best of his ability.

"We'll dock in half an hour," Lombe said as the Xi-Trang moved toward the door. "Let the rest of the crew know. We have the illegal shit stowed where it won't be found but we still need to make a show of doing something here."

"And what did you have in mind?"

"I picked up a couple of items on Mugh-9 that will bring us a small profit from one of the legal buyers here, so they'll come around. Make sure everything goes well when we dock. They're already waiting for us."

"Will do, captain."

Jozzun knew it wouldn't take much to convince their new clients that they needed to get in and out of the ship as quickly as possible. They did business on the Medusa Station, which meant they would know exactly what kind of business had brought the *Atalanta* in. All Lombe wanted was to make sure they didn't get a peek at something that would prompt them to alert the authorities in the hope of some kind of reward.

There was truly no honor amongst thieves but they could still do business with them as long as they understood what the rules were. Whatever profits they made from this small legit business would probably be enough to pay for them to resupply and refuel before their next trip.

He could hear movement in the cargo bay, which meant Daria was probably still drilling with the Hounds, getting used to them with their new and improved software. Of course, she would also use the opportunity to get to know the one that appeared to be a little more than the others.

It was interesting to see how curious she was about the one she liked to call Specter. *Maybe it's an appropriate name. Humans have a history of calling something they didn't understand in software the "ghost in the machine."*

No, he thought, that was something else. He'd read about it somewhere but the concept didn't come fully to mind. It was on the tip of his tongue, though, which meant he would recall the object of it eventually.

For the moment, it was important to work out what Daria was doing with the bot she was so interested in. Jozzun didn't need to watch them going through the drill to know that Specter, in particular, was sharper than the other Hounds. They were all designed for combat, which meant upgrading their combat software was the basic equivalent of adding five or six years of training to a combat specialist's repertoire.

However, there was a reason why organics were still used for most operations these days, and it wasn't only because a handful of civs out there had something against bots and AIs in general, although that was a factor.

Organic fighters had something like intuition. He

thought of it as experience over years of combat that enabled them to look into a field of battle and all but predict what their enemies were doing. This, in turn, would mean they could intuitively take a few steps ahead of those enemies and cut them off before any plans could be enacted.

It was more or less what he counted on when he looked into the minds of the people he was fighting to anticipate what their moves would be so he could jump farther ahead than them.

Lombe called it prescience and other people called it luck, but in reality, Jozzun knew it was merely using an organic's intuition against them. And maybe a little prescience, but that was a whole other matter.

There was a reason why rogue AIs were such a danger of course, but they didn't have the same thing organics had, especially when it came to combat. It was logical given that humanoid organics had evolved their abilities to fight whereas most AIs were only a few years old by the time they reached the decom pile.

They tended to learn and get better but there wasn't much in them that allowed them to grow and learn to any significant degree. Organics could transfer their knowledge to their offspring through DNA and simple instruction and let it grow with them, while AIs generally couldn't. The knowledge—both useful and not—and learning would continue to grow to the point where most humans would leave their knowledge intact in subsequent generations after they died.

This ability was mostly denied to AIs. They would go "crazy," wreck a couple of ships, and maybe even take over a planet or two but in the end, they would never be able to grow exponentially the way organic creatures did.

It didn't mean they weren't still a threat, of course, and in the end, aggressive machines usually terrified people the most. Humans as a species tended to be affectionate creatures, even to items in their lives that weren't alive. He remembered a young couple he'd traveled with in the past who put a pair of animated eyes on the side of their toaster oven, called it Toasty, and treated it like it was somehow alive.

Daria has clearly started to develop some kind of affection for the Specter bot, as evidenced by the name she's given to it. If it proves to be the kind of AI that develops on its own and in a way that cannot be controlled by experienced professionals, no one can realistically predict what it would develop into.

The fact that they sent it into battle with a coil rifle and advanced combat techniques in its programming was probably the type of thing that would get the advocates against AI even more up in arms.

It was probably good that he wasn't that kind of person. Jozzun leaned against the railing and watched the troop run a pincer movement. This sent the Hounds around to attack a fictional adversary from both flanks while Daria maintained the central position.

She fired quickly and precisely before she ducked behind cover but held the attention of the enemy bots controlled by their engineers. When she was sure they were fully engaged, she sent the Hounds in to finish the fight off with surprising timing and precision.

"I think I'm getting better at this," she announced, stepped out from behind her cover, and checked the batteries on her casters before she slid them smoothly into their holsters. "Seriously, give me five or six months of training and I could probably lead a full fucking army of these creatures, no problem."

Kleiz laughed. "I think you're ignoring the fact that the complexity of leading them grows more with every bot you add to the network. I think your limit would be... maybe thirty of the Hounds before you were a little overwhelmed."

"Psh, you underestimate me. More importantly, you underestimate what I would be able to do with thirty Hounds. It might be as good as having a full fucking army out there fighting with me."

The engineers didn't have much to say about that and they began to set up the Hounds that acted as the enemies in their little practices, although it looked like they alternated them between the bots. Predictably, they didn't add Specter to this group, and it remained close to Daria's side and didn't stray farther than one or two paces from her while it stayed out of her way at the same time.

"What's up with that one?" he asked. "The one with the...uh, the mark on its chest?"

"Specter?" Daria asked and patted the bot without even needing to look to see where it stood. "He has some kind of advanced software in his system, which means he's a little quicker than the others. It's always good to have that on your side in a fight—ain't you, big boy?"

The bot appeared to answer and nodded its head gently in response to her words. The gesture was odd enough on its own without taking all the other oddities into account.

"Have you been able to pin down exactly what has

caused it to act so intuitively?" Jozzun asked and masked his suspicions carefully when he spoke to the three engineers.

"Nothing stands out."

"Might be something with the hardware, so we might need to take him apart to see if there's something that we can replicate with the rest of the Hounds."

"Of course, if we do that, we might accidentally do away with what made him so special in the first place, so it's an experiment we'll put on the back burner."

The fact that they all referred to the bot as a male was an interesting development as well but he decided to put that down as something to be addressed later.

"Hardware?" Jozzun approached the bot in question and ran his fingers over the welding scar that had been left on Specter's chestplate when it was hacked into by the same sword their first officer now called her own. "What makes you think it's not something to do with the software?"

"That was our first thought," Daria answered. "But they ran a reboot on the software when they installed all the new combat directives and the signs were still there. It means it's probably hardware."

Either that or the AI inside knew how to stay hidden and prevent itself from being reset. There were many ways to do it, of course, but Jozzun felt he was likely being a little paranoid in this respect.

"Interesting. It's always good to have primo tech on our side in a fight." The Xi-Trang nodded and turned away. "Lombe wanted to let you know that we're coming in to Medusa and have some clients coming in to pick up those crates over there."

"We should probably clear out the rest of the items so no one else sees them." Kleiz realized immediately what Lombe wanted from them.

Or, Jozzun thought, it was probably Kleiz. "At least until we get some official markings on the 'quik we have in there," he agreed as the bots were quickly redirected to the work of moving the crates.

Daria stepped closer to him, her eyes narrowed and her voice low. "Is there nothing else you wanted to get off your mind?"

He turned to look at her, curious as to how she could have keyed in on his AI misgivings with her favorite bot. "I...I'm not sure what you're talking about."

"What? Why the sudden confusion? Didn't you want to talk a little more about the Red Crows given that everyone knows they have a presence on Medusa?"

The Xi-Trang sighed inwardly with relief. That made more sense than her suddenly developing psychic abilities and immediately divining what was on his mind. She would know he was worried about something easily enough, either through an empathic burst he'd emitted accidentally or simply through her keen eye for body language in the people around her. Her question also told him that she felt guilty enough about him having brought up her connection with the merc corp that it was where her mind jumped to.

And it was a logical assumption too.

He committed to a shrug. "As you know, Lombe is a good man and a good leader, but he also respects his crew's privacy in these matters. For myself, I happen to catch a couple of glimpses without meaning to here and there due to my species' talents. I thought you would feel better if I were honest about what I'd gleaned instead of pretending I don't know. I guess you could call it my way of showing that I care."

"How's that worked out for you so far?"

"Sometimes, people thank me for my honesty. At others, they feel…a little like you do now. You should know I have every intention to respect your privacy, but I think it would be for the best to share your past experiences—and not only because it might be a vital part of how we can avoid entanglements with the merc corp in question. I've learned that humans in particular take great benefit from 'talking things over,' as you say. Given that your species requires you speak in order to share your thoughts and feelings, it makes sense."

Daria nodded and folded her arms. "I'm a little curious, though. When did you pick up on the fact that we might have had a history together?"

"I… Well, it was immediately obvious when you engaged the Red Crows group in the North Pole city, although I couldn't make out any real details, merely a past association. I still don't know much since I was entirely focused on distracting them when they tried to board. If you are willing to share your history with me, I am always willing to listen, even if you aren't ready to share it with the rest of the crew. I might be able to determine which parts you might want to leave out when you discuss the matter with the others."

"Don't get me wrong," she interjected quickly. "I do appreciate your respect for my privacy and all that shit. I'm only…well, you're all like a family to each other, but it doesn't feel like I'm quite there yet. And I probably won't be for a while either."

"I understand."

Daria shook her head and moved to some seats in the corner of the cargo bay while the bots were moved the crates around them.

"You remember how I was caught by the XTA, right?" she asked and raised an eyebrow.

"Of course. You were doing some business in their space and when their law enforcement arrived to stop you, your crew left you behind to take the rap for their crimes."

"My crew were Red Crows. I hadn't been with them for long but they govern their people with some very strict rules, mostly to make sure they don't bother to try to narc on them, surrender, or lose face for the corp. I thought I was over them simply leaving me behind like that, but when I saw them... Well, I guess I'm not. I had some anger to get out so I provoked the fight."

That was about as succinct as she could be, and Jozzun appreciated that she was willing to share those details about her life with him. Since they'd likely been one of the reasons why she had such a difficult time trusting her new partners in business, he could understand why she could feel the need to lash out at them beyond only what she just mentioned.

Maybe it's her way to show them what they had lost out on when they left her behind to be killed or have her mind wiped by the Authority.

"Why were they chasing us, though?" Jozzun asked when he realized this was the next question he wanted to ask her before they moved away from the topic. "It seems that if they left you behind, they wouldn't have cared about committing those resources to getting you back. They talked about taking you alive, so I assume they were well aware of who they were chasing."

"You don't leave Red Crows," she muttered bitterly, likely quoting something she'd heard while with them. "Red Crows leaves you but you don't leave them. I can only assume they wanted to use me as a way to teach a lesson to the rest of their crew. It would no doubt be a brutal, graphic lesson seared into the minds of all those present for it, and that requires me to be alive and present for them to deliver it."

"They would put that much effort into making a point?" He frowned as he considered this kind of extreme paranoia.

"Reputation is important to the bastards, but everyone knows that reputation is only gossip, spread around like grams talking in a knitting circle. People hear about what happens when they leave the corp and for many of them, that's enough. But when they have the chance to make a show of it, they're eager to take that opportunity. It confirms what happens beyond merely the reputation they have."

"I suppose that is why you made a point of executing those who tried to surrender?"

"It wasn't a real surrender," she insisted bluntly. "They realized they no longer had the advantage and looked for a way to survive long enough to turn the tables on us. The chances are they had some weapons implanted subdermally that they could use once we had our backs turned. So yeah, killing the bastards was the best way to make sure they knew I wouldn't go back to be any kind of object lesson for them."

Jozzun nodded. Truthfully, it explained a lot. Daria was efficient and sometimes even brutal when she needed to be, but the point was that it was only when she needed to be. Those kinds of decisions were made without her being able to look into the minds of the people around her like he could. She made the decisions in a split second and she stood by them, whether he or even Lombe agreed with her or not.

"What do you think you would do if you ran into more of them who recognize you on the station?" he asked.

"I'll walk past them if they let me. I vented all my aggro on them already. But if they want to start a fight, I'll be there to finish it."

"Noted."

CHAPTER ELEVEN

The business they had scheduled was accomplished quickly. It looked like either their clients were desperate for what Lombe was selling, or the captain had already worked through pricing and haggling before they landed. Whatever the reason, they arrived, collected their merch, and left little more than a word or two between them.

Better still, the money appeared in their account a minute after the transaction occurred, which meant they were good for the creds too. Business was rarely ever that smooth in their line of work, but Jozzun was always happy for it in those rare instances where people came to buy and paid for what they walked away with without putting up too much of a fight.

It was enough for them to top the ship up with fuel and supplies, and Lombe left the work of loading those to his first officers while he headed out to deal with their contact.

"What's the situation with this Malova anyway?" Daria asked and raised an eyebrow once the captain had left the ship. "And is there any reason why Lombe is heading out to deal with her without any muscle?"

"You're forgetting that he is enough muscle on his own," he pointed out with smirk. "It might be that the captain is soft on her. From what I understand about humans, she is quite attractive and virile despite the fact that she's over eighty years old."

Daria leaned over as he showed her a quick view of what the woman in question looked like on his tablet and both her eyebrows rose in response.

"Shit, that's not a bad look for eighty," she whispered and shook her head. "How does she do it?"

"Everyone has a different theory about it." Jozzun pocketed his tablet again. "Genetics, implants, something like that. Some people think she's not pure human and has something else mixed in there that slows the aging process. For myself, I like to think Malova might not be the same person she was when she originally started. She's an institution among smugglers, so there's a good chance someone else stole the role, or maybe it was passed on from one to the other. If so, we might be looking at the third or fourth Malova. Either way, it doesn't matter. She is very selective about her clients and her connections, which means anyone who gets to work with her comes away happy, for the most part."

She tilted her head and nodded. "I approve. And I guess that would be why I've never heard of her before, especially if she keeps to herself. I doubt I would have ever been considered as someone she would want to do business with."

"Why is that?" He was genuinely curious.

"You already know that the crowds I've run with have never been the classiest."

"I'm sure you'll get to meet her someday but for the moment, I think she wanted to meet only with the captain. If all goes well, she'll send people with the markers for our product and he'll return with a name, a contact point, and a possible client in human space that should be able to take what we're offering, no questions asked, and for a decent price to boot."

"One can always hope."

She seemed settled enough to wait for the people to come, but Jozzun knew better than to think she wouldn't be ready to jump into action at a moment's notice. Her hands rested near her casters and if someone came in a little too close, she didn't even need to draw them. The sword would be much faster and cleaner in close quarters anyway.

Fortunately, it didn't seem like she would be needed for the moment. He could detect no foul play intended by the people who delivered their fuel and supplies, and all they needed to do was keep an eye on the situation from above while their engineers did most of the work.

It wasn't even work, honestly. They simply directed the bots to carry and push the crates from one point to the other, made sure everything was delivered as promised, and sent the delivery men on their way.

A short while later, another group arrived. They were dressed like an inspection team but Jozzun had seen the group before. They worked for Malova directly and they focused immediately on the crates that contained their illegal merch. Working quickly, they went over them with what looked like scanners until the devices attached to them had a registry that included purchase orders from non-existent sellers.

He knew better than to think it would stand against rigorous scrutiny, but that wouldn't happen unless they sold their product to a military corp directly. Malova would make sure they didn't land in that kind of situation. Not only would it ruin her reputation as a solid middle-person, but it would also risk having those assholes learning about her, directly or not. The best way for a business like hers to operate was to restrict her connections to the people she knew would do business well together.

Of course, it didn't mean there wouldn't be problems now and then, but it did limit the possibilities of shit that could go badly.

"Those military guys must be Malova's people," Daria commented, tilted her head, and leaned forward.

"What… How do you know they're military?"

"Not any one thing, but they've all laced their boots in the same way, their hair is in the same style, and their clothes are neatly ironed. All those little things point to about two or three years of a brutal boot camp that would have drilled everything the military needed them to know into them before they sent them to a colony planet to kill as many people as possible."

"It sounds like you've run into their type before."

"You see them here and there and once you remember the details, you see them more frequently, even those who might be trying to hide among the local population. Do you think Malova might have some military intelligence connections who do all the researching she needs?"

That was a possibility that hadn't ever occurred to him. "It makes sense. She maintains a ridiculously small footprint on the galaxy while being one of the most knowledgeable. It isn't something you can do unless you have the right connections."

"I'm not sure if I like working with or for the military," Daria muttered and rubbed her jaw a little irritably. "Then again, I am a little biased in that respect. I guess if the captain trusts her, we should all trust her."

"It still can't hurt to dig a little deeper."

"That's where you're wrong. If she's military intel, it could most certainly hurt us to dig a little deeper. I maintain that in much of the shit that goes on around the galaxy, ignorance is bliss. Lombe doesn't want us to go around killing people at random, but who the hell do you think will buy this much resin and 'quik from us? Charities that work to maintain native flora on terraformed planets?"

She'd made another good point that had failed to occur to him. *Maybe it's time for me to stop observing her so much and learn from her instead.* It was an oddly challenging thought.

The remarking of their merch didn't take long and if the "inspectors" responsible for the change heard what they had talked about, it didn't seem like they cared enough to show any sign of it. Less than ten minutes later, Lombe returned to the ship and took a moment to check the crates to make sure the alterations were complete and accurate before he turned to the rest of the crew.

All of them waited patiently for what they hoped was good news.

"We have a buyer," he said with a grin and clapped briskly. "It's already set up and they are waiting for us to arrive in human-owned space. I say this is cause to celebrate. They have a multi-species watering hole here on the station and I have every intention to find out how many species they cater to before we ship out tomorrow morning with the worst hangover of my life. How would you all like to join me?"

"I don't know," Daria muttered. "The worst hangover of my life was…uh, when I was fifteen and I got my hands on a full case of bubbly I couldn't sell so I decided to see how many bottles I could drink."

"Yeesh." Ishima shook her head. "Bubbly is the worst and proven to be so because the carbon dioxide that gives it all those bubbles helps it to absorb into the blood faster."

"And that is why I can't ever come within ten meters of bubbly wine before I feel like I need to puke. It means I will pass on that, but everything else is fair game. Will you join us, Doc?"

"Of course. I've always wanted to know what you all are like while you're out drinking."

Daria grinned. "You've had the opportunity before, you know, except your drinking got in the way."

Ishima sniffed disdainfully. "I'll have to make sure I abstain this time."

"No. No writing on your tablet or recording us in any way. If you come with us, you'll drink as much as we all do. You'll get stupid and tell us stories about the crazy shit you did in med school."

The woman shrugged. "I suppose I can't argue with that."

Jozzun already knew he was going, and Daria probably did as well, which left only three holdouts—their engineers.

"Ship needs repairs before we head out."

"Still too much work to get the shuttles into working order."

"And...well, there's not much of a chance that they'll stock anything we can eat or drink anyway. Euchriens are too rare for anyone to stock what we need."

Lombe nodded. "Of course. And I think the three of you would be much happier to be comfortable with the ship in your hands and only yours for the night."

"Yes," they all replied in unison.

"Well then, I wouldn't dare to tear you three away from a fun night with your own company. The rest of you, let's get the fuck out of here and give them full range of the place. And...uh, please don't ever tell me what the three of you get up to when the ship is all yours."

"We would never, Captain," Kleiz answered with a laugh, adjusted his mask, and waved the rest of them out.

The whole station was practically a small city. It was nowhere near as large as the one they had blown up, of course, but still large enough to house at least twenty thousand people. Atmo generators would have been imported during the mining period and left in place because moving them off would have been too expensive. This meant there were probably enough of them to keep the whole base running on automatic for at least a decade.

Of course, the asteroid was old, which meant the atmo generators would be as ancient. If someone took control of the base and ruled over it, their first order of business would be to have a veritable army of engineers working to maintain and replace the generators. Failure to do so would mean the whole place would go up like so many other stations before it.

Of course, there was no guarantee that the people running it would do anything of the sort, even if it was the smart play in the long-term. Anyone who took over locations like the Medusa Station never had anything even close to long-term vision.

The bar looked like it was more than willing to cater to about as many people as were in the station, which meant it was booming with activity when they stepped inside. Jozzun felt the barrage of uninhibited emotions from all around him, closed his eyes, and forced them all out for the moment. Once he was a little more relaxed, he would be able to feed into the sensations, find out what was happening, and try to protect himself from being overwhelmed again. For the moment, though, closing himself off felt like the most sensible choice.

He wasn't surprised to find it far more vibrant than most establishments they'd been to. They'd come to the Medusa before, but there had never been time to settle in and relax. Lombe was always on the move and always planning their next gambit, their next heist, or their next score and never took a moment to pause, reflect, and enjoy what they were doing.

Maybe this was the result of having a first officer he trusted to keep her head at all times, even when drunk and throwing punches at random people for the sheer fun of it. Sharing the leadership load seemed to have had a good effect on the captain, which meant it was probably a good thing for the rest of the crew.

He wasn't surprised when shouts erupted from the other side of the bar, and Daria was the first one to look up from the meal and drinks they'd ordered for themselves.

"It looks like some kind of sporting event going on," she muttered and settled into her seat. "I've never seen that particular kind of sport before."

"Not violent enough for you, is it?" Ishima asked. She had been through three shots and two stouts and still didn't look like it had affected her. Jozzun still wasn't comfortable enough in the room to peer into her mind to see if she was faking it or if she had some kind of tolerance to the poison they fed into their bodies.

Of course, he wouldn't need to tell them that the drinks he ordered for himself didn't have the same effect as alcohol had on humans. Alcohol, as he understood it, was basically poison that they fought their livers over to enjoy the state of being poisoned because it gave them a sense of exhilaration. Ishima had explained the process to them when they got their first round of shots, but he hadn't taken much of it in.

What he drank helped him to relax, settle his thoughts, and put his mind in a better state of focus. Xi-Trang had ways to lower their inhibitions, but they were smoked, not drunk. Their bodies had too many filters in their digestive systems for a poison like ethanol to have much of an effect. It wasn't that he couldn't drink it, but it didn't do much and he would end up pissing it away.

The lungs, on the other hand, was where most of the

sensors were without any filters. This meant that if he wanted to get nice and fucked-up, a bowl full of the right herbs set to a slow blaze was just the trick. Inhaling the vapors through a water filter was the way to do it, but there weren't many places that offered it for Xi-Trang outside of XTA space, and there were a handful of planets where it was illegal.

He drank because it was the companionable thing to do but the drinks he ordered weren't for the purpose of lowering inhibitions. Instead, they settled his body, cleared the tension, and let his mind be all it could be. It was similar to the effect cocoa had on humans, he supposed, although not quite the same.

Ishima would have been very interested to discuss the similarities between human and Xi bodies, but that was a topic for another time. The doctor was in the middle of explaining the one time when she and her fellow students in med school had been a little inebriated.

"No, no," she said and shook her head. "No, I was an army medic for...three or four years before they paid my way through med school so I could get a proper medical doctorate. Anyway, once I was there, this was the first time I realized they were paying for my scholarship through a good school. Farasa Medical School on Tempest. A whole horde of rich brats attended and ain't none of them seen anything like combat before, so they take me out to play paintball."

"Paintball?" Lombe asked.

"Yes—an old pastime for the rich and famous. I forget where it started. Anyway, little paint pellets are launched forward by a weak coil propeller, which fires them and plasters your friends with bright paint that stains their bodies for days afterward and bruises them something good. They'd played this fucking game since they were kids, but the moment I join them, they're covered in paint before any of them can blink. I hit them from the sides and I hit them from the back. They might have been good shots with those useless coilers, but I was all over them when it came to positioning. I could have fucked them up myself and they didn't even get a shot on me until three hours in."

"Three hours?" Jozzun stared at her. "How long do these games last?"

"They rent out these little obstacle courses, meant to simulate a tiny little battlefield. These come in all shapes and sizes, and the rich fucks always get thousands of the little pellets. Now let me tell you, they spend hours of their weekends on it, but...well, there's nothing quite like the real thing. Once you have to staple some asshole's stomach while mortar shells explode all around you, paint pellets ain't fucking nothing."

The Xi-Trang leaned forward. "You were in the military then?"

"Where else will you find an army medic? Shit yeah, I was in the military."

"You know, Daria has something against the whole concept of military people. We were talking about it while on the ship, and she—wait, where is Daria?"

"We might have lost her for the night," Lombe pointed out and directed their attention to where people were still shouting about the sports game. "It's not a particularly violent sport, but she said that was where the truly interesting fights happen. In the violent sports, people get their aggression out vicariously, but the peaceful sports is when the fans have all this pent-up belligerence that they start to take out on each other. It means that they're more likely to —oh, there we go."

The first blow of the fight was thrown where Daria looked like she attempted to egg people into the fight, and the first punch was leveled at the man who stood beside her. She twisted her body, hammered the man who threw the punch with her elbow, and hurled him into a group behind him as the rest of them began to get involved.

It looked like a battle from ancient times. Probably about a hundred people were in the tavern area and half of them had watched the sports match. This meant that those fifty were anxious to be involved in a battle over the honor of one team over the other.

"I think you might be right on that score," Jozzun whispered. "Daria might not have the worst hangover of her life but what's the effect of mixing alcohol with painkillers?"

Ishima shook her head. "Usually not the best, but I have some moderate medication that she can take without risking the dangers of mixing the two. It wouldn't be as effective as something a little more powerful, but I think the alcohol will dull the pain too, at least until it's out of her system."

Their first officer sent another man to the floor with a firm kick to his knees before she was tackled by three other sports fans, although one fell away almost immediately. It didn't look like she was in any immediate danger, though, and she soon wrestled herself into a more advantageous position. Her right eye had begun to swell from where someone had already managed to land a blow on her, but she had one of the sports fans in an armbar using only one hand while the other beat the other woman back.

"Do you think she needs a little help?" Lombe asked and pushed from his seat. It felt important to note that he had left his cane and pulled his hat off as well, which was all the indication Jozzun needed that he intended to join the brawl instead of ending it like he had the last time.

"I do believe our captain is buying into some of Daria's philosophies," Ishima shouted, stood as well, and rolled her shoulders. "Getting into fights simply for the hell of it does have a way of releasing all manner of stress. Not as much as sex, but there are similar hormonal releases between the two."

"You know, I think she said something similar." Jozzun pushed to his feet as well. "And I am curious to find out if that philosophy plays true for Xi-Trang as well as humans."

"Hey, look at that. I wondered the same thing."

"No one's surprised by that, Doc."

It did not have the same release effects on him. Or maybe he simply wasn't cut out for this kind of activity. His species were inherently empathetic. It was a part of their nature, which meant throwing his fists at people he didn't know had no beneficial results that came to mind immediately. Jozzun knew he could hold his own in a fight, but it was generally only put to the test when it was necessary.

Recreational brawling merely wasn't for him and all he was left with was an aching jaw and fists. Although he did feel a twinge of pride in knowing he had downed three of the brawlers before the fight had eventually wound down. Lombe and Ishima both looked like they'd taken about as good as they'd given, with bruises and cuts across their fists and faces, but they looked much more elated than Jozzun felt.

Maybe it was the alcohol. He would have to find somewhere that sold his particular form of inebriation before he joined another fight to see if that affected how he felt about it afterward.

"I guess I'll get all of us some painkillers," Ishima shouted as she returned with ice packs for the group from the bar once it opened up again. "Ten minutes on and ten minutes off should help with the swelling. For you too, I think."

Jozzun assumed he was referring to him, although he noticed she'd picked up one too many ice packs.

"Who's that one for?" Lombe asked when he noticed it at the same time the Xi-Trang did.

"It's for Daria whenever she comes back to the table. Have you seen her?"

Jozzun looked around and tried to make sense of the mess that filled the bar after the fighting had calmed. "I...I can't...see her. But I can't feel her either. Do you think she went home with someone?"

They all looked at one another and shrugged. It was certainly a possibility. Their first officer was no nun and she had some unhealthy associations between sex and brawling.

"We could check the sec feeds and see if they picked up who she left with," Lombe suggested, stood, and kept the ice pack pressed to the side of his head. "With any luck, we'll be able to track them to wherever they went and we can wake her and drag her back to the ship when we need to leave tomorrow."

That seemed reasonable. It wasn't so much about invading her privacy as making sure they didn't have to wait for hours before she came back to her senses. There was no point in delaying their trip when they already had a buyer on the hook.

Fifty creds was all they needed to pony up to access the feeds, and Lombe whipped his tablet out and scrolled through each of them. Daria wasn't hard to find, given that she was generally at the center of the fight.

"Shit." Jozzun narrowed his eyes and realized he'd been distracted by another feed a little behind than the one Lombe watched. He focused and picked up one of the feeds by the door that showed Daria leveling two brawlers when three came up behind her. She knocked one of them down without even trying, but the other two had their casters drawn and stopped her in her tracks.

They were sharp enough to keep their distance and clearly not drunk. The one she knocked down threw up before he pushed up and took her weapons from her.

"Who the fuck are they?" Ishima asked as she leaned closer.

"It's the Red Crows," he whispered and felt something painful sink into the pit of his stomach. "The Red Crows have her."

CHAPTER TWELVE

It was the kind of news that sobered them quickly, although Lombe was the first to start prepare the copious amount of coffee they needed to get them back to fighting strength when they got back to the *Atalanta*. Their engineering crew was already up to speed by the time they returned.

"Can't find her anywhere on the station," Kleiz noted once they were all gathered in the cockpit. "Looks like the Crows know exactly where the feeds have blind spots. Might have put those blind spots in themselves to make sure they could move around the place without being detected. Doesn't matter either way since they've already reached out to contact us."

It was weird to hear only one speaking without the other two constantly adding something or finishing each other's sentences like they all shared the same mind. All three were focused on finding Daria, and their focus meant only one needed to do the talking.

"They reached out to contact us?" Lombe asked and leaned forward.

"Must have noticed the *Atalanta* was the ship she traveled on and wanted to make some kind of point about taking her, I'd imagine."

Jozzun shook his head. He couldn't imagine the kind of mindset Daria must be in by this point, but she would know they wouldn't leave her behind. *Whether she trusts us or not, by now, we are the kind of family that stuck together.*

"They sent an encrypted message," Kleiz explained and called it up.

"Shoddily encrypted, but I don't think they tried to show off their tech skills."

"Might be that they only wanted to make sure no one tapping the broadcast line would be able to see what was happening."

"Either way, it works out well for us since we can track the message source."

"Do that," Lombe whispered with a scowl. "What does the message say?"

"We haven't looked at it yet."

"Thought you'd want to be the one to look at it."

"We've backtracked the message in the meantime. They bounced it around on a couple of channels, but not very well."

"Left a path like a scar across the broadcasting channels. We'll let you know if we find anything."

"And in the meantime…"

The footage appeared immediately on the screen and looked like a live feed from the point of origin. While reasonably sure it was indeed live, they couldn't tell what kind of lag came from the feed bouncing around.

Jozzun let the pained feeling in his stomach twist a little when they saw Daria held up by chains. She'd taken a beating, although it hadn't been enough to knock her out. Her face was swollen, and blood seeped from wounds over her right eyebrow and cheekbone as well as from inside her mouth.

Still, it looked like she was laughing, goading the rest of the Crows as she snapped her head forward. It made two of them flinch and back away, which drew another laugh from her.

"It looks like she still has her spirit," Lombe whispered and leaned a little closer to the screen as he tried to tell himself something acceptable or give himself some good news. It didn't appear that there would be much of it as the feed continued.

The lower-level Crows who had worked her over backed away as three others approached. They were in full armor and looked like they ranked above the grunts she had intimidated before.

She showed no sign that she would be intimidated by them either and spat a mouthful of blood on the ground in front of them.

"What the hell do you think you need that armor for?" Her laugh was almost a cackle and her voice slurred a little. "Are you that scared stiff of little old me getting back o—"

Her voice cut off when one of them stepped in from behind, tapped her between the shoulder blades with a shock baton, and made her jerk against the chains. Her body sagged slightly.

"I guess you bitches don't know how to work me over with only your fists then, huh?" she muttered and struggled to recover as a second baton hammered into her ribs.

Jozzun could feel the whole room flinch with each strike that came in to interrupt her before she could speak again.

Another character stepped into view next to the three armored ones. He had his helmet off but he wore the same red armor as the other three, although his was more impressive. Gold and silver tassels over his shoulders indicated that he was some kind of ranking officer.

Anger was building among the *Atalanta's* crewmates, but Jozzun didn't do anything to try to calm them. That was usually what he was supposed to do—make sure that calmer heads prevailed every time as much as he could—but something else was involved now.

He had begun to get angry too, and the fact that they had stopped flinching after the first couple of shocks only confirmed that they were getting too pissed to look away. Lombe and Ishima both vowed some kind of vengeance with each stroke, and Jozzun couldn't help but join in. It was all he could do to keep himself under control without riling them up with him.

Every time Daria tried to talk, they cut her off until she finally sank against her restraints, breathing heavily and with blood still dripping from her wounds.

The officer hadn't said a word yet, but it looked like he was prepping himself to since the rest of the Crows were present for the example being made. There was no cheering or jeering from the group. Jozzun couldn't see into their minds, not through a broadcast, but it seemed like this was a solemn moment for them. They were being taught a lesson. It was not a celebration of any kind.

"When word came to me that a deserter attacked our people on Mugh-9, I knew there was only one person who would have the kind of gall to turn her back on her brothers and sisters, siblings forged through fire instead of the water of the womb, and then turn on those she once stood side by side with. She was a problem child we accepted into our fold anyway, thinking we could show her a better way, and this is how she repays us."

Daria's response came in the form of spitting red on the man's uniform. A grotesque grin showed on her features.

"Deserter?" She hissed in fury. "You and your inbred shitheads left me to take the rap because none of you had the fucking guts to fight back when those Xi—"

She was interrupted again, this time by two shocks. They made her go limp and possibly unconscious, but another of the Red Crows approached and woke her with what looked like a stim to the neck.

"Dozens are dead because of her treachery!" the officer continued as though she hadn't spoken. "Dozens more in trying to take her alive before she could compromise our efforts on the planet further. Killing her would be a kindness in light of this level of disloyalty to her family. But allowing her to live any longer would put those she betrayed in further danger. I would not allow this to happen to my people."

He drew a caster from his hip and pressed it to the side of her head, but Daria still didn't show any sign of being intimidated by their efforts.

It will happen eventually when they push her beyond control, but I imagine her time spent in a Xi-Trang prison will have tempered her against the pain somewhat. There, all manner of unpleasant tortures had been projected onto her mind for hours and even days at a time. She hadn't been conditioned quite to the point where she wouldn't feel it, but she'd certainly felt worse.

Xi-Trang prison guards knew how to break their prisoners, especially those who were as unruly as Daria tended to be. He didn't even want to imagine the kind of pain she'd gone through to be able to grin at this kind of torture.

Still, it doesn't look like the spectacle is for her benefit. She was right about that too. It is all intended to set a very powerful example to the rest of the Crows to make sure they know what will happen if they ever turned their backs on their so-called siblings.

It was all crap, of course. The Crows' leadership clearly had nothing against leaving their members out to hang given what they'd done to Daria.

And she was still there and still defiant. She spat in the man's face again and forced him to take a step back and clean himself with a handkerchief while she was hit with the prods three more times. There was no more flinching from the *Atalanta* crew members, but Jozzun did pick up on Ishima's plans to get her hands on one of the prods, insert it into the officer's rectum, and turn it on.

That was enough to make even him flinch. Not that it wasn't entirely deserved.

"But I am nothing if not a businessman," the officer said once he'd cleaned the spittle and blood from his face. He now spoke directly into the camera that was casting the footage. "And if you are willing to keep a treacherous bitch alive on your crew, I am willing to make a deal. Money is to be sent to the families of those she disrespected. The word in the market is that the crew of the *Atalanta* is carrying a heavy load—something that is meant to be sold in human space."

He approached the camera and leaned a little closer. His proximity revealed that his hair was a wig he wore to cover his balding head, likely in an attempt to keep the fact that he was aging from being picked up by the rest of the crew. Soon, he would need to wear a helmet full-time if he wanted to keep that embarrassing fact a secret for much longer.

"The full haul is the price demanded in exchange for her life," the man continued. "And ten percent on the top as a fee for the inconvenience caused by fleeing the planet instead of facing her retribution with honor."

"Fuck you in the ass with a horse cock, you piece of shi—"

More shocks silenced Daria, but they had been a little slower in coming. Jozzun had no connection to them, but the body language from the mercs showed that they were confused by what sounded like mercy being shown to the so-called treacherous bitch instead of killing her outright.

Still, they knew better than to question their leader in front of the whole crew. They would no doubt question him later about why he had chosen to put creds over values. True believers were the easiest to fool on these matters, though, and all it would take would be a few empty promises of retribution to come to calm them.

"I will not have you delay, try to negotiate, or make things more difficult than they need to be. Any message sent by you will result in her execution. In six hours, if the promised riches are not delivered to us, she will be executed—and you can be sure we will come to take what is owed, with interest."

The footage cut out and left the cockpit in silence for a few long moments while the crew looked at the deck and considered what their next move would have to be.

Of course, they all immediately turned to Lombe in the expectation that he would make the decision. Jozzun knew he would look to them for some kind of guidance but in the end, the decision belonged to him as to how they would get their crewmate back.

The captain sighed, ran his hand over his face, and looked like he was physically trying to calm himself before he faced the rest of the crew.

"You heard the man," he whispered and his voice shook with barely contained rage. "He says he'll give us Daria if we pay him everything we have and a little more besides. Of course, the chances are he thinks he can get away with almost anything, which means he'll probably take the payoff, kill Daria anyway, kill us, and steal our ship to make a point. Everything I've seen and heard about the bastards says they can't be trusted."

Jozzun could tell that he would probably try the peaceful option if they had to and if there were no other options, but he also agreed with the captain in his assumption that the Red Crows would probably simply kill them and take their ship out of spite—and because there was no authority in this region of space for them to call on to stop them.

They were very much on their own, and whatever decision was made at this point had to be made with that knowledge in mind. Taking insane risks was essentially what they did as a group, but there was generally something desperate that pushed them to make those decisions when they were out of most other options and had to do something unexpected if they wanted to survive.

We'll reach that point soon but need to make sure we have no other options available to us first.

An unsettling moment of silence continued through the cockpit. It felt like the images of Daria strung up, battered, and bleeding but still shouting insults to the people who tried to break her spirit would be the deciding factor. *All of us are more than willing to sacrifice for someone we care about, but even she would make the choice to fuck the enemy up rather than give them what they want. There is no point in rewarding that level of disrespect.*

"I have a feeling I know what we will do," Ishima stated and raised an eyebrow. "But it should be noted that if we are planning some violence, the one person most talented for that kind of operation is the one we have to rescue. As much as we are all skilled fighters in our own right, we might want to consider giving them what they want and setting some kind of trap for them that would allow us to reclaim it all."

Lombe shook his head. "They'll expect that from us. I wouldn't recommend it since they would probably kill her immediately if they got a whiff of foul play and we'd have already handed the ransom to them. We'd have to be very, very sure about our play in that case."

"If it helps, we were able to track where the signal was coming from," Kleiz commented and raised a hand for attention.

"First step was determining that there's no signal of that weight leaving the station, which means it's restricted to an internal cast."

"That narrowed it down. A lot."

"Nothing else for us to do but pick up on the transmitters capable of putting that kind of cast out and that narrowed it down further. Then we found ourselves a location inside the station that saw many changes over the past few years."

"An old aux fuel station but they've been upgrading the already reinforced bulkheads, fashioning it into a type of compound the Red Crows appear to operate out of."

"I'd bet that you'll find they went on a shopping spree and picked up all kinds of defensive knickknacks," Lombe whispered and shook his head. "We have less than six hours to find a way in there."

"Especially since they'd probably outnumber us at least ten to one, even if we bring the Hounds in," Jozzun added and looked at their three engineers. "You can control the Hounds, right? Get them into fighting formation and start them shooting at people, that kind of thing?"

One of them shrugged. "Theoretically?"

"We've played around with them for much longer than Daria has, so we know how to get them to do what they need to do."

"In practice, things are different."

"Because we've only ever practiced with them. Daria's the only one who took them out into combat."

"And even then, from the ins and outs we've picked up from their sensors, it looks like they might outnumber us even if we do have the Hounds."

The Xi-Trang nodded. "Like I said, they have a superior force and a superior defensive position in there."

Lombe looked like he might have come up with some kind of plan. Jozzun didn't like the familiar expression he saw on his face, even though the captain's brain jumped all over the place and made it impossible for him to pick up anything other than the vaguest of ideas.

It's not anything we wouldn't have ended up thinking of anyway if we put our heads together, but it is interesting to see how quickly he considered our options. He might as well be a computer in his own right.

"The Red Crows have a presence here, right?" Lombe said finally and looked around. "It means there are other merc corp on the station too—those that wouldn't mind putting them in their place if they ever had the opportunity. It'll be a long shot, but we might be able to convince them to join us to kick their asses if the going gets a little too rough. Try to find which of the corp the Crows have been in spats with already and make sure no amends have been made. I don't want anyone who thinks they can get an in with them by sharing that we're looking for connections. It might be a good idea to see if they have their defenses networked too."

"Do you think we might be able to turn their turrets and drones on them?" Ishima asked.

"Well, we'll never know until we try. We have six hours

and I intend to use every fucking second of it. Let's get moving."

This is better. Lombe is in a mood and he has a plan. It wasn't the best of plans and if we had been given more time, he would probably be able to devise something better.

But at least we won't charge into the compound headfirst. Jozzun would take that particular win.

CHAPTER THIRTEEN

"Knockout gas?" Lombe scowled a little as he attempted to grasp what the doc was saying.

Ishima nodded. "Technically, I did say...uh, *sticky* knockout gas. But I guess you can use the shorter version of it as long as we make sure we don't miss any of the important details."

"You do know that most mercs these days have armor that comes equipped with respirator suits that are also meant to filter out anything that might be dangerous to the user from the outside, right?" The captain took a sip from the coffee that had kept him awake since they left the tavern and winced at the bitter taste. "The damn things are meant to help them survive in a vacuum so I can't imagine they would let their people be swamped by gas that would cause them injury. We might catch a couple of them when they aren't ready for it, but the rest of them will catch on and they will cause us trouble."

"Do you think I don't know about that?" Ishima demanded and looked mildly offended, although the response might simply have been irritation from the stress. "That I haven't picked those armored suits apart more than enough times to get to the people inside them that I wouldn't know how the fuck to get around the filtration systems?"

"So you do have a way around the filtration systems?" Jozzun asked and narrowed his eyes. He hadn't picked up anything like that yet, but he was giving himself a break on what he considered non-essential input. They were in a tight spot, after all, and his focus was already spread across multiple fronts.

The doc nodded, leaned forward, and showed them a depiction of the filtration unit's structure on Lombe's tablet. "Again, it's the sticky part that's important. It's an old development from my time in the military—the way they fought against soldiers being able to breathe in the battlefield. Yeah, yeah, I know. It's horrifying shit but I replicated the formula. Okay…uh, I worked out the formula a while back and I know it works the way it's intended—do you remember those guys on Fenton?"

"You—that was you?" Lombe asked and shook his head. "I thought it was Jozzun making them lose their shit."

"Me too," the Xi-Trang interjected. "I was surprised by how effective my mind games were on them."

"Well, there was a little extra outside help—from me, most specifically. The idea is that the gas would not only render a target unconscious if it comes into contact with moisture—think mucus membranes and the like that most humanoids have around their respiratory systems—but if it doesn't come into contact with something like that, it clumps on a surface. It means that on dry surfaces such as the respirators those mercs will be wearing, it'll gather on and create all kinds of problems in the mechanisms and clog them too, even if they do have a closed system."

"What kind of time will it need before it starts to help us?" Lombe asked and flicked through the doctor's notes, which were practically illegible to Jozzun. The captain looked like he was able to read them, albeit with a little trouble since he muttered under his breath.

"Oh...minutes. You don't need much to clog the inner workings of an air filter in armor suits like that. Ten minutes at the most if they have an isolated O2 source, but you'll be able to see those easily enough. There aren't many of them among the grunts in the merc corp these days, and they'll be the zero-g suits. They'll have to get their helmets off and clean the filters before they can be used again, which will put them in the path of the gas' real intention. I'll have to find a way to get it in their atmo scrubbers, but that won't be the hard part, will it?"

Lombe shook his head. "We might be able to put it into some grenades we can use in case you're not able to slip it in their atmo directly. Do you think you'd be able to do that?"

"Probably. I'll need help from Kleiz to adapt some of your grenades. In that case, it'll work much faster but it'll have a smaller area of effect."

"What stops it from affecting us?" Jozzun asked.

"Please. I've already inoculated all of you when I tried it the first time, and I slipped it in with Daria's mandatory shots too so there shouldn't be much of a worry of it affecting her either."

"I..." Jozzun wanted to complain about her experimenting with the team without telling them but in this case, it happened to help them. *It's certainly something I will have to address with her later. If I'm not allowed to peek into the minds of the crew, she isn't allowed to treat us like lab rats either.*

"What kind of luck did you have with the other merc corp?" Ishima asked and looked at Lombe as he dropped into his seat.

"Well, I don't think anyone will be shocked to realize that the Crows are less than popular with the rest of the corp, especially around here. They have a habit of bullying and pushing them around, and there have been skirmishes between them a couple of times in the past few weeks. With that said, none of them want to get involved in what is being touted as an internal issue. We don't have any proof to support Daria's claim that she was abandoned by the Crows so the other groups are more than content to leave them to their infighting. They did wish us the best of luck in our efforts, though."

"Of course they did," Kleiz muttered.

"They assume that if we're successful, it'll weaken the Crows on Medusa, but they don't want to start a war on account of someone like Daria." The captain sighed and rubbed his temples before he took another sip from his mug. "It looks like we'll have to raid the Crows on our own for now. Maybe, if we start putting some holes in their numbers, the others might end up joining the fight. Everyone's opportunistic around these parts."

Their engineers exchanged a few looks.

"Well, there's nothing for it but to make sure we can rely on only our talents," one of them commented. "We've looked through the blueprints of the area, and there are some points we can access that'll get us to the compound's bulkheads. We can rig up some breaching charges which could open the bulkheads without causing too much damage to the surrounding structure."

"Be sure about that. The last thing we need is to accidentally blow another asteroid station. That would be enough to establish a reputation for us and we'll be locked out of docking with any of them ever again."

Lombe joking like that was probably a good thing. It raised all their spirits and gave them some hope that there was a chance they would walk away from all this alive. Still, Jozzun knew that while his captain put on a good face, a twitching, aching despair had begun to wrap around him and squeeze painfully.

More plans were pulled together. They had three hours until the deadline, and their leader wanted to be ready to act at least an hour before that in case something fell through and they had to take some kind of action to make sure Daria wasn't executed out of hand.

It gave them enough time for prep work, but Jozzun doubted that they needed his services to prepare the shit required. He didn't know much about chemical weapons or explosives. Most of his work would happen when they were in the chamber with a clear line of sight on the bastards in question.

He felt confident in his ability to prevent Daria from being killed by anyone around her, either with casters, rifles, or knives, but he wouldn't be much help to the rest of the crew while he worked his mind games on them. Lombe could probably protect him and the Hounds would be there with them as well to make sure the room was filled with as much chaos and fighting as possible to keep the focus from falling on any one member of their party.

The Xi-Trang realized that he'd walked to the cargo bay, where the Hounds were all out of their harnesses with their weapons in hand and ammo connected and ready to enter combat.

Given my ability to predict what would happen in a battle like this, it might be possible for me to take control of the neural interface the Hounds are on. If so, I could make them react to whatever the Crows happened to do with valuable seconds to spare.

This was an advantage he generally provided their ship's AIs with when the *Atalanta* did most of the fighting. In that case, though, he fed his predictions in manually and let the AI process them and make the decisions. The Hounds were controlled on a neural network, however, something that worked rather well for humanoids who had no psychic links.

That wouldn't be the same for him, of course. Jozzun could do it, but connecting with bots on that level was uncomfortable and it could even get painful and feel like he was sticking his feathers into their gears and letting them churn over his mind.

Still, it's worth a try. If Daria can endure the pain she's been subjected to, I can surely overcome anything if it helps to rescue her.

He collected the node from where it hung on the wall—down low where the Euchrien engineers would be able to reach it without too much trouble. He'd tried to link to the Hounds before and while it had played out well enough, it had been an uncomfortable experience. Xi-Trang were connected to living things more than anything else. Forcing a connection to bots, even through tech, felt unnatural—like carving new pathways into his mind that he didn't want there.

Maybe this time, it will be a little easier. It might be that the pathways are already forged and I simply have to work with them. He connected the node to his temple, closed his eyes, and felt the foreign channel invade his consciousness to make it difficult to focus on much of anything else.

When his eyes opened, every one of the Hounds looked intently at him. They held their weapons at the ready and looked like they were waiting for instructions. *They want me to tell them what to do.*

Not vocally, of course. That was the point of a neural network. It allowed the commander to direct his soldiers from one point to another without needing to talk about it.

But something else was at play, although he wasn't sure what it was at first. A human's consciousness would only be allowed a glimpse at what was happening. His heightened senses, however, let him feel everything the Hounds experienced instead of simply picking up the sensors the way the humans would. Human senses were much less refined than his, which was proving to be both a blessing and a curse.

Everything about it simply felt wrong. Jozzun wasn't sure how to explain it but it grated on his senses and made it difficult to focus on things. He knew he had to restore some measure of control, though, because something reached out and tried to push into his mind.

Startled, he turned and noticed that one of the Hounds

was out of position. It approached him and looked concerned.

His mind backtracked in an effort to keep up. *Nothing is wrong with the Hound itself but the sensory perception I have collected from it is beyond anything I've ever seen in a bot before, combat or otherwise.*

It took him a moment to realize that this was the Specter bot—the one Daria had started to show so much affection for. He had been dubious about it but as he pushed a little deeper, he began to pick up what could only be the beginnings of conscious thought.

It was very similar to the kind of thinking processes he noticed from Daria, which meant it was clearly learning a great deal about itself by looking through her eyes and emulating elements of her thought patterns through the neural connection.

Maybe that is why we haven't noticed anything about it before. Its mind was already starting to become aware but it requires a compatible mind to connect to before it could truly awaken. Now that it was linked, he could see the mind had begun to reach out to connect with others.

Specter wasn't quite sentient yet, not by Jozzun's standards, but it was close—almost like a canid, smart and sharp in its own right and intuitive to the people around it.

I can now understand how she would have forged a connection with it.

"We'll save her, you know," he whispered, unsure if the bot could even understand him. "It'll be a little difficult but we'll get her out and you'll work with her again. I merely need you all to be at the peak of your abilities to help her yourselves."

Its head tilted to the side and looked even more like a canid in the way they cocked their heads in a similar fashion.

"Can you understand me?" the Xi-Trang asked and stepped forward. "It's not the highest of standards for sentience but...you do understand."

Specter took a step forward and the screen on its face displayed some static for a moment before it finally showed him words that were fragments of language but clear.

"Yes." The screen went blank for a few seconds. "Understand." Another blank was followed by another word. "Some."

Of course, most computers are capable of understanding what is spoken to them, usually by installing a few different preset commands in the software. It's new to see one that teaches itself the commands based on what it hears, though.

There were many ways for an AI to develop and while he'd never seen it happen, Jozzun could imagine that this was probably one of the most significant steps that would lead to the next few and allow the intelligence to continue to grow.

"You know who Daria is, yes? You can understand the difference between myself and her?"

Specter studied him for a moment while the screen continued to show signs of its attempt to communicate.

"Yes. Daria. Not here."

"She's in trouble," he whispered, took another step forward, and stood directly in front of the Hound to watch intently for all the signs that would confirm it to be more than merely another bot. "Daria has been kidnapped and we need to rescue her. Will you help us?"

Another pause made him hold his breath but the words now flowed a little easier like it had begun to get the hang of this whole communicating concept.

"Daria. In danger. Help?"

The question mark seemed to indicate that it tried to work out how it could help her not be in danger—like it attempted to assess the whole situation from the outset.

"The enemies who took her have a base here on the asteroid. We'll find a way get Daria back and maybe make them pay for injuring her."

Jozzun realized that the processing took a little while longer this time as it struggled to understand something he'd said.

"Pay how?"

He ran his fingers through his crest and tried to push past his mental protests. *It's utterly insane that I am communicating with a sentient creature in its earliest stages of consciousness. I know this might not be an entirely good thing since we cannot predict the outcome, but it is certainly intriguing and even exciting.*

"You remember how Daria attacked the pirate who cut into your chest?"

Specter seemed to understand that, although it looked like it was still confused as to why she had reacted the way she did.

"Kill. Equals. Pay?"

"Kind of. Killing them ensures that they will not try to hurt her ever again."

That satisfied Specter somehow and he reacted by nodding his head slowly.

"Make them pay. Kill them all. Soon?"

"In a couple of hours."

"Ready when you are."

Something was chilling about the way Specter voiced his determination. Anger was something most AIs were never programmed to feel—or maybe they tried and determined that as an impulse reaction, it didn't have much use.

But Specter felt angry. The Xi-Trang wasn't quite sure how that was possible and it didn't have the same reactions to the impulse as humanoids would have. Then again, why would it?

The unsettling nature of the bot's determination was what made a tingle reach down Jozzun's spine as Specter dropped back and fell into formation with the rest of the Hounds. It had an attachment to Daria, maybe sparked by the way she'd reacted when it had been attacked before.

Emulating her reaction is appropriate, and given how connected she is to the bot, it is very evident that she has been the catalyst for Specter's development beyond merely a regular combat bot. He is something new and he wants Daria back alive. And he is willing to carve through as many Crows as get in his way to save her.

"Weird," the Xi-Trang muttered and shook his head. *At what point did I begin to refer to Specter as he instead of it?* It was a worrying development since it suggested he was now starting to develop some affection for the Hound as well.

That is interesting—and ridiculous. Maybe I should put

animated eyes on my electronic appliances, give them silly names, and treat them like household pets.

If we survive rescuing Daria, perhaps this is something I could do to remind myself how foolish this affection for mechanical devices is. It would certainly make me smile if nothing else.

CHAPTER FOURTEEN

As plans went, there wasn't much for them to work with. Lombe had done about as much planning as he could manage in the short time they were allowed, but there was still far too much shit that could go wrong for them. As the rule of the universe said, anything that could go wrong inevitably would, which meant they had to make allowances for that kind of downside.

The simple truth is that it's the best plan they can come up with and none of us is prepared to leave Daria to die at the bastards' hands. Them wandering into the lair of the enemy was probably not the action that would encourage the Crows to feel a little more relaxed in the certainty that the *Atalanta* crew would cooperate.

It was a good assumption, especially when they approached the doors leading to the compound. They could see the turrets and drones were all set up and ready to attack, although no attempt to do so had been made as yet.

Lombe looked the part of the captain. His suit was a

bright silver that matched his top hat and his boots were shined to the point where a reflection could be picked up from them. He grasped his cane with the confidence of a vain man who knew he was better dressed than almost anyone else present.

His caster was ready but remained holstered on his hip, and he showed no sign of drawing it yet when he stood his ground despite the Crows gathered in front of him. They were all armored, armed, and appeared ready for a fight while he looked like he was dressed for a social engagement or even a party.

Jozzun didn't look like a fighter and neither did Ishima, and they were followed by Forrest and the other bots that piloted the mule that brought the crates in.

The captain of the Crows stood in front of the group, dressed and ready for battle, but it appeared that he wasn't quite sure what to make of the man who stood in front of him.

"Put your weapons down," he snapped finally and motioned for them to comply. "Hand them to us and we can do business."

Lombe shook his head. "We won't put our weapons down."

"What?"

"See, you're the ones with all the guns pointed at us. You're holding one of our people hostage, and you have turrets and drones ready to gun us down at the slightest provocation. If we lower our weapons, it means you can simply kill us and take everything without even needing to worry about us retaliating. Us handing our weapons to you will be your statement that you intend to murder us, and if that's what you have in mind, I choose to die with a weapon in my hand and a handful of you fuckers dead with me. So what will it be, baldy? Are you here to start a fight or do some business?"

This is the part I've been concerned about since everything hinges on this. I know the captain's purpose is to keep their attention focused directly on him so they won't pay attention to anything else that happens around them. Pointing out that their captain is as vain as he is and bald on top of it is certainly a good way to ensure that.

It would probably end up drawing fire much faster too, but it seemed Lombe was willing to risk that. He'd done all kinds of shit that most people would consider stupid. Still, he had a way about him that suggested he would bend the odds in his favor no matter what. The fact that this came soon after breaking into a prison to break someone out was the kind of nuts Jozzun had come to expect from his captain.

"We're here to do business," the Crows leader answered with a smirk and removed his helmet. "Keep your weapons if you like. Is that our merchandise? It doesn't look like much."

"We transport considerable merch here and there to make sure people think we're a respectable business enterprise. But this is what you heard we're transporting and it's far more expensive than anything else we have in the hold."

"That wasn't our deal."

Lombe snorted derisively. "Did you want us to carry a full fucking cargo bay's worth of crates here? I suppose we could probably make five or six trips, but if you wanted to alert the rest of the merc corp to the fact that you have expensive shit in your little compound, that would be a very good way to do it. This is easily worth at least a million credits—more if you can find the right buyer. Humans are putting a shitload of creds into 'quik these days, trying to outbuy the rest of their competitors."

"You're negotiating even with your comrade's life on the line?" the man demanded incredulously.

"I might be, but at least I'm here for her. From what she told me, it doesn't sound like you or your people did the same. It's kind of a pity that you set the leadership bar so low for me that it made it incredibly easy to take your place. She's one of the best shooters I've ever seen, and all she expects from me is that I don't leave her behind. I guess I should thank you for that shit."

"You're pushing your luck. It's almost like you want me to gun you down."

Lombe tilted his head and studied the other Crows. Jozzun was hard at work to calm them, relax them, and generally distract them from the kind of focus they should have if they expected a fight.

The Xi-Trang had certainly succeeded in this responsibility but he took care to not smirk. He'd managed to bring them to the point where they wouldn't pay attention, no matter how much noise was made in the maintenance tunnels above them. Out of sight and out of mind seemed an appropriate summation, although he wasn't entirely sure where the expression had originated.

A trickle of sweat worked its way down Jozzun's back and followed the trail of his spine, but he held his focus and worked as hard as he could without making it apparent that he was toying with their minds. They'd likely seen his kind before and if they saw his feathers start to glow, they would know something was up, no matter what games he played with their perceptions.

"I'm sorry—what kind of luck do you think I'm pushing here?" Lombe asked, took a step forward, and placed both hands on his cane while he looked at his counterpart with a small smile. "A less trusting man than I might imagine that people like you, in a location where you command the largest fighting force and with no real government to hold you back, would think you don't need to do business with puny freelancers like us. A less trusting man might see all these guns aimed at him and think you had every intention to kill us to a man and then steal everything we own, simply because you can."

The Crows' captain backed away and narrowed his eyes. His plans were fairly obvious but he was a little thrown by the fact that Lombe knew what they were and was still willing to provoke him and speak out, seemingly without fear. The *Atalanta's* leader was no psychic, but he didn't need to be to know that the man he faced was a coward to his core who wouldn't like the feeling that he hadn't accounted for something in this perfect little plan of his.

It was only too easy for the Xi-Trang to intensify those feelings and push him to the point of paranoia that made it impossible for him to think of anything but his survival. This wasn't the kind of leadership that inspired his people. They were already distracted, unfocused, and seemed uncaring about how things were going.

The node attached to Jozzun's head showed him where the three engineers were hard at work. Lombe had stalled long enough, and it looked like they were set up and ready for their part in the battle. The captain sighed, closed his eyes, and calmly let the chaos continue to build around them.

"Open those crates!" the Crows leader shouted. "Show us that they're not…not some kind of trap!"

His anxiety was very evident and his men stared at him like he had gone crazy. They seemed to try to understand why their brave and powerful captain, in an advantageous position with both firepower and numbers over the puny freelancers in front of him, acted squirrely and unsettled.

Lombe shrugged in response. "We have no problem there. Would you two help me with this?"

Jozzun nodded. He and Ishima moved with him to the crates but rather than work to open them, all three ducked behind them and kept their heads down as the timer triggered in the HUD that came with the node attached to his temple.

Closed eyes and covered ears still didn't seem to help much. He felt the impact when the explosives detonated and made the ground shake, although that was merely a matter of the grav generators being affected by the blast. The sound of stones and crumpling plastic was loud and the whole area filled with a smoke cloud. Forrest and the rest of their bots that also had hidden behind their cargo jumped up immediately and began to pull the tops off the crates.

These contained no 'quik. All things considered, it would have been incredibly dangerous to expose the volatile and expensive merch to the kind of fight they would engage in. Lombe straightened on the other side of the crates and looked like he was in the mood for a brawl now. Jozzun was in the mood for it as well, but he had to make sure the Hounds were liberated from where they had been carefully concealed in the crates.

Specter was the first one out. He vaulted smoothly from his hiding place, his coil rifle already in hand, and opened fire on the Crows who were still on their feet after the engineers brought their gates down on their heads.

Timing had been key to ensure that everything outside went boom at about the same time that Ishima's gas was released inside. There was no telling how effective it was, but there was no point in worrying about it now. They had the element of surprise, both with the explosives and the Hounds coming out shooting. Even the engineers picked off a few of the mercs when they could without giving away their location in the tunnels above.

"Make pay."

Jozzun shook his head when he realized that the mechanical voice echoed from Specter through his feed with the Hounds and the bot immediately guided them into a combat position. They closed rapidly on the mercs who still tried to regain their bearings. It was terrifying to watch mechanicals guided with the kind of decisiveness, precision, and deadliness that directed them to cut down twenty of the mercs within seconds of the engagement's beginning.

Especially since I'm not controlling them and another bot is—with the kind of intuition we would normally expect from humans.

The mechanicals cut away and the Xi-Trang tried to point to where the sporadic retaliatory fire came from when he picked up what the mercs were doing. All he needed to do was show Specter what was happening and the Hound snapped into action. He directed the other Hounds to kill another dozen or so before the mercs remembered they had guns, armor, training, and experience and began to fight in earnest.

A couple of the Hounds took some damage but unlike the mercs, they didn't seem to mind. Specter guided them perfectly, and even though the enemy outnumbered the bots despite their heavy losses, they were still pressed back into the opening that had been made into their compound.

It wouldn't last, however. The Crows' captain had already vanished from the battle and had likely run to where he could observe the fight from a distance. *Or simply run, the cowardly bastard.* His mercs, however, were trained and skilled enough to deliver a barrage to slow the advance of the Hounds.

"That would be my cue," Jozzun whispered and drew out the two grenades he carried.

Ishima had warned him to handle them with gloves and make sure he didn't breathe in too deeply while around them. He primed them carefully before he lobbed them into the group that had begun to gather and organize themselves to mount a counterattack.

"Grenade!" one of the men shouted as the devices arced in over their heads. The mercs dove out of the way and separated a little as both devices detonated and eliminated a couple of them with the blasts alone.

That wasn't all they were meant to do, however. A light cloud of gray particles suddenly spread over the area and the enemy began to reach for their helmets. A couple who already had breaches in their armor fell to their knees, affected almost immediately by the gas. The others struggled to draw air in as it began to clog their breathing apparatuses and forced them to take their helmets off in an attempt to help their lungs. As planned, they breathed deeply and inhaled the knockout gas.

The cloud didn't spread very far and it wouldn't last very long, but it did significant damage and halved the mercs numbers again. More of them felt the effects of it and they struggled to breathe even though they weren't in the cloud yet. They noticed what was happening and warned their men to stay away from the gas hanging over them.

All of them were sharp and even they realized that they needed to change the situation to something a little more in their favor at this point. The alternative would put much more at risk than only one of their compounds.

Lombe moved forward as they tried to step back through the shattered gates and the man shouted something Jozzun didn't understand. His cane crackled with energy as he drove into those closest to him and swung the cane like a maul and with similar effects. One was struck directly and his chest caved in. His armor crumpled and crushed everything inside it with enough kinetic energy to hurl him into the group that tried to retreat.

Ishima stepped in as the captain peeled away to let his cane charge and she caught one of the mercs before he even saw her. She held a combat knife in one hand and a caster in the other. The former weapon slid into the weak points in the merc's armor and she thrust hard and viciously until she found something that spouted blood from the gash.

She held the knife in place to position the merc in front of her like a shield as she snuck her caster around him to shoot at the others and prevent them from getting inside the compound.

Jozzun nodded, maintained his grasp on the minds of those mercs who were still in the area, and made them feel like they couldn't breathe. It wasn't quite as effective as making them think that they could fly, but it was enough to keep them distracted while Specter and the Hounds closed on those who had been knocked out with the grenades.

"Make. Pay."

He shook his head and looked away when the Hounds unleashed a volley into the unconscious mercs to eliminate them in a way he could only describe as exactly like Daria. *It seems Specter has begun to take after her a great deal, and even Lombe looks like he isn't sure if the execution was quite the right choice to make.*

Still, they were in the middle of a battle—or a skirmish, or whatever the proper term was. They could address whether all their actions were righteous or just once they were all on the *Atalanta* again.

Still, I can't help but feel like I unleashed some kind of monster when I spoke to Specter before the fight began. It wasn't a matter of principle for him since he'd seen humanoids do much worse than what AIs were generally criticized for. *I suppose it's more to do with the fact that it would always be an unsettling sight to see something so completely foreign begin to take matters into their own hands.*

Specter was angry and he made the monsters pay for every blow they'd inflicted on Daria.

The last of the mercs still outside of the compound were dispatched and they scanned the area to make sure there was nothing else for them to do before they started heading deeper inside through the hole the engineers had made.

The three Euchrians realized that the danger had mostly passed and they scrambled down the rocks to where the rest of the squad waited for them and checked their weapons.

"All in all, I think we can say that went better than expected," Kleiz commented. "We fed the doc's little potion into the atmo inside, so I guess the fact that no one has rushed out to help their friends is a good thing, right?"

"Right," Lombe answered and stared at the bodies of the mercs the Hounds had executed. "Our bets were on the hope that they would all be affected before any of them could take the opportunity to kill Daria. Let's see if we were right to gamble with her life."

He motioned for them to follow and stepped through the rubble into the compound.

The massive area was capable of storing hundreds of tons of fuel and half a dozen different chambers would have allowed it to include different types of fuel without needing to worry about mixing them. None of it was left, of course, but the smell still permeated the whole space, something Jozzun hadn't noticed before.

Reinforcements all around looked like they had been put in place to prevent anyone from trying to tunnel in, but none of them expected anyone to know much about the maintenance hatches the Euchriens had used to go around them. Their whole plan had hinged on having a way for the engineers to get in. Of course, they could have been smuggled in the same crates they'd used to ferry the Hounds and then blown their way in.

That would have called for another distraction, however, even once they'd released the knockout gas into the atmo. Jozzun would likely have been called on to use his imagination on that particular score.

"Daria!" Lombe shouted, looked around, and strode toward the groups of mercs that had struggled to breathe and finally simply pulled their helmets off and lay down for a nap.

About fifty of them still inside were affected by the gas. Ishima had said it would take about ten minutes for their bodies to process the poison, which would either kill them or let them wake up. It was sufficient time if they knew how to use it, and it didn't look like Specter or the Hounds had any interest in killing all of them.

They didn't have the time for it now.

"Over here!"

Daria's voice was weak but it echoed well through the chamber and led them to one of the larger sections where she had been chained.

They hurried to liberate her from the restraints and she located her weapons—stupidly tossed in a pile nearby—and strapped them around her waist. While she put on a good show of looking like she was still in fighting form, Jozzun could tell that it took all the effort she still had in her to stand on her own two feet.

Her fingers were numb from being chained and her

knuckles swollen from the brawl. Her face was every imaginable shade of black and purple but the bleeding had stopped for the most part. This indicated that the Crows had at least stopped punishing her while they waited for a response to their demands.

"You look like shit," Lombe whispered and scrutinized her carefully as she struggled to tighten her belt.

"Yeah, well, this has to...be the worst hangover ever," she answered, her voice dry and raspy. "Still, when all these assholes started to drop for a snooze, I assumed you had something to do with it."

He let her finish buckling her belt before he extended a hand to support her.

Jozzun ached simply from looking at her. *Of course, things could have gone worse, but it looks like there are certain lines even the Crows aren't willing to cross when they have business in mind.* The chances were that the captain had ordered no further violation until they had what they wanted from the *Atalanta* crew.

This was confirmed by Daria's thoughts. The possibility had hung over her head like a knife the whole time she was being held, which explained why she needed to make a show of being strong and vital when all she wanted to do was settle in with enough painkillers to kill a horse and sleep for a week.

But Lombe wasn't the only one who waited to greet her. Specter stood nearby and moved closer when Lombe finally looked around to try to find out where the Crows' captain had made off to.

"Yeah, I missed you too, buddy," she whispered and patted the Hound on his chest plate. "I hope you haven't caused any trouble while I was gone. Still, I guess I'd know about it."

Specter stared blankly at her for a moment before he stepped forward and offered his arm to support her. Images flashed across the screen on his head before they finally settled into two words.

Made. Pay.

"Yes, you did, buddy." Daria was a little too exhausted to fully comprehend that the Hound was speaking to her, and Jozzun approached quickly from the other side. He helped to keep her on her feet until they reached a few chairs where she could sit and Jozzun took the node from his temple and pressed it to hers to hand control of the Hounds to her.

It isn't like I did much other than direct them on where not to go. Specter was responsible for most of what they had been able to do and he acted almost independently. It was like he understood that I wasn't quite cut out for the job but was still willing to let me look good for the battle.

He turned to the bot, tilted his head, and smiled. "That was well done. I didn't think I would live to see the day when a handful of bots could engage a full troop of trained mercs and win. You made them pay for their shit."

Specter nodded his head slowly the way he did when he understood what was said.

The Xi-Trang turned and realized that Lombe was studying the interaction closely with a curious look on his face before he finally shook his head. The captain had no doubt decided that his time was better spent addressing other matters. They still needed to get out of the fucking compound before the other mercs came to—

or worse, the rest of the Crows on the asteroid decided to join the fun.

It was now apparent that it had been the captain's intention all along to leave his men behind to die. Although a smart plan, it was probably not the bravest. Still, the only Crows who had witnessed his cowardice were now all dead, which left him the job of twisting the narrative to make him come off as a hero.

It might be a little more difficult to sell it to the rest of his people but it isn't like they would believe the word of smugglers who hired traitors and deserters over one of their respected captains—the kind who has a full head of hair and everything.

Ishima approached Daria, who looked like she was about to fall over, and pressed something cold to where the bruising was worst. The doc was quick and precise with her movements and made sure that she treated her as efficiently and fast as she could while still keeping in mind that they were on a tight schedule.

"Only one...condition, Doc," Daria whispered as she straightened suddenly and her eyes closed for a moment.

"And what would that be?" The woman's voice was calm, collected, and almost emotionless as she tapped her patient's arm before she slipped in a shot of painkillers that made her relax almost immediately.

"No...no experimenting. No making new additions or anything like that. I'm good the way I am, thanks."

"I make no promises. In fact, you'll want to keep an eye on me through this entire process to make sure I don't try anything stupid."

Daria smirked but immediately erupted in a coughing fit. "Shit...it hurts to laugh."

"You might need to avoid that too. Jozzun, hold this."

She held what looked like a bandage pressed to the patient's cheek and eyebrow where the larger cuts were. He was careful to not press too hard as he didn't want to start the bleeding again. It smelled like a disinfectant and an anti-inflammatory had been applied on the bandage, and it was unnaturally cool to help with the swelling and seal the cuts.

"I'll need to stitch them and I want to give her a proper scan when we get to the ship," the doctor stated and scrutinized the first officer carefully. "There might be some nerve damage from the shocks, and I want to make sure nothing is bleeding internally. She's a tough one, though, to survive all that."

"Shit," Daria muttered and pushed slowly to her feet with Specter's help. "I've been through worse. Spend six months in a prison where the guards are sadistic psychics who can make fifteen minutes feel like days in the worst torture chambers in the world, and a good sound beating won't be anything by comparison."

"Unfortunately, she is right in that respect," Jozzun commented as they began to move in a group retreat to the ship. "You don't hear much about it because the prisoners are rarely ever released with their memories intact, but the few who are often talk about how fucked-up the prison wardens tend to be."

"Like I said," Daria whispered. "Still...feel like I should probably take things easy. No more brawls for me. Not for a few weeks anyway."

"No drinking either," Ishima warned in a growled tone as they exited the compound and moved back the way they'd come. Daria was thankfully deposited on the mule where the rest of the bots waited to ferry them to the *Atalanta*.

"What?"

"Alcohol is a blood-thinner and a diuretic. Given that you'll need as much fluid in your body as you can get, alcohol is utterly forbidden."

"Well...I would say I'd prefer to go back to prison but they didn't let me drink there either. I guess you'll have to claim second prize to their cruelty."

"I know, I know. I'm the worst, trying to keep you all alive and healthy. Sadism in its purest form."

Ishima patted her gently on the shoulder as they hurried forward. They avoided the path that led them through the city inside the asteroid and instead, headed directly to the docks. If the Crows were gathering for some kind of counterattack, the city was likely where they would wait. There was no reason to stay on the asteroid any longer. They had the merch, they had Daria, and it was time to leave and let the Crows deal with their weakened numbers and wrecked compound.

Like scavengers, the other merc groups would catch the scent of carrion in the air. They would make sure the Crows paid for keeping them under their boots, even if they hadn't been willing to help with the rescue in the first place.

Their hasty rush to the *Atalanta* was uneventful. The Hounds escorted them carefully and remained alert for any sign of an attack from the enemies but none came. Maybe, Jozzun, thought as he considered this, the Crows simply didn't have the local numbers to start another fight.

Except that reasoning doesn't sound right. We eliminated a good number of them but nowhere near the army of easily hundreds they were reported to have on the asteroid. It continued to nag at him until they reached their destination.

Still, now that they were back on the ship, it wouldn't take long to get moving again. There wasn't much in the way of a port authority to stop them from leaving anytime they wanted, and Lombe moved directly to the cockpit to get the process started.

The Xi-Trang, for his part, helped Daria to their medic's chamber where she was settled for a sensor reading to make sure that nothing was broken inside that needed to be attended to immediately.

While their first officer still looked like she needed rest, she certainly seemed better. Ishima was three or four different kinds of nuts but she knew what she was doing, especially when it came to treating wounds inflicted in a fight. The cold press was doing its job, both by cleaning impurities from the wound and making Daria's face look like it hadn't been run over by a tank.

She wasn't quite at full fighting strength yet, but the scanner didn't immediately pick up anything that needed to be addressed by surgery. The doctor made a note of some broken ribs and a few points that appeared to have sustained some nerve damage that could be corrected easily.

"How does she look?" Jozzun asked when the patient finally settled into sleep, although Ishima would still keep an eye on her for the moment.

"Not many people I know would survive a beating like

this," the woman admitted in a low tone. "That includes most soldiers. I'd like to see that kind of inner strength in far more people on my side, but...well, I guess this kind comes from a lifetime of tough experiences, so maybe not."

Jozzun smirked and nodded, but before he could answer, his comm keyed in to tell him that Lombe was reaching out to him.

"Aye, Captain?"

"I need you in the cockpit."

The man's voice was terse and he knew better than to delay. He nodded his farewells to Ishima before he hurried to the cockpit where the captain appeared to have avoided any delay in getting them ready to leave. The Xi-Trang had been worried that he would want to speak to him about the Hounds, but it was immediately apparent that something a little more important was on his mind when he called the situation up on the screens.

"I guess we know why the Red Crows didn't make any move to stop us getting to the ship," Lombe whispered and displayed the sensor data of the docks around them. Fifteen ships had already left and more were about to, all carrying the Red Crows' mark.

"They plan to cut off our exit from the asteroid field," Jozzun whispered and ran his fingers through his crest. "Couldn't we wait them out and let them play in the rocks for a while before they need to refuel?"

"What's to stop them from simply swooping in and hitting us while we're docked? I imagine they'd probably have to pay some kind of fine for the effort but in their minds, it would be worth it to get rid of a threat."

His logic made sense. They didn't want to have to wait

out a siege anyway since more Red Crows could be waiting for them on the asteroid to cut them off from supplies and whatever else they needed.

"What's the plan now?" he asked once he'd assimilated the facts

"Now?" Lombe shrugged. "We put as much fuel as we can into the thrusters and see if we can outrun them before they cut us off completely."

"I like that plan. It's better than the last one, anyway."

CHAPTER FIFTEEN

"Why haven't we left yet?"

Jozzun looked away from where Ishima explained some of her work to the small cot Daria was resting on.

"You should be sleeping," the doctor said and approached the scanners that provided them with second-by-second updates on the status of their patient. "There's no need to be a hero at the moment."

"Fuck that. I'm always a hero."

"The definition of a hero is the kind of person who gets other people killed." Ishima pressed the back of her hand to Daria's forehead to make sure she didn't have the beginnings of a fever. "Either that or the kind of person who ends up on my table whether they like it or not. So settle back in the cot or I'll give you something that'll do it for you."

That drew a smirk from the Xi-Trang as he approached the patient, who complied reluctantly.

"What? So you can start experimenting with me?" the

first officer whispered and glowered around the bandages that covered the right side of her face. "I know what your game is, Doc. It's the reason why I was still standing when those Crows assholes were all dropping for no fucking reason. You did something to me without telling me and now, you expect me to trust you."

Ishima smiled and even she could tell that the woman didn't mean what she was saying. She merely felt a little contrary because of the situation she was in. *I sense something else, though, but it's deep-felt and complex and a little difficult to understand. Even in her drugged state, I'd need a little more context to know exactly what she's trying to keep hidden.*

"Yes, all kinds of experiments," the doc answered with a small smile. "You shouldn't be surprised if you wake up and realize that your hands have been replaced with coil cannons. Your eyes will be fitted with plasma launchers, and you'll have four legs, ready to charge into battle like a fucking tank because you'll have subdermal armor implanted too."

Daria rolled her eyes but still relaxed on her cot. "You're not fucking funny."

"I like to think I am."

The first officer looked to where Jozzun stood. "You didn't answer my question. Why are we still docked? I can't hear the engines moving us out of here."

"There have been some…uh, developments. Lombe is pushing to get us out, but we're opening some pathways to make sure."

"What happened?"

"The Crows still on the station boarded their ships the moment we removed you from their little compound.

They have a small fleet out there getting ready to block our attempts to reach any of the Lanes and escape. Given the chaotic nature of the asteroids in the field around us...well, it's taking them some time to get into place."

"Why does everything we do always devolve into this kind of fun? More to the point, why aren't you up there with Lombe to find out what exactly we have to do when we get into the field?"

"I've already done my part and picked up what they intend and which avenues of escape they will focus on. We have a plan—which, it should be noted, is a fairly terrible one—but he doesn't need me to help him pull it together for the moment."

"And he was needed here for a while instead," Ishima interjected. "You were having fits in your sleep and I needed him to calm you. Otherwise, I would have had to restrain you to prevent you from damaging your body any further. It's been tremendous fun so far, but it looks like you'll make a full recovery. The worst of it was some nerve damage from the shocks you took, but your recovery is well on the way."

Daria smiled and groaned softly as she closed her eyes. "I...appreciate it, Doc."

"Of course. You're a part of my crew and I will always fight to make sure you're at the peak of physical condition, no matter how you feel about me." Ishima pulled a few strands of bright red hair tenderly from the patient's face. "So if you put your recovery at risk, I'll be right here to call you an idiot over it. That means you'd better get some fucking rest before I knock you out myself."

Jozzun smiled as he watched them interact. *It seems this*

is what weighed heavily on Daria. She is used to having people leave her behind but has far less experience in dealing with people who come back for her.

Deep down, something in her mind said she didn't deserve to expect anyone to return specifically to help her because they hadn't done so reliably yet—and certainly never simply for her. They would always have some kind of reason and agenda.

She wasn't quite ready to make the commitment herself but she had begun to realize that the relationship she was in with the crew of the *Atalanta* was more than only a business relationship. There was no telling what it would take to finally crystallize that realization in her mind, but he was comfortable to let her reach it in her time. Until then, they would all continue to fight together, find new and interesting ways to run headlong into danger, and hopefully get out of it again.

"She's sleeping," he said quietly.

"I appreciate your help, Jozzun."

"Anytime. Do you think she'll recover?"

"Assuming we don't get blasted to pieces in the next few hours, she should make a full recovery. I'll keep her under observation for the time being, though, to make sure she doesn't do anything to endanger her recovery."

The Xi-Trang nodded. That was all they could hope for. Still, given that they anticipated a serious fight ahead of them, he wished the doc had come up with some specialized treatment that would have Daria up and on her feet before they needed to fly out.

But that was purely wishful thinking for what amounted to magic at this point. As knowledge and understanding of the universe continued to grow, there were fewer gaps for that kind of foolishness in the general consciousness.

He stepped out of the medical room and left Ishima to do her work as the ship began to shift and shudder when the engines came on. They engaged fully to pull them away from the dock in a slow, deliberate sweep.

Lombe gestured for him to take the co-pilot seat without looking up from his screens. "How's our first officer?" he asked.

"Recovering—full of piss and vinegar as usual. We were a little foolish to think a beating like that would be enough to keep her down for long."

The captain smiled and nodded. "Good. She's an inspiration to all of us."

"Do you think we should be beaten simply to see how quickly we'll recover?" he asked in a deliberately offhand way.

"You know I was thinking metaphorically."

He snorted. "So you want us to be beaten...uh, metaphorically?"

"Shut up."

The *Atalanta* disconnected from the docks and cut the link to the network the docked ships were in, a process that handed full control of the ship to the pilot again. Lombe was ready and began to ease the vessel out from the tunnels they had been docked in. There weren't many chances for them to battle in some kind of debris field in space, but at the last two locations they'd been in, they'd fought in both.

Maybe it was time for them to stop visiting asteroid

and debris fields in general. Or, at least, they needed to make a few preparations for when it happened again. The Xi-Trang considered the possibility of activating their ship's coilgun and finding projectiles for it to use.

While it was expensive and would just be a drain on fuel most of the time, having one or two rounds for the cannon would make sure they had enough firepower to punch through situations like this.

Instead, they headed in with a frigate-class ship without its primary cannon. It hadn't been designed for this kind of warfare but Lombe had pulled the *Atalanta* through quite a few similar scrapes before.

It didn't mean that he had to like it, of course, he thought ruefully. And it wasn't like they could simply assume everything would work out in their favor either.

"So," the captain whispered as they slipped out of the asteroid and finally obtained readings on what was happening around them. "What the hell kind of odds do we have to beat this time?"

"It doesn't look good, even from the outset. The asteroids make it difficult to pinpoint exactly how many vessels are waiting for us, but the count—at least as far as I can determine thus far—is about fifty individual ships. Most of them are freighters and repurposed shuttles with guns mounted on their backs—mainly plasma cannons, although a few possibly have a couple of one-use torpedo tubes set up."

Of course, all of them would have some use in a fight, if only to add to the mayhem. Still, there would always be an order to the chaos and that was what they would take advantage of. Jozzun could predict what would happen based on the actions and reactions of the people in the battle. These came to him in a wave of sensations he could feed into the AI's reaction protocols.

This was a powerful edge and one the team leaned heavily on when they fought battles where the odds weren't in their favor.

But when things were neat, orderly, and going according to the plans of the people they were up against, there was little point in him knowing what would happen or even if they would be defeated. At that point, he carried the responsibility to cause some trouble.

In these kinds of battles, subtle influence was all he could achieve over the distance and sheer number of people around them. Still, subtle influences were sometimes all they needed.

He still didn't know what he would do to help, but inspiration would strike when he had to act. The whole point of being able to look into the minds of the people they fought was that he could tap into what would get the best reaction out of them.

"What exactly do you see out there?" Lombe asked as they began to approach the enemy positions.

"Mostly civilian ships fitted with bits and pieces of weapons and armor that might help them in a fight. A few dozen 'vettes in the mix could cause us trouble, though. They have three frigates, like the *Atalanta*—and armed about as well—and one cruiser in the middle of it all. That's the centerpiece of their defense as far as I can tell. The rest of the ships will fire at us, but they'll try to direct us into the firing line of the cruiser."

"Yes, I can read the sensors too. I was asking what you

can see in the Crows themselves. I know it's not quite…uh, as exact as any of us might want it to be, but any intel you can glean from them would be one hell of a help."

Jozzun nodded. He knew what Lombe was asking and had played it off as something else. In all honesty, he knew the extent—which included the limit—of his abilities. Some Xi-Trang could look over an entire battlefield, in space or on the ground.

They called it a battle hypnotic, where they could look into the bodies and minds of all parties involved and push their own forces to fight harder while they weakened the enemy forces, distracted them, and almost drove them mad.

Of course, there was always the option of the helmets that could stop the targets from being interfered with, but they wouldn't be able to pick up on what was being directed from their side either.

The Hypnos usually decided the outcome of most battles they were a part of, while the rest of the people involved were little more than pawns for them to direct. The most powerful were those who came away with the victory. The weaker ones were generally killed by the effort to keep up with their counterparts.

I wish I could forget those days when I pushed and drove myself as hard as I could and tapped into reserves of stamina I never knew I had.

Through these efforts, he'd discovered there were always greater lengths he could push himself to and new ways to reach into the minds of the people around him. Usually, though, this knowledge came with bitter disappointment when he realized he would never match the skills of the others. He would never be as good at it as they were.

The academy didn't like having failures on their record and when he left, he was mostly forgotten. *It was painful to realize that but honestly, I had nothing to go back for and nothing else to do but find work amongst the people who don't much care about my failures. It's perhaps the best thing that could have happened to me, although moving past the harsh truth was hard.*

Lombe had been the only one he'd felt comfortable revealing his abilities to—and the only one who had seen him in action—and as it turned out, it was still better to have him on the battlefield than have no help at all. The Xi-Trang knew he would be hopelessly outmatched if he was ever involved in a fight with a real Hypno. Still, until he ran into one of those, his skills and training at the academy had been useful in almost every fight they'd been in since they'd started working together.

"They aren't sure what they're fighting for," Jozzun said finally, closed his eyes, and rubbed his temples gently. "They were told they were being attacked, but they were also told it was merely a pathetic group of freelancers that had no ties to the area. This isn't the kind of thing they run from. While their leaders tell them they need to make a statement, they lost their compound and know something else is going on. Otherwise, they would have fought with us inside the asteroid. They are confused and unsettled but are following orders. Still, it's something I can probably touch on. If we survive long enough."

"Let's get to surviving then." Lombe turned to where Forrest was connected to a few of the systems to assist them with manning the point defenses and the targeting AIs for the torpedoes, although the command to release those was set to Jozzun's control panel. There were still a few ways for them to cause trouble for the Crows, even while they continued to gather and try to herd the *Atalanta* to where their heaviest guns were waiting.

The Xi-Trang tapped his screen to highlight the places where the Crows were hiding in wait. They acted more like wolves, knowing most of their ships wouldn't stand a chance against them. All of them must surely know that the *Atalanta* had been the only one to escape the derelict base when it exploded. In case they all didn't, Jozzun made sure those who did know began to share that information with the rest of their crews.

In minutes, the whole fleet would be abuzz with that knowledge and their members would try to understand how that could possibly play into how terrified their captains acted around it. It wasn't much, of course, but it was a seed planted in their heads toward a much longer game.

He estimated a couple of hours at most but it would all be for nothing if they ended up dead. Jozzun tilted his head and picked up a handful of 'vettes that had already begun to break containment and move through the narrow gaps in the asteroids. It was immediately obvious that their purpose was to try to flank the *Atalanta*.

"Point defense might be able to keep them off us," Lombe muttered. "But they're trying to push us to where the cruiser's waiting, and we won't stand a chance if we end up in its firing line."

"We won't make the gap they're using," the Xi-Trang

answered. "We know that and so do they. Plus, they're leaving charges on the asteroids to blow them up and make the path that much more impossible for us. Which means..." He frowned in thought.

There were two more paths they could take to avoid the heavier guns. While he had assumed they would cover them to make sure they weren't used, the chances were that they would simply blast them to pieces too.

"Forrest, would our shields be able to push us through the chunks and pieces of asteroid like that?" the captain asked and looked at the bot plugged into their attack systems.

"It's a possibility, although you might want to consider leaving it as a last resort."

"Yeah, I was afraid of that," Jozzun whispered as the 'vettes came into view and began to fire plasma rounds from the cannons under the cockpits. They were some of the only ships that allowed windows in their hulls and even put the cockpits out in front.

The reasoning was that it helped the pilots work better with less lag than when the visuals ran through sensors and cameras. Given how small they were, they couldn't be burdened with armor or even shields worth a damn, which meant the pilots had to be some of the best and possibly the craziest to even fly one.

'Vette pilots were paid some of the best creds in the mercenary business, although whether it was because it was never a guarantee that they would see their next paycheck or because they knew their value was a source of ongoing debate.

"Point guard triggered." Forrest alerted them and the

plasma cannons opened fire immediately to cut off all lines of attack before they could even approach. Lombe twisted the *Atalanta* and maneuvered her into the path of some of the smaller chunks that had been blown off the asteroids.

"Shields down fifteen percent," the bot warned calmly.

"Direct seventy-five percent of the power we have to the bow shields," the captain ordered and twisted again when a group of the freighters came into view. Jozzun immediately launched a volley of torpedoes and aimed them directly at the ships to ensure that they didn't think there was any chance for them to get a shot in before they were wrecked.

Still, one good shot to the *Atalanta's* flank would get through the thin shields they had left in place there for the moment. This meant they had to be far more effective at keeping the damn mercs off their shoulders while they continued through the field.

"We have hostiles ahead," Forrest informed them sharply.

"Shit!" Lombe swung the ship around and the point defense system delivered a barrage at a handful of 'vettes that had begun to close on their position. Unfortunately, there was little they could change since the situation meant only their weak shields were there to pick up anything the point defense wasn't doing on its own.

If they didn't keep full shields at the front, the bits and pieces of rock would begin to shred their ship's armor across the bow—or the knife's edge, as the captain called it sometimes—and that would weaken them a great deal more.

"Torpedoes away," Jozzun announced and directed

them quickly into the paths of the 'vettes. This forced them into evasive maneuvers, but one of the frigates came into view almost immediately and retaliated with a handful of torpedoes of their own.

The plasma cannons managed to tear into them before they could get close enough to cause damage, but Lombe had already yanked the ship behind a handful of the asteroids that were still intact and tried to find a way out in preparation to retreat.

A moment later, he shook his head and tried to bring the ship around again, and Jozzun realized that a volley of plasma rounds was closing in on them. They had been fired at from far enough away to give the *Atalanta* a decent chance to evade them, but the ship was being forced into the path they were trying to avoid.

"Whoever's running this operation knows what he's doing," the captain whispered and jerked them directly into the path of the 'vettes that had tried to flank them. He had no intention to try to avoid them this time, and the Xi-Trang flinched when they rammed through the smaller ships. The shields dropped by another thirty percent but none of the enemy craft were left.

"Drop shields and let them recover," Lombe ordered and turned to the him. "I know it's asking a lot from you, but we need something now."

The truth was that Jozzun did have an idea that had started to form, but it wasn't quite something he expected the captain to approve. *As much as I respect the man's taste for crazy plans, certain ideas are simply a little too crazy, even for the captain.*

"You've got something. What are you thinking?"

He cleared his throat, looked around, and scowled. "It… came to me when you moved the shields to the bow. It isn't the kind of thinking that would allow us to last for very long, but when I scanned through the ships… Well, the captain was there."

"The captain—oh, the one with the hair? Or…uh, without the hair, I guess I should say."

Jozzun nodded. "He's commanding the operation, and as much as we might not like to think about it, we might need to accept that we'll have to face that cruiser no matter what we do."

Lombe leaned forward in his seat, his eyes narrowed. "Go on."

That wasn't quite how he expected the man to react. "Well…they expect us to try to circle it and find anything else to do but face it. If we were to charge head-on, we would catch them by surprise and come in before they have any of their bigger guns prepped to fire. Once that's done, it's a matter of keeping their plasma cannons and torpedoes off us while we hope we have bigger balls than they do."

"You want us to ram into the cruiser."

The Xi-Trang shrugged. "Well…I want them to think we'll ram them. I've already planted the seeds of fear in their minds, and if we can get in close enough, it might be enough to make them blink first."

Even he wasn't quite sure it would work and there were numerous ways for them to assume that things would go wrong.

In all honesty, the only reason why he even entertained the notion that it would work was because the cruiser's coilguns still hadn't been activated. The Crows were arrogant enough to think the *Atalanta* would simply remain inside the asteroid field and try to find another way until they eventually had nowhere to go.

As much as he wanted to continue to play that particular hunting game in which they were the prey, he knew Lombe was thinking about how they probably wouldn't even survive that long.

Desperate is honestly the only play we have left. I also like to think it is exactly the kind of play Daria would suggest we make, and not only because she is straight-up nuts.

"Right," the captain whispered and immediately began to plot their path directly toward the cruiser waiting for them. "I have a feeling I'll regret this but hey, what's life without a few risks, eh?"

"I think you and I left a few risks behind many years ago," he retorted but it lacked humor.

"Many risks, then."

The shields had returned to their full capacity and it looked like none of the Crows would press toward their position yet. They seemed content to simply wait for the *Atalanta* to try something before they moved in to intercept, given that their early positioning allowed them to wait their prey out.

Lombe had already initiated their new course and it looked like none of the enemy 'vettes attempted to step in to cover their current trajectory. *It makes sense, of course, since this was what they wanted us to do, but none of them will expect us to be quite this fucking stupid.*

It was a last-resort plan but it enabled them to jump beyond the tedious feints and skirmishes to the end, press their luck, and hope their gamble paid off. If they survived this, Jozzun decided they were entitled to try one of the planetary lotteries to see how well that kind of luck would hold.

"They...haven't reacted yet," he whispered, keyed in the ship locations as he picked them up, and let the AI adjust the sensors to track them when they began to move. At the same time, they made sure they knew where the rest of the Crows were waiting.

Of course, they would run the flank when they realized what was happening but by that time, either the *Atalanta* would already be moving out of the asteroid field or the crew would be very, very, very dead.

The line of fire for the cruiser was immediately highlighted for them to indicate where the danger zone would be.

Lombe looked at Jozzun for a second to confirm that this was something they wanted to do before he activated the intercom.

"So...a fair warning to the rest of the crew," he called and paused to make sure he had all their attention before he continued. "We're about to do something extremely dangerous. Some people might even say it's stupid but at this point, it's our only hope to get out of this alive. With that said, I'm very sure everyone will want to be here in the cockpit, if only to make sure that if we take any damage, you won't be the ones who lose atmo."

"It's very kind of you to think of us, captain," one of their engineers called from a hatch on the other side of the room. "Lucky for us, then, that we are here already."

"I guess I have something of a reputation," Lombe whispered as he pulled them up and around to approach the line of fire of the cruiser. Jozzun still monitored the situation inside the larger ship, and nothing suggested that the Crows were even slightly alarmed. None of the torpedoes were in their tubes and none of the coilguns were warming up.

Time will be the major factor for the smugglers in this case and if we act quickly, they would push forward before their enemy realized what was happening. Arrogance, confidence, and probably the very reasonable assumption that no one in their right mind would do what we are doing will hopefully be enough to delay the response.

Ishima was the last one into the cockpit and there was enough room for her to wheel Daria in there as well, although the latter was still unconscious on her cot and looked like she wouldn't wake up anytime soon.

The captain rolled his neck and closed his eyes for a moment like he was coming to terms with the decision made before he began to accelerate the *Atalanta*. He pushed the thrusters to give them enough speed but held those on the side and front a little, enough to make sure they didn't charge headlong into an asteroid instead of the cruiser in front of them.

A surge of panic went through the other ship and as far as Jozzun could tell, it looked like they had watched the smugglers the entire way but had only now begun to realize that something was amiss. Alarms triggered and questions he had repressed now occurred to them as the *Atalanta* broke fully into their view, finally out in the open for them to see.

"That's right, motherfuckers," Lombe whispered and

increased speed as the shields were raised. He was completely focused on the bow of the ship as raced toward it.

"They've got torpedo locks," Forrest called.

"Why aren't they firing yet?" the captain demanded.

"It doesn't look like they have any set up in the tubes."

"We do, right?" he asked in sudden anxiety.

Jozzun nodded.

"Give them a volley—everything we can fire at them. I want them to start thinking they're fucked and there's nothing they can do about it."

That was all he needed to hear. Maybe Lombe had become a believer in their crazy plan. The cruiser, however, began to shift, pivoted into an attack position, and gave them a view of the dozens of plasma cannons that were not all aimed at them, although they started to fire.

This was the downside of having so many cannons on the ship, of course. They were great for point defense and meant it was almost impossible for the *Atalanta's* torpedoes to come anywhere close to testing the ship's shields.

But with so many rounds fired together over a long enough distance, they began to waver and interact with other rounds. This cooled them and spread them to the point where Lombe didn't even need to evade them. Instead, he simply let the heatwave wash over their shields with the familiar glimmer of silver for a moment, but with no real sign that the ordnance had caused any damage.

Through it all, the captain pushed the ship forward even harder. No asteroids lay between them and the massive cruiser ahead, which meant they didn't need to worry about dodging or twisting out of the way. Their thrusters were committed and so were the shields, which left only the point defense system and armor to deal with any attacks launched at them from the side.

Jozzun grasped his chair a little tighter and closed his eyes. He could feel the familiar prickle along his spine but especially around his feather crest. It warned him that he was pushing himself almost to the limit of his abilities and beyond what he was able to do.

The minds of the enemy crew were already in the flurry, but he continued his pressure to force those he could to panic. He caught glimpses of shaking fingers, mistakes, and distracted looks at monitors as they tried to determine what the hell a frigate was doing charging head-on at a cruiser.

Torpedoes were loaded into their tubes and the first volley was launched to join a round from the plasma cannons. The latter now worked in an alternating firing line to prevent the same thing from happening again so the rounds wouldn't be ruined before they could reach their target.

Lombe yanked them around intuitively and twisted the *Atalanta* into a corkscrew that brought them away from the trajectory of the plasma rounds while their cannons eliminated the volley of torpedoes.

More followed but this time, mistakes were made in the firing solutions and a handful of the torpedoes veered off and hammered into nearby asteroids instead. A large number of the plasma rounds linked up and lost their potency, but enough of them reached the shields to drop them to a dangerous level.

The *Atalanta's* captain showed no sign of being affected.

He controlled the ship masterfully and wove calmly through the fire they faced while still maintaining their velocity and a trajectory for a head-on collision with the cruiser.

It had been an easy approach, but Jozzun knew it wouldn't last, especially since the rest of the fleet had begun to close in. Panicked calls from the captain ordered them to try to intercept the frigate and keep the *Atalanta* away, and while it wasn't the best look for the man in this case, it wasn't the best for the smugglers either.

Jozzun's feathers pricked and almost felt like they were burning against his scalp but he held his focus and punched in the updates for Forrest and the AIs to keep in mind, marked off volleys of torpedoes, and let Lombe devote his singleminded attention to his evasive flying.

In that moment, the thought crashed into the Crows captain's mind. The frigate would crash into them. While the cruiser was two and a half times the size of the *Atalanta*, a solid collision like that would wreck it, drive directly through the middle, and split it in half. The cost of repairing it was one thought, but the other was that the inevitable damage would expose the whole ship to the vacuum outside.

This is what I've waited for. He pressed on it and made sure the man could think of nothing else. *It's inevitable. Nothing you can do will prevent it. You're dying while gasping for breath. The freezing temperatures outside turn your skin to paper while you watch helplessly. You can hear your silent screams in your mind but no one else can and no one will come to help you.*

He almost felt sorry for the man since he sent him the

kind of panic that would drive most people mad. The captain was no exception.

Almost was the operative word when it came to sympathy. All he needed to do was look at Daria's bruised and battered form to remind himself that mercy had never been an option in this fight.

The cruiser had already begun to change course. It shifted up and around in an attempt to avoid the *Atalanta's* charge. In a game of wills, Lombe had won—although he did have the help of a psychic, which had to be considered cheating.

The captain smirked as the enemy ship began to move away and tried to shift so it would be able to reposition itself to fire on the smugglers' vessel once it had passed them.

Other asteroids were waiting, however. The first impact looked like it destroyed one of their coilguns and immediately triggered alarms to blare across the ship while three of four sections of the cruiser were vented and locked out.

It was a good start and the ship continued to spiral out of control. It spun into a handful more of the smaller asteroids as the atmo vented from the chambers that had been damaged. This made their movement even more chaotic but still moved the ship out of the *Atalanta's* path as they barreled past.

None of them had expected them to get that far without being plastered across three or four different asteroids but thankfully, Forrest was primed and ready. As the *Atalanta* flashed a broadside across the cruiser, a barrage of plasma rounds and torpedoes was unleashed to add to the struggles the massive ship had encountered.

Their shields were already mostly down or weakened, which meant every last round and torpedo found its mark and cut smoothly through the heavy armor to find the fragile parts and pieces inside.

Of course, a ship that large wouldn't be disabled by only a couple of hits and collisions, although it did look like their thrusters were taking a beating. Cruisers were generally designed to play the part of a shield in an armada full of frigates that could send coilgun rounds but were comparatively easy to break apart.

Their troubles weren't over but they were out of the net that had been cast for them. A wave of relief washed over Jozzun and he smiled and allowed himself to enjoy the moment—very briefly of course.

They still had considerable work to do.

CHAPTER SIXTEEN

Jozzun knew they couldn't hang up the victory holos yet, but he had hoped that the Crows would be a little more stunned by how one frigate had managed to get past a cruiser and cripple it at the same time.

It soon became apparent, however, that the damage fell well short of disabling the massive ship, and it didn't take long for it to come about. Even worse, the rest of the fleet had already been converging on their position before they made their breakneck charge.

This meant they wouldn't pull up, especially when the orders came from their captain—no doubt desperate to show that some part of him wasn't covered in urine—to continue their pursuit of the *Atalanta* while the cruiser regained its bearings.

There were dozens of them, mostly 'vettes, and all eager to take a chunk from the ship. They began to break away from where their group and containment strategy had clearly not been successful and now tried to swarm them instead.

It was chaotic and full of elements for Jozzun to control, but he could now feel the weight and the fatigue as more of the ships approached. The 'vettes especially looked like they were less interested in tearing the *Atalanta* apart. They seemed keen to board them, kill everyone, and make sure they came away with a ship and everything on it.

That was assuming they could get around the Hounds. The Xi-Trang suddenly realized they were being controlled by Daria, who was awake and watched the fight from the cot. Whatever the doctor had given her, it appeared to have worked wonders and she looked like she was about to jump up and join the battle.

Then again, it's how she's always looked. Perhaps I'm merely reading a little too much into what the doc can do and ignoring our first officer's bloodthirsty nature.

"Well, that worked," Lombe stated finally and looked around to where they were now tagged by a group of the smaller, less combat-ready ships. He let Forrest take over flying the ship and manning the attacks. "I suppose I should ask around to see if anyone has anything else to suggest? I'm all ears over here…well, metaphorically speaking, of course."

A handful of the ships were caught in a broadside of plasma cannon attacks and the rest turned away quickly.

They had thought they would catch their enemies by surprise and they likely would have too if Jozzun hadn't picked up their intentions early on in the attempt. He'd alerted the AI to the attack and kept up with the movement from the rest of the fleet.

Enough of them remained to cause trouble, no matter what was happening, and as much as Jozzun tried to make sure they weren't caught in another net, it looked like they intended to surround them again. This time, there was no option of a retreat to base if things got a little too hot for them.

The chances were they would have to come up with another crazy plan to keep the Crows on their toes or whatever their appendages were. It looked like most of them were humans. There were a couple of non-humans on the ships, but mostly engineers and other staff and certainly not among the mercs.

He hadn't noticed it before, but maybe the Red Crows were one of those corp that hired only humans. It wasn't unheard of, even in areas outside of human space. A few of them practically expected it and talked about how it was a matter of trust, and no human would trust a Xi-Trang to cover them in a firefight.

Of course, the crew of the *Atalanta* challenged that notion, which could prove to be another reason why they had put so much work into harassing them.

"We'll be able to break free of the asteroid field," he commented in answer to the question Lombe had posed. "It doesn't look like they're too worried about us breaking out, and... Well, they'll be able to stop us from sliding into a Lane fairly easily. All they need to do is fire some plasma rounds and they will interfere with any attempts we make. Running away won't be an option until we can get them to back off a little first."

The captain nodded and looked like he had thought the same thing as they launched another battery of torpedoes when one of the frigates came into view. They were fast enough to make sure that the Crows were never able to get a lock on their position without exposing themselves for too long, but the unfortunate point remained that their ammo and shields wouldn't last forever.

"If we get out into the open," the Xi-Trang continued, we'll be able to outrun all the ships except for the cruiser. Even damaged, it has enough boosters to get them moving much faster than we can. That means they'll probably call the 'vettes in to ride in their loading bay and then they'll be able to maintain their attack no matter what."

"We won't have any cover out in the open. Then again, neither will they."

Jozzun looked around. "We have the advantage with cover. I can see their movements and make sure none of the smaller ships can get in for a clean shot. Sure, we'll be able to see them outside the asteroid field but they'll see us too. We'll lose the advantage."

The captain narrowed his eyes and stared intently at the screen like he tried to weigh their options, although the truth of the matter was that he knew what the best option was and he simply didn't like it.

In all honesty, the Xi-Trang wasn't much of a fan either. He had already started to breathe heavily and sweat trickled over his body and made it all far more uncomfortable than he liked. Still, the vacuum of space or a caster round lodged in his skull would be considerably more uncomfortable.

"We'll come about." Lombe almost growled the words as he came to the same conclusion and at almost the same time. "Jozzun, keep them thinking we're running right until the last second. I don't know what you were doing to their gunners in there, but if you keep that shit up, I'd appreciate it."

It wouldn't be easy to disable their stern thrusters and the Crows would realize what the *Atalanta* was doing almost immediately. But with the cruiser's coilguns out of the fight after colliding with the asteroids, the frigate wouldn't have to deal with anything that couldn't be handled by their shields, at least for a while.

The *Atalanta* groaned softly as the forward thrusters began to slow them and turned them to head back the way they'd come so their pursuers overshot them by at least a few hundred thousand klicks. There wasn't much out there to help them to stop, and given that they were deep in the asteroid fields and trying to stay in cover while they kept up with the *Atalanta*, the process of turning would be far more difficult.

It bought them maybe thirty seconds but that was all they needed at this point. Jozzun reached out and pushed the gunners on the support ships into anxiety and fear. His attempts were helped by the way they were being treated by their superiors as frustration began to mount. It was the kind of feeling that would drive almost anyone into making stupid mistakes like setting their torpedoes to detonate on impact instead of when they came into priming distance from their target or scatter-shooting their plasma cannons.

Everything would help them at this point. The Xi-Trang felt like his feathers were growing hot to the touch from the effort, but he maintained his connection with almost every Crow he could reach out to, gritted his teeth, and pushed the pain aside for the moment. If he continued, the pain would get much worse, but it would be a while yet until he had to reach into depths that would cause any damage to his body.

But they had a way in. The mistakes of the teams in front and behind them meant that both sides suddenly faced fire from their own people. The cruiser's shields took a beating, but the ship itself didn't sustain much in the way of damage. The same could not be said for the vessels that attempted to come around and find the *Atalanta* as most of their shots went well wide. Those that didn't were easily picked up by the shields or the PDS and the torpedoes were gunned down before they had reached an effective range.

Still, the closer they got, the harder it would be for them to evade the attacks. Lombe was grimly focused and pulled them around just short of engaging the cruiser before he snuck the *Atalanta* behind a handful of asteroids as a couple of shots came a little too close. They could feel the impacts now, which told them the shields on the starboard side were down to nothing and a few shots had come through.

They all held their breath and waited for the booming sound that would tell them they had lost atmo to one of the sections of the ship.

It didn't come, fortunately, so their armor was still holding.

"Do you have a plan for this?" Daria asked as she pushed up from her cot and looked stronger by the minute.

"Not really," Jozzun admitted and shook his head. "But the way I see it, there's nothing here that says that I have to engage these assholes in a fair fight. I thought I'd put them through a little fencing. The *Atalanta's* knife-like design means we can slip in and out of the asteroids far easier than their frigates, so we do what they've tried to do to us and…uh, you know, hope that they don't get wise to the plan."

She scowled as Lombe eased them out from behind the asteroids and their guns delivered a volley as they advanced on the cruiser from the flank where they could see that most of the cannons and torpedo tubes had taken some damage earlier. It wasn't the most elegant of all plans, but it made sure they were constantly on the move and harassed their enemies at every opportunity.

When the cruiser began to turn to where they could engage fully, Lombe slipped the *Atalanta* behind the asteroids and crashed through two 'vettes that thought they could flank them.

"Shields are down to critical levels," Forest warned after the impact. "Our armor is holding but only just."

"I can work with only just," Lombe whispered, entirely focused on keeping the *Atalanta* flying. He used the asteroids around them as an improvised shield against the ships that tried to sneak closer and get a shot at them while their shield generators worked to bring them up to full functionality.

"I have an idea."

Jozzun closed his eyes when he heard Daria say it. She was far from being back to full strength and while he applauded her recovery effort, it was a long reach from there to assume she was ready for combat. Still, it looked like she had a plan and they didn't exactly have much in the way of options at this point. There was no telling how long they would be able to keep moving and shooting before a lucky shot finally found them. It usually only took one, even if they did have their shields on.

"What is it?" Lombe asked but didn't look away from the controls.

"Put me on one of the shuttles with the Hounds," she suggested. "I've been aboard the *Vermillion Phoenix* and I know it inside and out. Play one of your thrusts before you pull out with a volley of torpedoes and we'll head out with them. If we time it right, they might not even put in the work to engage their point defense system and we'll be able to get in through one of the holes left by their collision. We can start to bring that fucking ship down from inside instead."

"It's risky," Jozzun protested. He wished he'd noticed the beginnings of the idea starting to form in the back of her mind before she'd voiced it. "You'll be in there with no support and we'll have to fire in your general direction the whole time."

"I know how to keep myself safe. There's nothing like having a mind inside that's working with you, right?"

It's was her way of saying I'm pushing myself to the limits. She isnt quite at a hundred percent but honestly, neither am I. That applies to almost everyone on the fucking vessel and shit, even to the ship itself.

They needed all the help they could get, and as much as he wanted to protest, they were not in any position to turn down help when they needed it.

"Do you think you can disable their guns and shields?" Lombe narrowed his eyes.

"Possibly. Or simply cause them trouble inside the ship

and keep their focus off you for a while. When you have an opening to hit the engines, let us know and we'll high-tail it off and get back here, no problem."

"And you honestly think it'll be that simple?" The Xi-Trang raised an eyebrow and ran his fingers carefully over his crest. The feathers felt like they were on fire but they were nowhere near as hot as that. It was merely a sensory overload on the less evolved senses attached to the base of the feathers.

"Fuck no. But keeping our plan simple is the best way to stop something from going wrong, right?"

Daria looked like she was well enough to fight again and all things considered, the Hounds would probably do most of the fighting anyway. She knew her limitations and for better or worse, they had to make some changes to the battle plan.

"All right," Lombe conceded roughly. "But no heroics. I'm trusting you to know when things are too hot in there and when it's the right move to get the fuck out."

"I appreciate that." There was no hint of sarcasm in her voice. Jozzun could tell that she had expected far more resistance to her plan because it must surely look as desperate from where she was sitting as it did to him.

And she did appreciate the trust that was being put in her, especially after all that had already happened. They wouldn't leave her behind but she was well aware that if they had an opening to get out of this part of space, they would take it. This was the last gasp of an organization that would face the wrath of all the other merc corp they'd bullied and abused while they were on top.

If the Xi-Trang had to guess, he would assume the

Crows still on the base were already being gunned down or finding new recruitment, depending on how many friends or enemies they'd made. The ships in the asteroid field would soon leave too, either to look for new employment or to whatever strongholds the Crows still had in their region of space.

Daria readied herself to leave and after another shot from the doc, she headed to one of the shuttles that hadn't been damaged during their last tango with the mercs. They would be out for blood this time, but so was she.

The Crows were a large enough corp that losing a base and a dozen or so ships wouldn't do much to their overall bottom line. Still, they would have one hell of a time justifying their reputation for efficacy when word got out that they'd run into trouble with a small smuggler group.

It was the beginning of the end and they knew it. She knew it too, which was why she looked forward to a little revenge too now that she was on her feet and energized by whatever the doc had given her.

"Locked and loaded, captain," she called from her seat in the cockpit of one of their shuttles once the Hounds had boarded.

"We'll head in for another attack," Lombe called back. "Forrest will take you out with the torpedoes, which should make it a little more difficult for them to notice you. It's not impossible, mind, so if they start shooting at you, he'll simply bring the shuttle back immediately."

"Roger that."

Jozzun had expected a little more protest from her, but she had been entrusted with her life, a shuttle, and most of their Hounds. This meant that even though she wanted a little payback, she wouldn't be stupid about it.

He hoped her determination would hold when she had to engage in a firefight. While he'd never known her to get so lost in the fight that she didn't know how to come out again, there was always a first time. With her hopped up on drugs, adrenaline, and fifteen different kinds of rage, this was as good a time as any.

"The shuttle is away," Forrest announced and looked at them with a small, yellow smiling face on the screen that should have been its face.

"I appreciate it," Lombe answered. "From this point forward, Daria, there's no communication to or from your shuttle aside from what Jozzun can send you. Good luck."

"I don't need luck. I have my casters."

That sounded like the Daria they all knew and even the captain couldn't help a grin as the comm connection flipped off. Her only link to the *Atalanta* was the Xi-Trang now, and he would make sure she knew she and the Hounds weren't alone over there.

It looked like the *Vermillion Phoenix* had tired of their interference and would start to take their approach seriously, although the captain didn't do much about it.

He didn't need to since the torpedoes were directed into a section of the cruiser that was too damaged for them to justify keeping the shields up around it. They blasted holes Daria and the Hounds were able to slip through. Jozzun's influence prevented the crew from any real concern about the extra damage but as it turned out, they were more focused on reaching the *Atalanta* than about the damage the smugglers caused to a sector they had already abandoned.

"They're in," he told the rest of the crew. "It doesn't look like they'll have much resistance there."

"Do you think Daria knows what she's doing?" Lombe asked, his voice still calm and collected as they slipped behind cover and a volley of plasma rounds missed them by a few thousand klicks.

"She knows where the thruster control ports are," Jozzun answered. "It looks like they're heading to one of those and if they hit it, they can start to disable the thrusters along the ship."

"Is there a downside?" The captain's tone said he sincerely hoped there wasn't.

"It's usually manned, which means taking over the ports will get loud and messy. There are upward of five hundred mercs on the *Vermillion Asshole* over there, so if they start a fight, a shitload of them will make things difficult for our team."

"I'd say that sounds like the kind of distraction Daria wants to cause," one of the engineers called from their control station on the far side of the cockpit. "I'll bet you fifteen creds that a whole horde of those fuckers goes down with sword cuts across the body."

"No bet," Lombe answered. "The *Bright Red Asshole* is starting its approach and they're blasting asteroids to reach us. It looks like they're done playing games around the other fucking shit and they want to get to us by the fastest route."

"What does that mean?" Jozzun asked and narrowed his eyes.

"It's time to run."

They still couldn't move faster than the cruiser, of course, but it had become clear that they didn't need to, not while they were in the asteroid field. The smaller, nimbler *Atalanta* could change direction and continue to move and prevent the larger ship from getting a firm lock so they wouldn't be able to target them effectively.

Unfortunately, it wouldn't last. Lombe had no doubt planned for when a clean shot—lucky or not—hit them and it was only a matter of time. A fleet of fucking ships out there still tried to corral them, and eventually, the smugglers would run out of ammo.

The Xi-Trang could feel the seeds of fear he'd planted in the enemy heads start to grow and fester and it made a difference in the other ships' decisions. None of them were willing to continue their participation and they were content to simply let the *Phoenix* battle it out with the smaller ship and land whatever strikes they could without exposing themselves.

Fear began to play into their natural instinct to preserve their lives and none of them wanted to be killed over a feud their captain had with someone.

Lombe pulled the ship around and kept their movements erratic and unpredictable as the *Phoenix* continued its pursuit. It could close on them quickly, especially since the cruiser simply blasted the larger asteroids out of its way and powered through the smaller ones to shatter them with their shield. They had covered considerable distance and it wouldn't be long until the smugglers finally reached an open area where they wouldn't have much cover to hide behind.

The rest of the fleet realized that something was happening and immediately started to move as if to try to keep up with the action, although it didn't look like Lombe was overly concerned about what they were up to.

He chuckled quietly, on the verge of full laughter, and shook his head.

"What?" The Xi-Trang asked

"You're supposed to keep track of what Daria's doing in the cruiser. Didn't you notice that half their thrusters are misfiring?"

Jozzun glanced around, narrowed his eyes, and realized immediately that the captain was right. It looked like half the ship wanted to move forward while the other half struggled to decide what it should do. A vessel that large had almost seventy thrusters spread across it to help it turn and adjust course in zero-g on top of six main thrusters in the back that gave them real speed.

Those thrusters would be maintained in the engineering room, which was probably protected and guarded at all times. Daria wouldn't be able to get anywhere near it so she'd opted for the next best thing instead. With the thrusters across the port side of the ship all firing, they had to slow dramatically before they plowed into asteroids they weren't able to blow up beforehand.

It was time for her to get off the ship. She knew that already and didn't need him to tell her, but it was good to know they were on the same page—on most things, at least. He sensed, however, that she was in an odd mental state. Maybe it was the drugs Ishima had given her or simply the way she usually was in a fight.

Whatever the reason, she seems cold and distant, much like Lombe is when he is in the middle of tricky piloting.

She hurried to the shuttle and it didn't look like she'd needed to go far before it started again. Forrest manned the damn thing, which meant they would only take off when they had a full complement. Still, it seemed that perhaps the bot wouldn't go out of its way to get every last Hound off the Phoenix intact, which was why she hung back to make sure she was the last one to board. Finally, the seals snapped shut again and the shuttle took off.

Her attachment to the bots was probably one of the most human elements about her and it was something Jozzun admired about her more and more.

"The shuttle is on its way," Forrest announced. "Daria should return to the ship in t-minus forty seconds. It is interesting that she chose to be the last one to board."

"She didn't want you to leave any of the Hounds behind," Lombe explained without paying much attention. "She knows your core programming is in place to protect the organic crew members above all else and she didn't want to risk any of her people being left behind."

"But they aren't people. They are bots like me."

"And now you know what lengths we'd go to in order to ensure that you always make it back home safe and sound."

The bot didn't seem to understand what he meant but it didn't look like he would ask any questions.

It didn't matter. Daria approached the ship again and as soon as the shuttle locked in, they accelerated away from the cruiser toward the edge of the asteroid belt as quickly as they could and easily outpaced the rest of the Crows fleet.

"Welcome back," Lombe called once the comms reconnected. "Did you have fun over there?"

"Of course," Daria answered and sounded a little winded. "The Crows don't like it much when people use their dirty tricks against them."

Jozzun smirked as the shuttle glided into the ship and the rest of the enemy fleet began to fall back intentionally. This wasn't because they were outpaced but because they had chosen to give up the chase. It seemed that without their cruiser and with their captain knocked out of the fight, they didn't want to involve themselves either.

They had bigger problems to worry about than a small group of smugglers and an alleged deserter. Of course, the Xi-Trang had planted thoughts in the minds of those in charge to start looking into why Daria had deserted and hopefully, that would stop the bastards from trying anything in the future.

It's no guarantee, of course, but it's hopefully something to keep them occupied.

"Forrest, what's your processing capacity at?" Lombe asked as they approached the outer reaches of the belt.

"Fifty-three percent, sir."

"Start working up a Lane for us. Those bastards are pulling back now but there's no way to be sure it will hold. I want us out of the system as quickly as possible."

"I'm already working on it, sir."

"Oh. Well, good job."

Jozzun nodded agreement and looked around. The captain's shoulders finally began to relax and he drew deep breaths as Daria settled on her cot for the doc to take a look at her. She didn't appear to have sustained any fresh injuries, but her old ones still had to be checked on. The first officer seemed to understand that but she was still annoyed about being poked and prodded for any reason.

"The Lane is ready and waiting," Forrest announced as they eased entirely away from the asteroids and Lombe cut their thrusters to let the Sidespace engines kick in.

In that moment, before they could get into the envelope, an alarm activated to warn them that they had been targeted. Something snapped from the asteroid belt, fired by one of the ships, and headed directly into their path. With the thrusters down, they weren't in any position to escape it.

"Brace for impact!" the captain yelled.

They all ducked into cover and waited for something to hit them, but all they felt was a resounding thud that seemed to echo through the entire ship's hull. After a few moments, they registered that there would be no loud noises to indicate that they had lost any sections of the ship and no explosive decompression.

Somehow, they were all alive.

"What the fuck hit us?" the captain demanded and scowled at his panel. "It doesn't look like it did any damage although it slipped right past our shields."

"Something's stuck on the hull," Klyz noted and scrabbled quickly onto what was usually Daria's chair. "Oh... Oh shit."

"What?"

"It's a tagging beacon." He called up one of the scanners and it immediately detected a pulse from the device, although it was an obscure frequency. "It's a quantum entanglement com. Cheap one from the looks of it but it'll broadcast our location to whoever hit us with it."

"Can we cut it out?"

"Sure—with a couple of hours and the right equipment. And no threat of being attacked while we're out there."

It wasn't the best situation to be in. One of the worst, frankly, but in the end, if they stayed in the system, they would be hunted and cut to pieces. They had to leave and Lombe knew it. He had to put their safety first and they would find a way to get the beacon out later.

"Let's get the fuck out of here," he whispered as the envelope collected around the ship and it moved into the Lane set aside for them.

CHAPTER SEVENTEEN

There wasn't much for them to do but wait and see what came next. They could have simply sat around and tried to disconnect the beacon, but that could have taken them hours—assuming they could even accomplish it. Lombe had made the right decision to clear out of the area as quickly as possible before the other ships began to swarm again.

No one argued that it was the right decision to make in the moment, but if they wanted to avoid ending up on the wrong side of another Crows attack, they needed ideas and they needed them now. It seemed like they constantly had to come up with ideas and new and better ways to survive because all the regular options were no use to them. They had to get as creative as possible and anyone who knew the captain could tell that he had at least the beginning of an idea brewing.

"We're out of the system," he announced once the crew had gathered in the cockpit again. He'd let them have a few hours of rest once they were settled into the Lane. They'd made a short jump to get them out of the system immediately and the next jump pushed them to human space where they would meet their new client, although it was probably for the best that they didn't plot a course directly to them.

Not if we are being tracked through space by mercs who want retribution for their perceived grievances. Jozzun had to push his frustration and feelings of helplessness down. *That would ring a death knell for the sale we need to offload this fucking cargo and earn something out of this whole nightmare.*

The crew remained silent and simply waited while Lombe decided on the right way to speak his mind. None of them were very sure what their options were since he was the only one who had spoken to Malova and knew who they would sell their product to.

Maybe they wouldn't care that the freelancer group were involved in a feud with a merc corp and maybe they could help. Of course, they all realized like the Xi-Trang did that there was always the possibility that they would simply drop the purchase altogether and leave Lombe with nothing but some very expensive merch for which they had no buyer.

"What kind of chances do we have to get the tagging beacon out?" the captain asked finally. It seemed he'd decided to focus on what they could do for the moment.

"Not particularly good," Kliz answered with a shake of his head.

"It's in deep in the port-side armor but no way to tell just how deep until we can get out there and have a look."

"Which isn't happening in the Lanes, I'll tell you something."

The captain scowled at the three engineers and nodded as he ran his fingers over the head of his cane that looked like a pair of ram's horns. "Yeah, I had a bad feeling about that."

"What other options do we have?" Daria asked. "We could always find a nice port, start running the repairs, and get ready for a fight on our terms."

"Any lawful port we could make would want to know why our ship is battle-damaged and carrying suspicious cargo," Jozzun explained. "Any that would let us make port without asking questions is likely to have a base for the Crows to operate from, and they would find us and turn any advantage we might be looking for into their own."

Lombe sighed, still toying with his cane. "It's a possibility but something closer to a last resort. Removing the tagging beacon won't be much of an option until we land. Space repair would be risky since we would have to stand here for who knows how long."

"And we don't even know if we would be able to pull it out," Kleiz noted.

"Don't know what kind of tagger it is."

"Might be that we can clip the outside of it off and that'll be the end of it, or the tagger itself might be a solid meter inside our armor. Won't know until we get a proper look at it, which we can't do while we're in the Lane."

"And if we stop at any point in space, they could scramble a small fleet to attack while we have someone on the outside of the ship," Jozzun added. "To add to all the bad news."

"Can't we use the Doppelganger Code to hide?" Daria

asked and looked around. "They'll be looking for the *Atalanta*, not some random ship out of the Vaster Nordens."

"But they'll still have the tagger in our ship. They know they sent it and it'll give off the signal they'll be looking for from us."

"Even worse, the tagger might be enough to disrupt the coding too."

Lombe looked at their engineers, his eyebrows raised. "What? Wait—how?"

"The signal it's emitting isn't compatible with our ship's signal, which means any transmission we send out would very likely be interfered with by the tagger. If nothing else, it'll get people to pay attention to us when we don't want them to."

"It might be that we'd want someone to pay attention to us," Daria commented. "If we get the attention of the right people in human space, they might not mind getting into a fight with the Crows because of us."

"That...that's maybe not the worst idea in the world," Lombe whispered.

"What? Yes, it is!" Jozzun growled a protest and leaned forward. "Not...well, not the worst idea, but if we call people in to deal with any Crows, they might be as interested in stealing what we've got in our hold almost as quickly as the Crows would. Have you thought about getting our clients involved in offering us some protection for delivering the items?"

"These aren't the kinds of people we want to get into bed with," Lombe told him bluntly. "It's a possibility but I would rather sell to these guys instead of getting into business with them."

"Right down there with landing and trying to win the fight on our terms?" Daria asked.

"Below that even. I don't want to be caught shit-talking anyone who doesn't need it, but suffice it to say that...well, these are very bad and very connected people. If we end up owing them any favors, we will learn to regret it."

"Fun times." Jozzun drew a deep breath and brushed his fingers lightly over his feather crests. "Wherever we go, we can expect heavy resistance and there's a better than likely chance that we'll be outgunned and attacked with extreme prejudice. Does that about sum our situation up or do we need to go into a little more detail?"

"Nope, that's about what we can expect," Lombe answered. "Waving a white flag merely means we'll die with a white flag in our hands at this point. It might not seem like it at first, but Daria's suggestion of deciding where we fight might be the best option."

It wasn't that he thought the captain or first officer were wrong in their suggestions. When it came down to it, the Xi-Trang's frustration was with himself. They had expected to be free and clear when they left the asteroid field.

I allowed myself to be distracted and didn't pick up whatever ship tapped us with the tagger. There is simply no excuse. I should have seen it coming and now, I'm also not able to pick up where we can expect their attack to materialize and what we can expect from the fight.

There wasn't much else to say on the matter, of course. None of them had anything to add to it and they had to turn their focus to the preparation for the fight that was inevitable.

There was no need to direct them since they all knew what to do. Jozzun's abilities were more useful in the moment of action and there wasn't much need for him to plan anything. He had to prepare himself, but that mostly meant resting, calming himself, and relaxing.

But how the fuck am I supposed relax when the whole ship is teeming with anxiety and it is all my fault?

The Xi-Trang didn't realize that he'd left the cockpit until he was already halfway down the hallway. He hurried to where he could feel the doc in her office breaking something out that wasn't known for its medical benefits. *Although there is something to the self-medicating aspect of it that most humans find appealing so she could argue in favor of its efficacy in this situation.*

He slipped through the open door and watched her pour herself a second serving of the auburn drink. She'd downed the first one in a single gulp, but it seemed like she intended to take things slowly for the next few hours. Then she would rest and get herself ready for the possibility that she might need to return to her combat medication training.

"Jozzun." She gestured for him to approach her desk. "Can I interest you in a drink?"

"I wish you could," he admitted with a small smile and sat in the chair offered him. "Sadly, I don't think you're equipped with anything I can use to take the edge off."

Ishima studied the bottle for a few seconds, read the recommendations for who could drink it, and finally reached the point where it said it was not suitable for Xi-Trang. Many things he ate and drank weren't suitable for humans either, which meant they always had to order special food for him.

"What's got you drinking?" he asked and raised an eyebrow at her.

"I never liked combat medicine. It's what got me into the business to start with and while I know I can do it, no questions about that, I always hated it. I like treating people, don't get me wrong, but that's not what a combat medic does. Mostly, it's...uh, making people comfortable for what comes next, and I always loathed that aspect of it."

The Xi-Trang nodded as she swallowed her drink in a single gulp again and poured a little more. She retrieved another glass and poured him some water to make it seem like she wasn't drinking alone. He could oblige her in that, at least. Besides, he was a little thirsty anyway.

"Do you honestly think there'll be much in the way of treatment going on?" he asked and made sure she sipped her third drink instead of guzzling it.

"Not really. If we choose to fight them in space, the chances are it'll all be over in the blink of an eye. One minute, we're all alive and in it, and in the other...nothing. And that's kind of peaceful if you ask me. If Lombe wants us to fight on the ground... Well, Daria will put up a good fight, so she'll no doubt need treatment. Once they're past her and the Hounds, though, probably not. I doubt it'll be quick but they won't be looking to torture. They only want to erase the embarrassment and move on."

He leaned back in his seat and studied her for a moment. Her mind wasn't usually one he wanted to look into for a variety of reasons. This was mostly because she had a great deal of personal information on the rest of the crew he didn't have the right to know.

Still, it looked like she would share her thoughts and he was there for her if she needed it. There was always the chance that it would help to change his mood too.

"There was this one fellow—Lieutenant Mark Hagan with the Flymmiens. He was a tough drinker that one and always came into my tent looking like he'd drunk too much and picked too many fights. A bit like Daria in that way, but he was…tall. I love me a tall man with nice broad shoulders. When I broke away and started working on the other side, he was one of those who arrested me.

"Fortunately, all the times I'd taken care of their medical problems paid off and they agreed to 'lose' me. The others left but we started drinking, one thing led to another, and next thing I know, I'm in an affair with the bastard for the next six months. I contacted him every time I came into that part of space, and we'd share a bottle of whiskey and find us the nearest hotel. I don't know why but I've thought about him often lately."

"Do you think we should head to Flymmien space when this is all over?"

"I think so." She smiled. "Still, I'm not sure why he's been on my mind. It's not like we were ever in love or anything but…" She shrugged.

"It sounds like you were a little in love with him."

"Maybe. Or I simply thought about what might have been if I had taken a job on the planet where he was. Maybe we could have found a way to be more than only fuck buddies."

It was a little too much information—more than he

would have liked to hear from her—but it was interesting to note that she was thinking back on her life as well, trying to consider what could have been for them.

"Wait—is this the same Hagan who saved your life all those years ago?" Jozzun asked and tilted his head.

"Oh...yeah. I was working a bootleg pharma deal when he showed up to stop me with a whole band of his goons. He took all my shit and impounded it, but I found out later that those shits planned to shoot me with a sharp from half a klick away before he arrived to make the arrest. I never could get a straight answer out of him as to whether he knew they had planned to kill me."

Her story sparked an idea. Daria had mentioned something similar before, but none of them had thought much about who they would bring in to help them if they had the opportunity to do so.

It would be a gamble, but it could be an answer. It certainly couldn't be worse than what we're facing now, could it? There would be no way to control it but maybe, if they found the right location, they would be able to make sure people were more interested in the Crows than them. That would give them the opportunity to escape and get the tagger out of the ship's armor.

"I'll be right back," Jozzun whispered, pushed from his seat, and took a moment to finish his water and leave the glass for Ishima. He rushed out of her office and returned to the cockpit where Lombe and Daria were discussing which planets they could possibly make landfall on that would allow them as much advantage in a fight as possible.

Both paused when they saw him and registered that he

was flushed and wore a mad grin they hadn't seen from him before.

"Do you have something on your mind?" she asked and raised an eyebrow.

"I have an idea."

"I hate the fact that we've constantly come up with ideas since we got into this mess," the captain muttered. "All it means is that we can't get shit done the regular way, which forces us to be creative."

"Well, creative is what we'll have to be for this to work. Daria, you suggested we send a signal that would get people to come in and fight the Crows for us, right?"

"Right." She nodded. "But...we walked away from that idea because we wouldn't know who would show up and what they would want from us if they survived the Crows."

"Besides, it would land us in the middle of a firefight that wouldn't allow us to get the tagger out, which would leave us right where we started," Lombe added.

"Well, yes." Jozzun smirked. "And yet, there might be a way for us to control the situation at least to some degree. If we were to find ourselves in Gallian Enterprise space, for instance."

The captain leaned forward, narrowed his eyes, and looked intrigued by where he was taking the conversation.

"Go on."

"My thinking is that we could change our code to one of a notorious vessel—probably a pirate since that's what gets people moving the fastest these days. I'm sure we can find a ship that's been on the top of their wanted list for a while now. If the tagging beacon does disrupt the signal, it's unlikely to override it completely. Enough of the code should get through even intermittently to suggest that the pirates are trying to disguise themselves or at the very least, that it's worth investigating.

"If we can find one that is enough of a potential prize, it'll bring a patrol running, so the more infamous the better. When the Gallian forces arrive, they'll arrest everyone on principle but we'd have a better chance to slip away if they're only trying to arrest people. And, of course, especially if it turns out we're not the ship they're looking for when we change our outgoing code."

Lombe leaned back in his seat and looked at Daria. "I don't know... I was kind of getting used to the last stand on a mountain concept, but it would better for us to get the Gallian fleet involved than to get into another slugfest with the Crows. They'd be likely to back down quickly too since tangling with a civ's official forces is far more trouble than we're worth, especially given the issues they're already facing on their own."

The first officer didn't look like she would be convinced so easily. "I'm not big on the idea of being arrested. And why Gallian space?"

"Our psychic here is a sly bastard." Lombe laughed. "See, my good first officer, the forward arm of Gallian Enterprise space is caught between both Angelos territory and known corsair space so they patrol that area in force. If we wave a notorious flag, we're likely to draw a heavy cruiser or even a full-bore battleship."

"And this is a good thing? What happens if they simply shoot us full of holes? That's what battleship captains are notorious for doing, right?"

"Indubitably, but so powerful a ship will expect compliance before a fight. And with that kind of power on display, the Crows won't want a fight either. They can't afford to lose any more ships at this point."

She still didn't look like she was on board with the plan, but it was clear that the captain felt it was the one with the highest chance of them escaping with their lives. That wasn't saying much, but it sounded like they were committed to making it work.

That meant she was too.

"Right," Lombe said decisively and looked at their engineering team. "Look through the database and find the biggest, baddest piece of shit out there."

"Already been looking, captain," one of the three answered and glanced up from the screen in front of them. "Picked one up too. A defector captain. Went rogue from the Angelos Dominion almost a decade ago."

"Captain Slate?" Jozzun asked.

"I heard they'd arrested him already," Lombe commented.

"They did," Daria answered. "He was in lockup for about a year before his crew got him out and blasted the prison from orbit so he's been out for five years now. I heard he went on a rampage. He took his ship the…uh, *Regents Favored Vendetta*, I think it was called, to sack a couple of stations, stole the data from their computers, and used it to find convoys in the Lanes and wrecked them too. He hasn't been seen since then."

"It sounds like the perfect ship to use for our little ruse," Lombe agreed. "Make it so."

"Already making it so, captain."

CHAPTER EIGHTEEN

"Do all their names have something to do with red?" the Xi-Trang asked.

"Most of them. Crow associations are in there too, although there was one called the *Nevermore* that I never understood. Someone told me it has something to do with an Old-Earth poet who liked to write poems about crows or something."

"Poetry?" Jozzun raised an eyebrow.

"I know. I was surprised too. Not many mercs have the time or inclination to run around with poetry books in hand. I saw a few of them openly mocked by their peers for going to the theater. Still, I guess the captains get away with more than the rest of the dumb shits out there."

"I guess that makes sense," Lombe whispered, a little distracted by his focus on the screen. "That's still a fucking armada waiting for us out there. Is anyone else starting to feel like this wasn't a great idea?"

Jozzun tilted his head. "Well…a little, yeah."

Daria didn't have anything to say and she looked at

where the captain was seated. Jozzun could tell that she considered asking him if there was still time for them to call up the Sidespace engines and escape. There must be a better location for them to start this fight, although it didn't feel like they would find one.

We can keep running if we want to and it might even work, but it isn't in the blood of someone like either the captain or our first officer. They will solve the situation instead of living their lives as fugitives. Still, that didn't mean the thought of running away wouldn't occur to them.

It was merely much easier for them to resist it.

"Right." Lombe cleared his throat and rolled his neck a few times before he grasped the *Atalanta's* controls. "What are we looking at here, Jozzun?"

It was clear cut from the display but he summarized anyway. "We're looking at fifteen gunboats in total. They have torpedoes, plasma cannons, and drone platforms—which is interesting because those were supposed to be exclusive to the military. Each one has no less than four corvettes running escort for them. It looks like an organized fleet, all centered around the main vessel, a Seahawk-Class Attack Cruiser enhanced and armed to a level way beyond what mercs are generally allowed. The sign they're using for it is *Blood Rook*. I guess this means the fuckers have some kind of military connections in this part of space who get them whatever the Gallians cast off as long as they pick fights with everyone but them."

The captain nodded. "That armor will be a pain in the ass to get through. And there's no chance we'll be able to pull the same stunt we did on the other cruiser. All their weapons are hot and ready to go, waiting for us to make the first move."

That was the interesting part. It didn't appear that these people cared much about Daria or her perceived treachery. They did seem to understand that there was a threat aboard the ship and some people wanted some semblance of revenge, but it didn't quite work out the way they wanted it to. Still, it looked like they were confident in their superior numbers and positioning, and their commander was a steadfast type of person who wouldn't be easily influenced by Jozzun, although he would try anyway.

They'd also heard about the damage this single ship had caused to one of their fleets, so the commander wouldn't commit his forces until he knew he had a real opportunity for a killing blow.

"Charging them headfirst is essentially suicide at this point," Jozzun continued with his assessment. "I'm working on them but I don't think I'll manage more than a slight influence. They're well-led and their commander has some battle experience, so I doubt I'll get him to do anything truly stupid."

"What I wouldn't do for a fleet right now," Lombe muttered. "Give me a couple of Aegis-Class Defense Cruisers, six frigates like the *Atalanta*, and I'd frag these assholes to kingdom come. It doesn't look like we have much in the way of a tactical approach to this battle."

"The guerilla approach served you well in the asteroid belt," Daria pointed out. "It might not be as effective here but since we're playing for time, we might as well...uh, you know, start running and see if they follow."

It was as good a start to their little skirmish as any. The whole crew was already in the cockpit to help with anything they could. The thrusters engaged and began to move them away from where they'd come out of the Lane.

"You know," the captain said to her as they began to move again, "I'm starting to wonder why these Crows hate you so much."

"Frankly, Captain," she responded easily, "I'm very sure you're the one they hate the most."

"What? Why? What did I do?"

"Well, you borrowed one of their flagship's codes for one thing. That probably opened them to sanctions from the Jindahin or even—which is unlikely, I admit—got them excluded from one of the most profitable places for mercs to fight in all of known space."

"Oh. Right, but besides that."

She'd made a good point. Jozzun hadn't even thought about it. *While she might have been the reason why they started fighting, Lombe is far from innocent in his dealings with the Crows. Since he is the captain of the vessel, he will be the one marked by them as the person responsible for everything that came after, including hiring Daria.*

"We need to start evasive maneuvers." He pushed his thoughts aside and alerted the captain. "They're starting to set themselves up for a fight and we don't want to be swarmed by them, not in this open region of space."

"Appreciate it, Jozzun," Lombe answered and began to pull the *Atalanta* around.

Daria had already loaded all the torpedo tubes and set all their weapons to hot, although her most interesting move was to highlight all the enemy gunships with torpedo locks. This set them immediately on the defensive as they pulled away from their starting formation. He had been right in his assessment of the battle-readiness of the Crows opposite them. They were well-trained, with good pilots and a solid plan in place.

They merely haven't ever met someone like Lombe before.

"They're heading off," the Xi-Trang noted. "It looks like they're a little jumpy about us opening fire on them. I guess our reputation precedes us."

"It's always a good thing to use against people as long as you don't buy into it," Lombe answered. "Daria, choose those that are following us the closest. The rest of them will hold back and wait for us to do something unexpected."

"It looks like we have five gunships ready to start the fight," she replied. "All of them have 'vettes running escort. They haven't locked onto us yet. What do we do?"

"We'll move away and get them to commit, then I'll turn and start a little fencing game with the big boy to see what they're willing to invest in this engagement."

"Do you think they picked up our code?" She frowned as if she expected this to be a stumbling block for them.

"Sure, but they'll probably think it's an error. Everyone knows the *Regent's* not a frigate. Hopefully, no one knows about the Doppelganger Code yet."

"We'll see," she responded with an edge of doubt still in her tone.

Lombe swung around and drew the first engagers into the open with them. He pulled them away from the rest of the fleet, who appeared to be content to stand, watch, and wait for further developments. It wasn't arrogance but the knowledge that he had proven to be an unpredictable and dangerous adversary against them in the past. It made sense that they wanted to keep all the fighting in front of them as much as they could.

It was a conservative approach but in this instance, they could afford it. At least they thought they could based on their knowledge of how the skirmish would play out.

"'Vettes are coming in hot," Daria announced. "It looks like they're a little tired of waiting around for us to do something."

"Do you have a lock on them?" the captain asked.

"Yeah."

"Hit them with only the point defenses for the moment and only if they get too close. I want them to think they have us on the run and we can do nothing else but evade them."

Jozzun wasn't quite sure how that was different than the truth but it sounded like Lombe planned to broadside the *Rook* at least once. He wouldn't let them sit and watch the battle from afar.

"The gunships are closing," he warned them. "They've got torpedo locks on our engines. It looks like they want to cripple and board us instead of blowing us up outright."

"Probably because they heard we have some valuable merch on board. Give them a nice wide target to see what they'll do." Lombe grinned.

It didn't take long for the alert to tell them the torpedoes had been launched from only about three hundred thousand klicks away. It was far enough away for them to maneuver but not by much.

The captain engaged the forward thrusters and

brought them as close to a dead stop as was possible in space before he shifted them down and around as the torpedoes were about to close on them. It was a tight maneuver and two of them detonated close enough to rock the ship, but it looked like the shields absorbed most of the damage. The others overshot them as the *Atalanta* twisted again. Its knife-like build made it harder to hit than most frigates, and he was quite skilled at evading fire by this point.

He spun the ship in an instant to face their adversaries and accelerated toward them while he directed all shields to the bow to "sharpen" the knife's edge, as it were. Daria was quick on the draw, as she was with most things, and unleashed five torpedoes. She aimed them at the 'vettes that provided the gunships with an added escort.

None of them had the time to move away or evade and the screens lit up with five explosions as the 'vettes shattered in space, vented atmo, and whirled uncontrollably to collide with their fellows.

The bits and pieces that were left weren't enough to pose a threat to the larger frigate. Lombe pushed through them and headed directly toward the gunships that were surprised to see the *Atalanta* now ready to engage them instead of running. The torpedo tubes were loaded again and fired as soon as they had something to shoot at. They targeted the rest of the escort as they raced directly toward a collision with the gunships.

It was the same kind of tactic he'd employed against the *Phoenix* but in this case, the gunboats were smaller and more likely to be wrecked if the *Atalanta* powered into them. The chances were that the frigate's design would protect them from any serious damage in that kind of ramming.

Before the enemy could react, the *Atalanta's* plasma cannons opened fire with enough of a barrage to prevent them from being able to stop the attack. It was pure brute force and a tactic they hadn't expected. Jozzun did his best to make sure they were stressed and unsettled so they either didn't get decent shots in or missed them outright. A handful of their plasma rounds even targeted their own 'vettes.

They had already begun to pull away when the frigate knifed between them, plowed through their weakened shields, and tore massive holes through two of them while the others barely managed to get out of the way. One of the gunboats hammered into another, which knocked two more out of the fight and left only one that was entirely intact.

All five of them suddenly faced the series of torpedoes that followed the *Atalanta*. Their shields were already down and each torpedo gutted one, ripped them to pieces, and killed all hands inside.

The last one was able to limp away, atmo still venting from where it had been hit by one of the torpedoes, but Lombe pulled them back from finishing it. The ship would be out of the fight for the most part anyway, and they didn't want the people they were fighting to think they were actually in a kill-or-be-killed battle.

His mindset—one the Xi-Trang made sure their enemies were aware of—was that he hadn't started the fight but he would finish it, for better or for worse.

They already had the *Rook's* attention, and Jozzun

narrowed his eyes as they exposed their coilguns to the vacuum. The heat register from the massive pair of guns was in excess of three thousand degrees and superheated the projectiles almost to the point of liquifying them.

"Captain..."

"I see them. I see them," Lombe assured him in his chillingly calm voice. He had already begun to maneuver the *Atalanta* out of the way of a clean shot.

It didn't mean they wouldn't shoot anyway, but it was standard practice to allow them some wiggle room when the projectiles were finally fired.

Jozzun could see the commander captaining the *Rook* was reevaluating his tactical plan. He was a little impressed by the balls it took for them to use the gunboats' torpedoes against them and he made a note to use that kind of tactic in the future.

He realized, of course, that he needed a particular type of ship and pilots to accomplish what he'd witnessed but it was still something he wanted to see from his people in the future.

"The guns are getting hot," Daria muttered. "Do you think we could hit them with a couple of torpedoes while they're heating up like that? The chain reaction would be enough to cripple the ship."

"It's a weakness they're well aware of in that ship design," Lombe countered. "It means they'll keep the shields on until the last minute before they fire, and their PDS will focus on preventing exactly that kind of attack."

It's an interesting tactical possibility, of course, but one we wouldn't be able to employ without three or four more ships to keep the attack cruiser distracted.

For the moment, all they could do was run when the coilguns finally fired. Their projectiles accelerated beyond what any other weapon was capable of, and the *Atalanta* dove and twisted away from the first round. A wash of heat illuminated their shields with a silver gleam but with negligible impact. The second round was the most important, anyway, since that was the one the commander seemed to think would strike.

It had targeted the *Atalanta* through its evasion and calculated its likely flight plan before it fired again.

Lombe showed no sign of being any more anxious about the attack than the others and slowed the *Atalanta* with an abruptness that jarred everyone in the cockpick. The projectile flashed past them faster than even the sensors could pick up but again, there was nothing more to it than a few percentiles taken from their shields' efficacy.

"How long until the coilguns are ready to fire again?" the captain asked and brought the ship into motion as three gunboats and their 'vette escorts broke away from the fleet's formation and rushed toward them.

"Three hundred seconds from what I can tell," Jozzun answered. "That's the official reloading speed for those guns, though. Since it's a merc vessel, it might be a little longer."

"Right then. We have to keep wasting their fucking time—and a few of their ships too."

The captain seemed to be in a good mood as he turned the ship and headed away from the new group of attackers.

CHAPTER NINETEEN

We will run out of tricks eventually. Even the captain can't possibly produce many more crazy maneuvers, although he's done better than I expected.

Jozzun sighed inwardly as Lombe navigated the *Atalanta* out of the way of the coilguns and still gave the rest of their fleet hell. They'd been lucky with the first couple of engagements but it had soon become apparent that they needed to run far more than they would fight.

Although the man finding a way to bait the *Rook* into firing their coilgun into a mess of their own gunboats had been hilarious to watch. The shots had only eliminated three of the vessels but it had pissed the commander off to no end and forced him to gather his people closer and keep them under tighter control.

With that, the enemy began to press their advantage, drove their whole fleet forward, and forced the *Atalanta* to back away and run much harder than before. The steady stream of fire from the attack cruiser made sure they couldn't remain in one place for long, and Lombe's good mood had disappeared around the fourth hour in which they had kept the evasive tactics up and hadn't returned in the two hours since. It wasn't like they could do so forever, but he had made sure they stayed out of the worst of it so far.

Daria's ability to discern the attacks that would compromise any powerful advance also served them well, especially with the limited weapons they had. Jozzun had managed to anticipate where their attacks would come from and made sure the 'vettes were mostly neutralized to stop them from getting in close enough to try to board the *Atalanta*.

But it wouldn't last. They were already all but out of torpedoes, their thrusters had begun to overheat, and the shields practically ran on empty as the relentless fighting continued. The engineers did their best to prevent everything from blowing, and they were also responsible for keeping them in the fight as long as they had been.

More importantly, Jozzun could tell that the commander on the Crows' flagship grew steadily more reluctant to commit his people to this kind of hit and run battle. They'd already lost far more than the *Atalanta* was worth, even with her cargo, and they were less determined to board the ship and more willing to simply scrap it and move on.

Lombe dripped with sweat and kept himself as focused on flying the ship as he could. He barely spoke and he became more fatigued as the battle dragged on.

Jozzun could empathize, of course. The fight had taken its toll on the whole crew and they became more prone to making mistakes with every second that passed. They'd barely avoided the last battery from the *Rook's* coilguns. It had wrecked their shields and overheated a handful of their port thrusters, which had certainly affected their ability to navigate the fighting. For now, however, all they could do was keep moving, keep fighting, and hope things continued to favor their efforts.

The Xi-Trang had worked to keep the crew calm and collected, but that effort on top of monitoring what the Crows were doing began to tell on him as well.

We won't last much longer, that much is clear.

"I'm picking up a couple more signatures coming out of the Lanes," Daria said suddenly and looked up from her screens. "Do you think they called in some reinforcements?"

"That's not the coding signature I'm getting," Lombe answered and looked at the engineers. "Speaking of which, what's our code looking like?"

"Already switched it to something a little more innocuous," Kleiz answered and glanced up from his panel. "Even better, it looks like that last hit from the coil guns knocked out the transmission on the tagger. We might be in the clear to get out of here."

The captain shook his head. "It's not likely. They're staying too close to us. If we stop long enough to get a Lane open, we'll be wrecked before we know it."

Still, with the new arrivals, things would maybe be a little more confusing for their enemies. Even if it was reinforcements, Jozzun felt confident that he would be able to keep them from coordinating easily with their command structure. This meant Lombe would be able to bait the attack cruiser into hitting a few of the newcomers too.

"Codes coming in," Klyz called, focused on his screen. "Gallian Enterprise Naval codes by the looks of them. Scout ships, which usually means something that can transport them through the Lanes is on its way."

"All ships in the quadrant," a shaky human voice said across the general comms. "Be advised, by order of the Gallian Enterprise Navy, you are to cease all hostilities immediately or be fired upon."

"Be fired upon?" Lombe hissed in outrage. "They know we're being attacked here, right?"

"It won't matter," Daria answered. "We're all out of torpedoes and our plasma cannons will barely be able to keep pace with the only PDS we have left. We've already stopped fighting at this point."

It was true and as much as Jozzun hated to think it, they were lucky someone else had intervened and demanded the attention of their enemies while they continued to move away from the attack cruiser.

Their sensors picked up something large emerging from the Sidespace Lane and it jumped into view almost immediately. They could see the ship itself over the distance of almost a million klicks without needing to rely on their sensors, although those told of a ship that practically bristled with weaponry. It carried five coilguns in total by the looks of it, dozens of torpedo tubes, and hundreds of plasma cannons, and drone stations protruded from almost everywhere.

"All ships in this quadrant," said another voice over the comms. "This is Admiral Bennet of the GEN ordering any and all hostilities to cease or you will be fired upon. This is your last warning."

His voice boomed in command and showed no sign of tolerance for their antics. The Leviathan-Class Battleship was one of the latest additions of the GEN fleet, and it looked like numerous strings had been pulled for this admiral to command one of them. They were made to transport entire fleets through the Lanes and once they were out, dozens of smaller ships broke away and formed up around it.

"It's about the size of a fucking city," Daria whispered and leaned closer to her screen. "I didn't think anything but the cruise liners ever got that big."

"Do you think the Crows will back down?" Jozzun asked but answered the question for himself when he turned his attention to where the enemy had paused their pursuit of the *Atalanta* for a second.

In the next moment, the *Rook* moved forward. It didn't engage with the GEN battleship but certainly disregarded the orders for them all to stand down.

"It doesn't look like it," Lombe muttered and shook his head. "I guess any fears that we would get caught in the middle of a battle between both sides are validated."

"I appreciate you saying so, Captain," his first officer responded with a smile.

They needed to keep moving, jump ahead of where they were, and stay ahead of the coilguns. There was no way to know how many rounds the damn ship had, but it had already gone through at least twenty over the past six hours. That said, however, it didn't show any inclination that it would stop anytime soon.

"The commander is looking for one last shot at us," Jozzun whispered, straightened in his seat, and clutched his chair tighter when he felt the burning in his scalp. "He wants to get in close and pin us down with one last broadside. They have the engines to catch up with us too, which means we'll have to try something interesting to stay ahead of them."

"Try something interesting," Lombe repeated slowly. "Well, we've been trying interesting things all day so might as well keep the tradition up, right?"

He began to move the ship, adjusted the power distribution accordingly, and made sure they didn't give the *Rook* any easy shots from its position.

All hopes that the fighting would stop when the GEN arrived were shattered, but if they could survive a little while longer, maybe the Leviathan—a ship named *Lyon de Rampant*, of all fucking things—would do their work for them.

It wasn't a guarantee but it was something for them to hope for while they ran for their lives.

"Jozzun!" He jerked in surprise and realized Lombe was staring at him. "Is everything all right?"

The Xi-Trang nodded slowly. "I'm…yeah. I'm fine, Captain."

Lombe didn't believe him, but he had to accept that he was still in working condition. They all needed to be at this point.

"I need you to look ahead and plot a course for us," the captain explained, his tone level and calm despite everything. "We don't know when the *Lyon* will start to fire, which means as soon as they do, we need to be between them and the *Rook*. Can you help me?"

A hint of desperation threaded his voice, something

close to begging, hoping, and praying that Jozzun was still in a condition to help them even though he had a hard time keeping himself upright anymore.

He wouldn't let his captain down, however, not until his body gave out under him.

"Yeah," he whispered. "I can find you a way. It won't be easy and it'll take balls and more than a little luck to prevent us from being blasted to dust. But I can do it."

"Let's get it done."

They moved forward again and he punched in the details of what they needed to do next. The first task was to power their shields down almost completely and only maintain enough so their armor wouldn't be compromised by space dust and particles. Aside from that, all the power was shunted to the rear thrusters and the bow plasma cannon.

Lombe's trust in him didn't waver for an instant, and he appreciated the captain for that. It was an honor that the man was willing to risk his life and livelihood on the word of their psychic. He didn't even need to be a psychic to see it, but all he could do was hope that he was worthy of that kind of trust.

Still, the engineers didn't sound like they were happy, and they grunted and groaned as they worked to stop the systems all around the ship from overheating. With only one blown fuse, they would be dead in the water at this point. They had the responsibility to stop the ship from killing itself like equines did when they were pushed too hard and ran until their hearts gave out.

For the first time since early in the battle, Jozzun heard Lombe chuckle softly. It sounded like he had embraced the madness of their situation, held it close, and engaged fully with it. He knew what they were trying to do as they turned and headed directly toward the cruiser where the first coilgun of the *Rook's* broadside was waiting for them.

"If we can pull this off, it might go down in naval history," the captain whispered and engaged the thrusters with as much power as he could risk without wrecking anything. The *Rook* came closer but Lombe kept the *Atalanta* at an off-angle to make sure the coilguns were never allowed a clean shot at them.

While they could try, all they would have was the knife's edge, the narrow bow of the frigate, to aim at and that allowed for comparatively easy evasion.

Still, with their shields down to paper, even the heat wash from a close call would be enough to knock them out.

Jozzun shook his head, forced himself to stay focused, and watched and waited for any reaction from the Crows. He was curious to see if they realized what was happening as the *Atalanta* closed on them at a breakneck speed. Collision alarms triggered when they came within five hundred thousand klicks of the cruiser and he tensed, ready for a reaction.

They were slow. Maybe they didn't believe the frigate was advancing with an attack in mind, but it didn't matter. They would think this was their chance. They expected some kind of mad plot like the one Lombe had devised against the *Phoenix*. A few of the crew wavered but their protests were immediately quelled by the captain, who shouted at them to prepare to fire the coilguns.

It will be close—too close. Jozzun's feathers seemed to

burn into his scalp and made him grit his teeth as he stared forward. He didn't have it in him to control or push anything at this point but he could still see. What he saw were thousands and even millions of different variables preparing them to fire their coilguns again.

His eyes closed and his fingers hovered over his board as he watched and waited for the order to fire. That moment—that split second—was all they would get. Milliseconds one way or the other could see the *Atalanta* perforated from one end to the other with superheated rounds fired at impossible speeds.

But they had their opening. The Xi-Trang sucked in a deep breath as the pain worsened. He knew his feathers now glowed outright and it was all he could do simply to watch for their moment and their opening.

Thankfully, it came almost instantly.

"Fire!"

Daria had waited for the order and she all but pounced on the button to fire their plasma cannon at precisely that moment. The Xi-Trang had accounted for the quarter-second of lag between his order and her enacting it. He'd also accounted for the lag between the enemy commander's order to fire and his crew following that order. Time felt like it slowed as their plasma cannon responded less than fifty thousand klicks away from the bow of their adversary—practically at collision distance already.

The *Rook's* shields lowered in the moment before the coilgun sent its deadly projectile into space. They'd timed it perfectly all day. The shield had lowered and the coilgun had fired like clockwork for the past six hours.

Now, the shield dipped but before the coilgun could go

off, the plasma round came in first. It punched hard into the gun that was about to launch its superheated projectile.

Plasma splashed across the white-hot depleted uranium round heated to a little over eleven hundred degrees and slightly shy of its melting point. The plasma catalyzed it and the surface melted off and bonded almost immediately with the rest of the coilgun.

Lombe had already slowed dramatically. Jozzun could have sworn he'd told him to do that, but it seemed not. His jaw no longer worked and he guessed he'd collapsed in his chair. He'd blacked out for a second but thankfully, the captain quickly realized what would happen and he drew the *Atalanta* away as the coilgun imploded on itself.

The explosion was as impressive as it was silent, and the Xi-Trang opened his eyes in time to see the coilgun contract and bring a chunk of the *Rook* in with it, followed quickly by a blast of white light that made the massive cruiser spiral out of control.

He couldn't tell if the ship still had a living commander on it. About two-thirds of the ship was still intact, and too many redundancies were in place for the whole vessel to go up in smoke from a single blast like that.

Despite this, it was beyond crippled. Its major weapons were disabled and the ship drifted, pushed more by the venting atmo than the thrusters. These all appeared to misfire, which indicated some kind of problem with the cockpit.

The *Atalanta's* crew should all be celebrating, throwing their fists up in the air at the impossible maneuver they'd accomplished, but none of them were. He realized that Daria propped him up in his seat and stroked his cheek gently. She said something but he couldn't hear her over the ringing in his ears.

What he could hear were the words of the admiral over the comms.

"That was some impressive flying there, Captain Lombe."

"I have one hell of a crew, Admiral."

"I hate to have to rain on what should be a celebration over pulling a bullshit maneuver like that, but I have to bring you in."

"We have no problem with that, Admiral. We've fought these assholes for the past six hours, and as long as you don't intend to shoot at us, I think we can tolerate the inconvenience."

"I appreciate that. I don't think the mercs you've squabbled with will be as interested in you but at this point, without their flagship, they won't have much of a choice."

"Capture them, blow them to pieces...whatever. You won't hear any complaints from me."

The admiral laughed. "We have you in our trajectory. AI's will take over the docking process in a moment."

Jozzun smiled, leaned back in his seat, and felt Daria's fingers stroke his feathers lightly. It wasn't quite the gesture he had expected from her but it was oddly soothing.

His eyes drifted shut but the last image he collected was the sight of one of the Crows gunships swarmed by drones. They immediately vented the whole ship while its 'vette escort was reduced to slag.

Not a bad way to end a day of work. Not bad at all.

CHAPTER TWENTY

They had a decent medical wing aboard the Lyon. It wasn't something people usually considered about the naval vessels, but they certainly put some effort into keeping their crew healthy.

He meant no disrespect to Ishima when he decided it was better than the one they had, although he doubted any apology was necessary. She'd explained it as an overabundance of caution as they helped him onto the stretcher. It didn't look like the staff were familiar with his biology but they at least knew better than to interfere with the treatments she had administered to keep him alive and more or less conscious. Even with those, he could feel himself fading in and out here and there.

His emissary paperwork was about a decade out of date but thankfully, that didn't show on their uplinks, which meant they were more than happy to help him in any way they could.

And that was the best part. Emissaries were granted diplomatic immunity for themselves and the crew of whatever ship they happened to be on. It was a nifty trick and one that likely wouldn't have helped them if they were in Xi-Trang space.

Maybe it's time to get my paperwork validated again. Or...I wonder if we can find a way to finagle the Doppelganger Code to get my paperwork into working order without needing to get the XTA involved.

Jozzun shook his head when he realized that he'd drifted out again. They were giving him fluids intravenously, which meant he was too weak to take them the ordinary way. That sounded about right. *Honestly, I feel like I could nap for the next decade too. Some sentient species out there hibernate when the weather got cold and I can certainly see the appeal of it.*

"Being unlawfully harassed by mercenary corp isn't as unusual in this part of space as you might think," someone said nearby, although he didn't have it in him to peer into their minds. He couldn't even bring himself to open his eyes and see who was talking.

"They must have tagged us at our last port of call and were waiting for us the moment we got out of the Lane." That was Lombe. He talked to the admiral of the *Lyon* like they were old war buddies. Some measure of respect remained for pulling that little trick off with the plasma round into the coilgun, but the man was a little less impressed when he realized a Xi-Trang was on board.

They'd called it cheating, although Lombe was quick to remind them that appearing with a whole fleet to attack a frigate wasn't exactly a fair fight either.

"We shouldn't keep you long anyway," the admiral said in answer to a question the captain asked that Jozzun didn't catch. "GEN has no intention to cause any diplomatic incidents with the Xi-Trang, not with how things are going in our little chunk of space. The least we could do was pull you out of some piracy, although I won't be allowed to offer any of our resources to help with your repairs."

"Our engineering crew is working to keep the ship spaceworthy, at least until we reach a port where proper repairs can be made. We don't want to cause any trouble with the Gallian Navy either. We might be hauling an emissary but we're still only a freelance operation."

It didn't take much effort to guide the admiral's mind to the kind of thanks he would get for pulling a Xi-Trang emissary out of the fire like that. Jozzun was surprised to find that he was still able to reach out, although it was only a surface probe and short-lived.

His eyes opened a little and he realized that Ishima was seated next to him and added a couple of interesting and unknown ingredients to the fluids going into his body. He had no idea what they were but he certainly felt better as a result by the time the captain and the admiral parted ways.

"Look who's finally in the land of the living." Lombe laughed as he approached his bedside. "I could have sworn you burst a brain vessel by peering into the future for us like that. But there you are, looking like you're a power nap away from being back to a hundred percent."

He didn't have the energy to explain the process of anticipation that came with his work so he smiled and relaxed into the hoverchair he had been placed in.

"How did things go?" Jozzun asked, his voice only a whisper.

"Well, the admiral was brought here by the promise of capturing some notorious pirate or another so he was a little disappointed. Despite that, he'll let us head off as soon as you're able to transfer to the *Atalanta*. We were all released about an hour ago when they picked up your paperwork."

"Yeah…" Jozzun looked at his feet and moved them a little to make sure there was no neural damage that needed treatment. "I guess he'll have to settle for getting our asses out of the fire instead."

"I'm sure he'll find some way to make that work for him," Daria noted, which drew a glare from Lombe.

Her anti-military stances were generally acceptable but they probably needed to be kept in check when they were aboard a navy vessel like the *Lyon*.

"It looks like you're about ready to go," one of the nurses told him and raised an eyebrow at the crew there waiting for him. Lombe, Daria, and Ishima didn't get much of a look compared to the three short engineers who stood next to his chair. "I'm sorry. This area is reserved for family only."

"We are his family," Daria snapped and took a step forward.

"Yeah," the Xi-Trang agreed with a small grin. "Of course. Can't you see the familial resemblance?"

"It's uncanny, truly," Lombe interjected.

The expression that came over the nurse's face reflected the one Jozzun felt come over his own whenever Klyz, Kliz, and Kleiz spoke in their rapid-fire way.

"Oh… Well…" She didn't look like she knew what to say. They had no doubt been told that the emissary was not to be interfered with in any way, and that probably included his family members too.

"We're about to return to the ship," Lombe told her. "We have some important business to tend to."

"I..." The nurse finally sighed and shook her head. Jozzun could tell that she thought all this was far above her pay grade, and she didn't need the trouble it would cause for her if it blew up in her face. "I'll get the release paperwork started."

"We'd appreciate that," he said with a small smile, relaxed into his chair, and closed his eyes.

Hopefully, they wouldn't run into any more trouble on the way. He didn't think he could accomplish any more impossible assaults. Two was about his limit.

"Come on, buddy," Daria whispered and patted him on the shoulder. "Let's get you home."

That is a very good idea. Home sounds perfect.

AUTHOR NOTES - MICHAEL ANDERLE

MARCH 4, 2022

Thank you for reading both this story AND these author notes here in the back! I am going to ask Alfonse the Idiot AI about Dr. Who's special screwdriver (it's Sci-Fi) but since I don't actually 'know' anything about Dr. Who – and wouldn't be able to confirm or deny anything Alfonse says I have asked one of my collaborators Sarah Noffke (Tiny Ninja™) to fact check Alfonse.

For those who haven't seen any Alfonse author notes, here is the background: I have been looking into technology for decades, and one of the items I've played with are AI tools to help build articles. To date, I have not been too impressed. Therefore, I finally decided to share some of my findings about:

Alfonse the Idiot AI™

Part 06 of ... who knows?

Subtitle: 'Why AI's Shouldn't rule the world...*yet.*'

Here is my story so far:

I decided Monday to make the trip up to the Great Oracle (otherwise known as Alfonse the Idiot A.I.) and ask him a few questions. My job is to decide if humanity should start packing our bags, and just move ahead to another world or we have a few years left of good living and to see if Alfonse has any favorite T.V. shows.

Upon making it through the metal detector, I was rewarded with an opportunity to ask a short question... for a large fee.

Alfonse is nothing if not a commercially motivated artificial construct.

My Topic: Sonic Screwdriver.
My Subtopics: Dr. Who.

Here is the Alfonse' response, and I just want to say that Sarah was NOT any help. In fact, her comment was: *"Lol. I'm thoroughly impressed with your knowledge of the sonic screwdriver. I can't find anything to add or subtract and may have learned a little something."*

For those who find ANY issues with Alfonse's response and corrections, please direct them to my esteemed inaccurate collaborator Sarah Noffke. She deserves all of the attention, trust me!

Michael: Alfonse – what is the Sonic Screwdriver from Dr. Who

Alfonse: The sonic screwdriver is an electronic device that allows the Doctor to control the TARDIS from a distance. Unlike the original sonic screwdriver, the sonic screwdriver is not made to kill, but instead to emit a continuous glow. Often referred to as a sonic cane, the sonic screwdriver features a metallic ball attached to its claws and emits a constant green light.

First introduced as a simple screwdriver, the sonic screwdriver is now capable of more advanced tasks. It can disarm robotics, repair computers, detonate bombs, and perform medical scans. In the new series, the screwdriver can even perform geolocation and track alien villains. Its versatility has earned the Doctor the right to be called the Doctor's 'Sonic Toolbox'.

The screwdriver is a handy tool that the Doctor often brings with him on adventures. The Doctor can use it to reattach barbed wire, light candles, and operate the TARDIS remotely. It can also be used to fix electronics, burn materials, and fuse metal. While the original Doctor Who series introduced the device in the 1960s, its uses were eventually eliminated because the show's creator, John Nathan-Turner, felt that it limited the show's scope. However, it did return in a 1996 film for the same character.

The sonic screwdriver first appeared in the serial, Fury From the Deep, written by Victor Pemberton. The Second Doctor first used the device in the fifth series, and it's now featured in all of the show's latest series. Its popularity didn't end there. The device has been featured in several other episodes, including the latest one. The new incarnation of the sonic screwdriver was unveiled at the 2013 San Diego Comic-Con.

AUTHOR NOTES - MICHAEL ANDERLE

Alfonse has left me wondering whether he has a fascination with the Sonic Screwdriver or Sarah is just a really poor fanatic of Dr. Who. Since he has done SO poorly with my other requests, I really hope some of you might mention (in the reviews for the book?) whether Sarah got her answer correct.

If she did? I won't be able (all of the time) to say…

Alfonse, you are an idiot A.I.

Have a great week or weekend, and join me in the next book where we talk more to Alfonse the Idiot AI™.

Ad Aeternitatem,

Michael Anderle

CONNECT WITH MICHAEL

Connect with Michael Anderle

Website: http://lmbpn.com

Email List: http://lmbpn.com/email/

https://www.facebook.com/LMBPNPublishing

https://twitter.com/MichaelAnderle

https://www.instagram.com/lmbpn_publishing/

https://www.bookbub.com/authors/michael-anderle

BOOKS BY MICHAEL ANDERLE

Sign up for the LMBPN email list to be notified of new releases and special deals!

https://lmbpn.com/email/

For a complete list of books by Michael Anderle, please visit:

www.lmbpn.com/ma-books/

www.ingramcontent.com/pod-product-compliance
Lightning Source LLC
LaVergne TN
LVHW091709070526
838199LV00050B/2331